A Rooted Sorrow

A Rooted Sorrow

Keith Francis

iUniverse, Inc.
Bloomington

A Rooted Sorrow

iUniverse books may be ordered through booksellers or by contacting:

iUniverse
1663 Liberty Drive
Bloomington, IN 47403
www.iuniverse.com
1-800-Authors (1-800-288-4677)

ISBN: 978-1-4759-8145-2 (sc)
ISBN: 978-1-4759-8148-3 (ebk)

Library of Congress Control Number: 2013904679

Printed in the United States of America

iUniverse rev. date: 04/22/2013

AUTHOR'S NOTE

To the owners and residents of the magnificent El Dorado building in the Upper West Side of Manhattan I must apologize for squeezing the insignificant and slightly seamy Benjamin Thompson School into their corner of West 90th Street and Central Park West. Worse things have happened in the history of the novel, however; in *Gaudy Night*, Dorothy Sayers constructed a whole women's college on the sacred cricket ground of Balliol College, Oxford.

A Rooted Sorrow follows the further adventures of a character from my *Death at the Nave* (Writers' Club Press, 2002) and *The Place of a Skull* (Iuniverse, 2013), but the story is perfectly self-contained.

A Rooted Sorrow

Macbeth: *Canst thou not minister to a mind diseas'd,*
Pluck from the memory a rooted sorrow,
Raze out the written troubles of the brain,
And with some sweet oblivious antidote
Cleanse the stuff'd bosom of that perilous stuff
Which weighs upon the heart?

1

"Susan, Susan . . ."

Jessica's screams reverberated on and on, as if trapped in a huge echo chamber, mingling with the sound of her body hurtling down an endless staircase, and continuing even after the terrible thud that ought to have ended everything. Now Susan was crying for her dead lover and her grief was intolerable. A truck made its slithering way along a narrow, muddy lane, and they were out of the echo chamber and into the open, where it was dark and raining. People were digging Jessica's grave among dead leaves and dripping trees. Phrases from the burial service struggled to penetrate the heavy, sodden air. "Earth to earth, ashes to ashes, dust to dust; in sure and certain hope . . ."

John Hume, who had once been Captain John Berkeley of the Royal Navy, awakened very gradually from a dream that he had endured hundreds of times. It took him a long time to realize that it was his own voice that had reached him through the dark rain and over the dark years. Jessica was in a real grave now, not in a home-made coffin among the oak roots, and not lying beneath the foundations of a jerry-built science building at the Nave School, where they had hastily moved her at the end of the war. Hume had taught chemistry there for twenty years, with Jessica's remains thirty feet below his lab, but the fire that had gutted the building had left its foundations open to the explorations of a group of curious schoolboys, bringing his long vigil to an end.

She's gone away and she doesn't know me any more, he thought. *So if the police decide they don't want me, there's no point in staying here.*

Perhaps if he were thousands of miles away, the dreams would stop.

"Well, Mr. Hume, now that the Chief Constable has decided not to prosecute, that's really the end of the matter."

So said Inspector Phelps, sitting at his desk in Gloucester Central Police Station in the West of England, on a cold, wet day in late December 1965. Hume, with his grey hair, his shabby blue suit and his scholarly stoop, looked like the archetype of the world-weary middle-aged schoolmaster that he actually was, and quite unlike the tall, vigorous captain of one of His Majesty's destroyers that he had been when King George VI was on the throne and the country was at war.

"Maybe it is for you. I'd almost rather you prosecuted."

"So would I, if you want to know the truth, as long as it's 'almost.' You've admitted doing something criminal and immoral and causing the death of a young girl, but apart from you and your wife we have no witnesses and no evidence. You won't tell the whole story because you don't want Mrs. Berkeley to be involved, and she won't say a word against you. And in any case, the C. C. thinks that having been torpedoed and half drowned gave you some excuse for going off the rails, added to which we're talking about something that happened twenty-five years ago. On the whole I think he's right."

Looking at the hopeless, defeated human being before him, Phelps asked, "What are you going to do now?"

"I don't know—settle some things with Susan and arrange a divorce, I suppose. Maybe I can get some kind of a job on a merchant ship. I'd like to be a very long way away from here. I'm going to continue being Hume, by the way."

"John Hume" was the name under which he had worked at the Nave while his secret remained underground, and it caused some difficulty at the American Embassy in London where visa applicants who had changed their names by deed poll were not often seen. So it was as John Hume that he arrived in New York

City on a Wednesday near the end of January, having worked his passage on a small cargo boat.

Having proved that he could still earn a living of sorts on the high seas, Hume pondered the only thing he felt qualified to do on dry land—namely to teach chemistry and, if necessary, physics or mathematics. On his way across the Atlantic he had found out where cheap lodgings were available, and on the morning after his arrival he sat in a coffee shop studying the Education Section of the *New York Times*. It seemed that science and math teachers were in great demand and, noting the qualifications required for public school employment, he realized that he would have to look for work at a private school. A good honors degree in natural sciences from Cambridge University carried a lot of weight in England, where there were still headmasters who preferred applicants who had not been corrupted by teacher training courses, but apparently things were different in New York. Fortunately there seemed to be a lot of private schools, and he noticed that there were several in Upper Manhattan on either side of Central Park. Manhattan seemed to be generally very noisy and very dirty, so the idea of being close to the park appealed to him. Nearly all the ads were for teachers to start in September, but the Benjamin Thompson School needed a science teacher with strong qualifications in chemistry to start immediately. Benjamin Thompson; that name rang a bell—something about an American who achieved eminence as Europe's leading military entrepreneur, bored a lot of cannon barrels and had some early inklings of the kinetic theory. Hume paid his bill, obtained a supply of small change and made for the pay phone just inside the door. Grades 7-12, co-ed—Hume had only the haziest notions of American education, but that obviously meant that unlike the Nave, this place would be full of adolescent girls as well as boys.

The Benjamin Thompson School consisted of Nos. 1 and 3, West 90th Street. No. 1 was a large converted town house on the corner of West 90th and Central Park West, with its main entrance a few paces along the side street. The large glass and metal front door, three steps up from the sidewalk, opened onto a wide space with two doors on the right, the first labeled "Headmaster" and the second, "Business Office." Straight ahead there was an ornate archway with an imposing oak door, behind which was an auditorium that could accommodate the school's one hundred and fifty students. On the left, opposite the headmaster's door, was a somewhat less impressive portal that led to the stairs to the basement and the upper rooms. A little further along was the reception desk and beyond that the doors to the back stairs and the elevator. The upper floors were devoted to classrooms and laboratories for the high school classes. No. 3, a smaller building with a separate entrance a little further along the street, provided space for the seventh and eighth grade classrooms, the school library and the faculty lounge.

While Hume was studying the *Times*, James Hamilton, Head of Science at the Benjamin Thompson School, was in conference with the headmaster. Looking up from the small pile of papers on the headmaster's desk, he said, "Nothing doing, and I'm not surprised."

Aloysius Thornbury stood at the open window of his office, puffing smoke from a cheroot into the frigid air of West 90th Street. Approaching sixty, he was tall and athletic-looking, and still possessed a head of well-groomed, dark brown hair. At this moment, however, his shoulders sagged and his conventionally handsome features wore an expression of extreme weariness and anxiety.

"Listen to this, for instance", Hamilton continued: "'My degree is in English but I have always been interested in chemistry and I would be willing to undertake any necessary additional studies if the school would pay the expenses thereof.' And here's a woman who studied agriculture for two years and would be willing to teach from three till six every afternoon and feels sure that we could easily rearrange the schedule. Well, what can you really expect with the salary we're offering—that and the acute shortage of science teachers?"

Thornbury crushed his cheroot and sat down opposite Hamilton.

"And the fact that it's the middle of the school year. Well, there's nothing we can do about the goddamn salary and the second semester starts next week, so it looks as if it will have to be plan B. How about it, Jim? You said you'd hold the fort till we got a replacement—what if we can't get one?"

Hamilton, who was a little shorter, balder, more solidly built and fifteen years younger than the headmaster, looked up wearily.

"You must be joking, Allie. That was before we realized that Herb was going to be out indefinitely. I'm overloaded as it is, and chemistry takes hours of preparation in addition to the actual teaching."

Herbert Weinstock, the Deputy Headmaster, had suffered a stroke a week previously and was still in the hospital. Hamilton was now sharing Weinstock's duties with Andrew Johnson, the business administrator, whose office was next door to the headmaster's.

"I suppose there's no chance of letting Miller come back", Hamilton went on without much conviction. "I mean with suitable cautions and undertakings."

"None whatever—we managed to hush it up, which is where half of this year's budget went, and you didn't hear me say that, but that only means it's quiet on the surface. Everybody knows what really happened."

"Everybody knows what Amanda Friedman says happened."

"We accepted her story because it was the only way of making the thing go away. Anyway, I think she's telling the truth."

There was a buzz from the intercom and Hamilton was silent. Thornbury ignored the buzz and lit another cheroot.

"OK—*officially* I think she's telling the truth. I know what you think."

Hamilton grunted.

"I think she's a goddamn liar."

"Yes, but what good does that do? It's so damn frustrating—here we are with a school named after one of America's great scientific figures and the best applicant we have is someone with a degree in farming . . ."

Hamilton laughed.

"Come on, Allie, nobody's ever heard of Benjamin Thompson. You know the story as well as I do."

It was said that the founders had originally named the school after Benjamin Franklin, and the sculptor had got as far as carving the first name on the stone slab that formed part of the building's rebuilt façade when someone pointed out that there was already a Benjamin Franklin School in the city. After a quick conference it was decided to save time and money by honoring Franklin's less distinguished contemporary, who had actually preferred to be known by the spurious title of Count Rumford and spent most of his life in Europe. In spite of this rather rocky beginning, the school had achieved its object of becoming known as a fine all-around institution with a particularly strong science program. Thornbury knew the old story very well and claimed that he didn't believe a word of it, but he took the precaution of making sure that all faculty and staff members knew enough about Thompson to answer the inevitable question.

The intercom buzzed again and a moment later there was a tap on the door, which opened a foot or so, revealing a young female head topped by a mass of curly brown hair.

"Excuse me, Mr. Thornbury, but there's a man on the line who says he's a chemistry teacher and can do general science, physics and math if they're needed. He has a degree from Cambridge University and twenty years' teaching experience. And he knows who Benjamin Thompson was."

"Ask him if he can come in at four o'clock for an interview."

"Today, Mr. Thornbury?"

"Yes, today."

The curly head came a little further into the room, supported by a small, slim figure in a tight red sweater and a black skirt of a brevity that was not yet fashionable but soon would be.

"But Dr. and Mrs. Friedman are coming at four o'clock. Wouldn't you like to talk to him now?"

"No, I wouldn't, but I don't want to let him get away. Put the Friedmans off till tomorrow . . . No, that won't do—we already put them off once. The PTA officers are coming at two—Oh I hate this job—what's this fellow's name?"

"John Hume."

"OK, Sally, tell him to come at three fifteen. He'll have to fight his way through the crowd around the front door, but you never know—maybe he likes kids."

Sally Evans departed and, turning back to Hamilton, Thornbury added absent-mindedly, "Some teachers do, you know . . . Now how are we going to explain why we need somebody in such a hurry?"

"I don't know, Allie, but if you would close the window the cigar smoke would stand a better chance of hiding the smell of scotch, and our applicant won't think he's freezing to death. Are you fit to do an interview today?"

"I'm perfectly OK, and if you start fussing I'll schedule you for chemistry whether you like it or not."

"And if you don't get your act together pretty soon you may find yourself looking for two new science teachers instead of one. There's still some dignity attached to being head of science at the Benjamin Thompson School, and you're a good headmaster when you're sober, but the way things are going . . ."

"OK, OK, I was only joking."

Thornbury lit another cheroot while Hamilton left the room without saying whether he was joking.

2

Hume had brought only what he could pack into two medium-sized suitcases, and the only respectable clothing in his possession was his old blue suit. He hadn't expected such a quick response to his phone call, and there wouldn't have been time to go out and buy something even if he'd had the money. Fortunately he had a clean shirt, a decent pair of shoes and a fairly presentable overcoat, so he thought he might just pass muster as a transplanted English schoolmaster. What concerned him more was the problem of concocting a suitable story to explain his presence in New York. Why would a fifty-five-year-old teacher with a good position at a good English school decide to uproot himself in the middle of the academic year and arrive in Manhattan with not much more than the clothes on his back? His connection with the young girl whose skeleton had turned up under his old lab in Gloucester had never been made public, and the two people at the Nave School who knew the truth could be trusted to keep it to themselves, so he was free to make up any story that seemed plausible.

He was still trying to think of something that an intelligent person might possibly believe when he emerged from the subway at West 86th Street and had his first view of Central Park. Walking up Central Park West, with some fairly posh buildings on his left and trees and open space on his right, he began to have a better feeling about Manhattan.

On reaching the corner of West 90th Street, he saw a crowd of teenage boys and girls milling around, and the fact that he had realized theoretically a couple of hours earlier became concretely visible. Ever since the dreadful episode with Jessica he had done his best to avoid the company of women under the age of about twenty-five, not so much because he was really afraid of anything like that happening again as because the memory was so painful that he couldn't bear having it stirred up in any way. As he worked his way through the crowd he thought they seemed very young and harmless enough—healthy boys and girls glad to be done with lessons for another day—so perhaps it would be a good thing to deal with his anxieties head on and dispose of them. Jessica, he reminded himself, had truly been one of a kind, and he had been quite a young man at the time. Switching his mind back to the impending interview, he remembered another thing that would have to be explained; why his Cambridge degree was in the name of Berkeley.

"Mr. Hume?"

It struck Hume that the receptionist's cheeky smile had something to do with the stocky, middle-aged man who appeared to have withdrawn rather hurriedly into a corner. She didn't look much older than the high school girls on the street, and Hume was surprised and slightly alarmed to find himself taking note of her obvious attractions. Well, he was starting a new life so maybe it wasn't such a bad thing as long as it didn't get out of hand. He smiled back.

"Yes, John Hume. I believe the headmaster is expecting me."

"I'll look in and see if he's ready".

Thornbury was still wreathed in smoke when Sally's familiar curls reappeared in his doorway.

"Mr. Hume is here, Mr. Thornbury."

Thornbury took a couple of extra-large puffs on his cheroot before putting it out and hiding the ashtray. Hamilton, who had come out of his corner and followed Sally into the room, took a deep breath and went into a violent fit of coughing.

"OK, Sally, count slowly up to twenty and then bring him in."

"Don't you think it would be a good idea to open the window for few minutes first?"

"No, just for God's sake do as I say."

He slapped Hamilton vigorously on the back.

"Come on, Jim, pull yourself together."

"OK, OK, I'm alright—it's your disgusting cigar. I hope he doesn't take one sniff and walk out."

"Mr. Hume", Sally announced as Hamilton went into another fit of coughing. "Oh, Mr. Hamilton, would you like a glass of water?"

"Yes, please", Hamilton croaked.

"Welcome to the Benjamin Thompson School, Mr. Hume. I am Aloysius Thornbury and I have the honor to be Headmaster. This is James Hamilton, the head of our distinguished science department."

Hume peered through the blue haze and took the headmaster's outstretched hand. He was about to greet the science head similarly but Sally had re-entered and a glass of water materialized in Hamilton's proffered hand, so the men sat down, Sally left and Thornbury started on his prepared speech.

The whole scene had only lasted a minute, but during that time something had happened to Hume's perception of the situation, something about the quality of the people he was meeting. Thornbury was speaking, but Hume was only half listening, hearing an undercurrent of anxiety to please and impress, and wondering why an interview would be conducted in such an overpowering fog and whether the slight tremor in the headmaster's grip had anything to do with the trace of alcohol in the air. It was almost as if twenty-five years were rolling away, and he was once again a naval officer assessing the state of one of his men. Hamilton would probably turn out to be all he should be if only he could stop coughing, and Sally seemed efficient as well as intriguing, but there was something not quite right about Thornbury.

"We understand that you are a graduate of Cambridge University and taught for twenty years in England. Since our need is quite urgent there won't be time to check on your qualifications and references before deciding whether to hire you, but we shall, of course, need all the details. I assume you have a *curriculum vitae* with you.

Hume had never heard of a *curriculum vitae* but he remembered enough Latin to figure out what it probably was.

"No, I haven't. I have second class honors in the Natural Science Tripos, and I prepared pupils for General Certificate and college entrance exams in chemistry at the Nave School in Gloucester. You could telephone my college and my former headmaster in Gloucester, but apart from that I'm afraid you'll just have to take my word for it—or not, as the case may be."

Hamilton had stopped coughing and grunted disapprovingly.

"To put it bluntly, Mr. Hume, you don't seem very well prepared for this interview."

"That's true, Mr. Hamilton, but I am very well prepared to teach chemistry. I made the decision to come to this country rather abruptly and it never occurred to me to ask for references. Perhaps you would prefer to terminate the interview at this point."

Hume started to get to his feet but Thornbury was quick to interpose:

"Oh no, Mr. Hume—as you say, a couple of phone calls will give us enough to go on for the time being, and an English second class degree would be called *magna cum laude* in this country. But you will understand that we really need to know why you left your previous position so abruptly."

Hume had still not made up his mind how to deal with this question, so he said the first thing that came into his head. This had the advantage of containing a few grains of truth.

"Well, if you must know, it was the result of an intolerable marital situation and a messy divorce. I certainly don't intend to go into the details, but my wife and I were both at fault and once we had agreed about the way it would go I made it easy for her to divorce me. The official record of the divorce isn't available yet but it soon will be. I had been a naval officer in the war and I wanted to get a long way away, so I got my visa and worked my passage to New York. While we're on the subject of sudden departures, am I to take it someone left here in a hurry?"

Thornbury was no more prepared for the question than Hume had been for his. His mouth opened, closed and opened again.

"Well, you see . . ." he began and looked appealingly at Hamilton, whose relative sobriety allowed his wits to work quicker.

"Our previous teacher, Peter Miller, had to return to California on urgent family business."

"I see. Are you expecting him to come back at any time? I mean are we talking about a temporary position?"

Thornbury and Hamilton both started talking and appeared to be contradicting each other, so Hume butted in.

"At this point it doesn't matter to me whether it's temporary, permanent or something in between. I can assure you that my lab technique is excellent and I know much more chemistry than anyone in this building is ever likely to need. If you take me to the lab I'll show you."

This produced a long silence, eventually broken by Hamilton.

"That's a good idea. It's on the third floor and I'll take you up now. There's no need for you to come, headmaster—I know you have a lot on your plate just now."

3

Hamilton took Hume up to the third floor in a small, old-fashioned elevator with noisy, hand-operated doors that opened onto a wide space from which five more doors led. Two of these were to the front and back stairs, two were to classrooms, and the remaining one, on the left as they came out of the elevator, was the lab door. The lab looked well organized, with stools, workbenches, sinks and all the usual chemicals, glassware and burners. The demonstration bench was to the left as they entered, and in the opposite wall there was a door leading to an office and a small room where chemicals and apparatus were kept.

"This is really a general science lab", Hamilton explained. "Everyone does general science in the junior high grades. Then there's biology in the tenth grade, physics in the eleventh and chemistry in the senior year. I have a bio lab directly above here and some of the general science is taught there, too. It's very different from the British system as far as I understand it."

"I'm willing to teach whatever is needed and I'd be quite happy with a temporary position—would you like me to do a demonstration for you?"

"I don't think that's necessary, Mr. Hume. As you say, a couple of phone calls will verify your qualifications."

"Then I'd like to know more about the school and what really happened to Mr. Miller."

This was a shot in the dark but it seemed to hit some kind of target.

"Well, you do come straight to the point. The fact is nobody's quite sure about Miller, but I'd better give you the official version and then I'll tell you what I know. If you're going to be here you'll get all the other versions within the first forty-eight hours. Miller came to the East coast two and a half years ago with a degree from Caltech and a job at G. E. in Schenectady—that's upstate New York. Apparently they didn't hit it off too well, but we gathered that he had left of his own accord and he brought satisfactory references. His version was that he had always wanted to teach but wanted to get some experience in industry first and make himself financially secure. It hadn't worked out the way he had expected and he thought it was better to make the break sooner rather than later. He was twenty-four, tall, dark and handsome and we thought there was probably more to it than met the eye, but with our budget and the enormous difficulty of getting any kind of science teacher we decided to go ahead—well, Mr. Thornbury did and I backed him up."

Hume smiled.

"And now you're in a similar position with me."

"True, but unlike you he had no teaching experience and he was young and very attractive to females of all ages. There were some disciplinary difficulties with the younger general science classes but he knew his subject inside-out and he really hit it off with the senior class."

"And that, if I may guess, was the cause of the trouble?"

"Exactly. It wasn't only that he was good-looking—he has a sense of humor, a faintly provocative manner and a streak of the kind of idealism that appeals to teenagers and might just be bogus. So there were starry-eyed girls swooning over him and finding all kinds of reasons why they needed to spend time talking to him at recess, lunchtime and after school. With a lot of help and good advice from me he managed to survive his first year, but one of the eleventh grade girls already had her eye on him and started writing notes to him. When we came back in September there was a lot of gossip. He admitted that he was attracted and that they had met surreptitiously a couple of times over the summer, but he swore that nothing serious had happened."

"And you believed him?"

"Not exactly—there was really no way of knowing, and we obviously didn't want to stir anything up, so we decided to let it go. Amanda Friedman—the girl in question—was quiet about it at first and just went around looking like the cat that had swallowed the canary, but unfortunately for her she had a rival. Her name is Jill Davis, and by Christmas it looked as if Miller had really fallen for her—enough, at any rate, to put Amanda's nose out of joint. I talked to him, of course, and once again he swore that there was nothing in it. But over the vacation Amanda started telling everyone who would listen that Miller had taken her out in his car and had sex with her on the back seat and furthermore they were still lovers. We had anxious calls from a lot of parents and it seemed that the only people who hadn't heard the story were the Friedmans—or so they said when the shit finally hit the fan."

Hume grunted and Hamilton said, "Oh, I'm sorry—excuse my French!"

The Englishman smiled and said, "I like your French—it's just that they didn't teach us that particular idiom at school."

"OK, one day we must swap idioms. Anyway, the denouement took place a couple of weeks ago, and in my opinion it was a frame-up. Regular classes end every day at three o'clock and then we have various clubs, tutorials and so on. Well, about 3:30 last Thursday, Amanda came running down the stairs. She looked very disheveled and claimed that Miller had tried to rape her. She said that she went along at first but changed her mind and told him to stop. He wouldn't stop, she said, but she struggled free and ran downstairs. I happened to be at the front desk talking to Sally. No one else was around, so we came up here and found Miller back there in the office, doing some correcting. Everything seemed to be in order, except that his tie was crooked and there was a pair of panties under his table where he couldn't see them. I told Sally to pick them up and take Amanda to the bathroom—Sally's very quick on the uptake. Well, to cut a long story short, the panties were Amanda's. Miller said that he had been working in his office and Amanda came in to ask him something about an assignment.

She sat with him for a few minutes while he explained it and then she threw her arms around his neck and tried to kiss him. He said he managed to get her to stop and leave and that was that. He seemed astonished when Sally fished the panties out. Anyway we had to call the Friedmans in and they convinced us that they would call the police unless Miller was fired immediately and a suitable payment was forthcoming to compensate Amanda for her trauma. And the fact is that as far as the school's reputation is concerned it doesn't make a hell of a lot of difference whether the story is true or not—as soon as it gets out there people start nodding their heads and saying, 'Ah yes, that's the sort of thing that goes on in these fancy private schools.' So the whole thing was more or less settled within twenty-four hours and the headmaster is just putting the finishing touches on it now. All we need to complete the deal is a new chemistry teacher—except that I don't believe Amanda's story. I think she set him up."

"Do you have any concrete evidence of that?"

"Not exactly, but the whole thing seemed very fishy. She obviously had a severe crush on Miller and put about all those stories about having sex with him. Then someone else comes along and pushes her out and she hits on a way of getting her own back. It's exactly the kind of thing I might have expected Amanda to do. She's a very manipulative child with a knack of getting her own way somehow or other and if she can't get it she's apt to get nasty. Another thing is that apparently she hasn't said a word to anyone in the school about the incident. Part of the agreement was that the thing would be kept strictly within the small group of people who were directly involved—that's Amanda, Miller, Sally and me. It was just our good luck that no one else was around at the time, except for poor old Herb Weinstock, the Deputy Headmaster. He came out of his office to see what was going on and promptly had a stroke. But I just can't believe that if Miller really tried to rape her she wouldn't have told a few of her closest friends—in strict confidence, of course, but we know what that means. They tell their friends in strict confidence and within a few hours it's common knowledge. But if she set him up she might have thought that it was safer not to talk about it."

"Was she wearing shoes?"

"Good question—as it happened, it had snowed the previous day and then thawed overnight so she had left her wet shoes in her locker and gone around all day in knee-socks. So maybe she had the whole thing worked out beforehand."

"And you're telling me all this because you think I may get some of the backwash from it?"

"Well, frankly, we're in pretty much the same position. We need a teacher and you need a job. We have something to hide and so have you. Not that I think you told us any lies—you just left something out—the real reason why you couldn't stand being in England any more. Yes, I have one or two colleagues who will take you aside and whisper in your ear that there are certain things that you ought to know in your own interest. And the same ones will talk behind your back about this odd Englishman who appears in the middle of the year and won't say anything about his family or his background. Don't get me wrong—I don't have that kind of curiosity. As long as you can teach chemistry I don't care if you're a Russian spy or the Emperor of Siam."

Hume didn't reply. Hamilton had touched the fringe of his secret and sent him back twenty-five years and three thousand miles for an involuntary re-enactment of the terrible scene—Jessica running away from him, calling Susan's name, falling down the stairs and lying in a pool of her own blood, with Susan weeping over her; it still seemed so odd that he and his wife had both fallen in love with the same girl. He wrenched himself back into the present but didn't trust himself to speak.

"Look", Hamilton said, "I can see I put my foot in it. As long as it wasn't something vicious or criminal it's none of our business here. I can tell a good man when I see one, so let me give you some brochures and take you on a tour of the school. The headmaster is busy with the Friedmans right now—just the finishing touches I guess—but as far as I'm concerned the job is yours if you want it. And if your qualifications don't check out we can fire you."

Hume had to work hard to overcome an impulse to tell Hamilton the whole story, to acknowledge the viciousness and criminality of what he had done. He tried to regain the poise and confidence that he had begun to feel a few minutes earlier.

"All right. I think I can tell a good man, too. I'm not running away from the police but there is one other complication. I took my degree at Cambridge under the name of Berkeley and changed it to Hume after leaving the navy in 1945."

"I guess I shouldn't ask why."

"No, please don't. I might be tempted to tell you."

Aloysius Thornbury saw the Friedmans to the front door and went back to his office. Sally had left for the day and there were no students around, so he left his door open, opened the window, lit another cheroot and took his bottle of Johnny Walker out of the file cabinet. Hamilton and Hume must be in the building somewhere, but what the hell—he had to do something to relax. The PTA officers had been very officious (Come to think of it, wasn't that what officers were supposed to be?) and had asked him for a more detailed explanation of Miller's sudden departure, which struck them as very fishy although they didn't say so in so many words. They remained unconvinced by the official explanation and wanted to know what the school was doing about a replacement, so Thornbury was very relieved to be able to tell them that a highly qualified applicant was being interviewed that very afternoon. They viewed the developing hippie movement with great alarm and were very concerned about dress regulations, drugs, sex and rock-and-roll, demanding all kinds of assurances about order, discipline and appropriate behavior. They complained bitterly about the way Sally dressed, and it looked as if he would have to speak to her about it, which would be a pity.

And then the Friedmans—well, they had the upper hand and they weren't likely to let him forget it. Mrs. Friedman was big, buxom and blustery, a type that Thornbury knew how to handle, but her husband was small, bald, beady-eyed, soft-spoken and slyly intimidating. The school's legal advisers and the executive committee of the Board of Trustees had signed off on the agreement, so as far as Thornbury could see, the only reason why the Friedmans had insisted on another meeting was to keep stirring the pot and make sure that no one felt that the school was off the hook.

"Don't forget", Dr. Friedman had said as the headmaster held the door for him, "two hundred grand is just a token compared with what we could get if this came to court. We expect only the best for our daughter from now on. You think about it."

Knowing exactly what this meant—an easy ride, straight A's and an outstanding college recommendation—Thornbury had gone back to his office and thought about it. So far he had managed to keep the lid on the story so that the school's outer image had not yet been tarnished. The glory days might be over but it was a good image—a decent, middle-of-the-road private school staffed with competent teachers in a good location where children were as safe as they could be in Manhattan. But it was a hell of a strain even when things went smoothly, and there was the constant fear that the scandal would become public property. Miller, of course, had not admitted guilt and had threatened legal action, so to make the thing work he had had to be schmeered pretty heavily too. He probably wouldn't talk and Sally could be trusted, so it all depended on Amanda and her parents keeping their side of the bargain—but the girl was a blabbermouth and her parents would take advantage of the situation in any way they could. Hearing voices, he took another nip and put the bottle away.

Hamilton came in and closed the door.

"I don't think there's any point in beating about the bush. He's the only genuine applicant we have, and I think we should ask him to start next week so we have him for the whole second semester. We'll have all day tomorrow to check up on him. And I think we should offer him the regular salary because he may be really good and he may want to stay."

"In other words, we give him a contract for the rest of the year and take it from there."

"Exactly."

"OK. Well, there is one way of saving a little money. I don't suppose he's found anywhere permanent to live yet."

He rolled his eyes meaningly in the direction of No. 3.

"That's good idea."

At the top of No. 3, West 90th Street, was a furnished room with a kitchenette and bathroom attached that was available for visiting dignitaries and guest teachers. This was strictly illegal as it was accessible only by a single staircase and off limits to students and teachers, but no one stayed there for more than a couple of days at a time and no questions had ever been asked.

"We can't officially make him pay rent but we could make an arrangement with him and reduce his salary accordingly."

"Are you going to tell him it's illegal?"

"I'll think about it. Let's have him in."

Hume was quite happy to agree to any contract he was offered. He realized that there might come a time at which he would have second thoughts, but at that moment the only pang of regret that he suffered was caused by the thought that he was substituting the cigar-smoking, unsteady, faintly alcoholic Aloysius Thornbury for his old headmaster at the Nave School in Gloucester, the impeccably honest, straightforward, clear-headed Colin Woodcock.

4

In the early afternoon of the following day, Colin Woodcock received a buzz from his wife, who happened also to be his secretary.

"There's a Mr. Thornbury from New York on the line. He's the headmaster of a school in Manhattan and it seems that John Hume has applied for a job there."

This was something that Woodcock had not expected, being under the impression that Hume intended to restart his maritime career.

"You'd better stay on the line", he said, and made up his mind to give the most positive impression possible. He assured Thornbury that Hume had been a very good teacher, had been at the Nave for twenty years and that his sudden departure was not due to any problem at the school.

"He told us that he had been involved in a difficult divorce", Thornbury said.

"That's true. It seems that things became very difficult in December and during the Christmas holidays he told me that he needed to get away. He was very apologetic about it."

"Rather an extreme reaction, wouldn't you say?"

"Yes", Woodcock replied, trying to think of an explanation that would sound satisfactory without bending the truth too much. "I thought that the whole thing might have been a regrettable misunderstanding, but it seems that he and his wife agreed that they were incompatible and there were some incidents that left them both deeply hurt. He said that he realized he was reacting more like a twenty-year-old than a fifty-five-year old but he couldn't bear the thought of remaining among the surroundings where he had been so happy for such a long time."

This last sentence was complete fiction, as contrasted with the previous one, which had been about fifty-fifty. It was true that the divorce had recently been finalized, but Hume and his wife had separated in 1941. Thornbury said that he couldn't help feeling there must be more to it than that and Woodcock agreed that there might well be, but it was a question that only Hume could answer.

"Can you confirm that he was a naval officer and holds a degree from Cambridge University?"

"Yes, he was captain of a destroyer and served throughout the war with great distinction. Naturally we check up on all these things—he took his degree under the name of Berkeley, by the way."

"So he said. Was there ever an explanation of that?"

"Not that I know of—he was appointed by my predecessor in 1945."

"Well, thank you very much, Mr. Woodcock. You've been very helpful."

"Well done", Mrs. Woodcock commented. "I didn't know you were such a good liar."

5

No. 3, West 90th Street, was a narrow building with two rooms on each floor. Hume was very relieved to be able to move into the apartment on the fifth floor—not that he had much to move. The elevator went only as far as the fourth floor, where the school library occupied both rooms, and the third floor was devoted to the faculty lounge and the art room. The seventh and eighth grades were housed on the first and second floors. Teachers were not usually given basement keys, but Hume's set included both a basement and a front door key so that he would be able to reach the back staircase by entering through the basement door and get to his apartment unseen by anyone in the building. The thick steel door at the foot of his private staircase could always be opened from the inside but was kept locked from the outside during school hours. Once past it he felt as if he was in a world of his own; he would miss his books, his piano and his records but at least he was assured of peace and quiet.

He looked at his schedule and reviewed the situation; general science classes with eighth and ninth grades, algebra II with the slower half of the eleventh grade, chemistry with the twelfth, calculus with small group of seniors and study hall supervision three times a week. Miller had left no reports of any kind in his precipitate departure, so the only recourse would be to familiarize himself thoroughly with the textbooks and rely on the students to give him an idea of how far along they were. Well, perhaps he could get Hamilton to select a couple of dependable students from each class and he could talk to them before the lessons started. Meanwhile he needed some new clothes. Teachers were paid in advance and he already had his February check in his wallet, but today was Friday, January 28th, so he wouldn't be able to draw on it until Tuesday. He really couldn't go on wearing his old blue suit much longer and felt relieved to see that the school provided long white lab coats. At least he would be able to cover up to a certain extent.

A quick look at the textbooks revealed that the work was on a fairly simple level compared with what had been the norm at the Nave, so Hume spent his weekend wandering around the city, prey to all kinds of uncomfortable thoughts. Rushing off to America had seemed like a good idea, not because he really thought it was possible to leave the unbearable past behind but because it would provide him with a set of distractions and perhaps lead to a future without painful associations. Saturday seemed interminable and there were moments when he heartily wished he were back in England, where the sedative qualities of his familiar possessions and his comfortable landlady would have been available. He had kept his flat in Gloucester and paid six months rent in advance, which was why he was so short of money now. If he wanted to he could just change his mind and run back again. There was no official record against him and science teachers were just as much in demand in England as they were in America. But that kind of retreat was impossible; maybe later but not now. He had made a commitment and had a check in his pocket to prove it. If he could get through the next few months successfully he might feel like going back. He'd have to wait and see.

Sunday was sunny and relatively warm. The Natural History Museum and the Metropolitan were both within easy walking distance, but Hume didn't feel like museums, so he decided to walk through Central Park, down Fifth Avenue and take a look at the fabled Carnegie Hall on the way back. Working his way diagonally toward the East Side, he came to the Alice in Wonderland group and the small pond where children would be sailing their model boats in the summer. On this occasion there were no boats, but the fine weather had enticed enough people into the park to give the feeling of an early spring day. Parents sat on the benches watching their offspring playing around the statues, and Hume found something almost heart-easing about the scene. He sat for a moment and was slightly surprised to see Aloysius Thornbury in earnest conversation with a girl of seventeen or so. There was no reason why Thornbury shouldn't have a daughter of that age, but there was something business-like about her attitude that gave a different impression. She was wearing a down overcoat but no hat, and her long blonde hair concealed most of her face, so that she had to keep brushing it back from her eyes. Thornbury was well muffled up in spite of the mild weather, but when the sunlight fell on his face Hume saw a look of mixed anger and desperation. The girl appeared to finish what she had to say, but as the headmaster turned away she added two words that were plainly audible.

"I'm serious."

Thornbury took two more paces before looking over his shoulder.

Hume wasn't quite sure what he said, but it sounded like, "You stupid little bitch!"

The girl shrugged and walked in Hume's direction, automatically pulling her hair away from her eyes as she did so. He decided to make himself scarce but not before he had a good view of a pretty face with something as hard as nails underneath. He thought he could make a very good guess as to her identity.

6

At three o'clock on the following Friday afternoon, Hume was sitting in the office behind the lab, waiting for Hamilton to show up for a discussion of his first week's work on American soil. He had already developed a good working relation with the Science Head, who was always ready to help him out with information about the way things were done in American schools and advice about dealing with anxious parents. However, when Hamilton did appear he seemed to be in a hurry.

"Sorry, John, I can't talk much now. You look healthy enough so I guess things haven't been too bad."

"Beginner's luck, probably", Hume said. "I do have some questions for you but nothing that can't wait until Monday."

"Tell you what—why don't you come to supper tomorrow? My wife didn't like Miller—she thought he was a fake—but she's very anxious to meet this mysterious Englishman."

Hume hesitated, nervous about the possibility of being quizzed about his past. Hamilton sensed what the problem was.

"Don't worry—we'll be very tactful. Come at six o'clock and you and I can talk shop for a while and then try to forget school for the rest of the evening."

Hume agreed and Hamilton left him to do his own review.

On the whole it hadn't been too bad. The eighth-graders were a bunch of chatterboxes but he had found the ninth grade unexpectedly serious-minded and the eleventh deeply concerned about the rapidly approaching SAT's. Chemistry with the twelfth grade had gone quite well and he thought that Miller must have been a very good teacher, whatever his other faults might have been. There had been a certain amount of good-natured teasing about his English accent, and he had found it unwise to crack any but the most obvious jokes, since American students didn't seem to be tuned in to the kind of verbal and situational humor that was the staff of life to the English schoolboy. It wasn't due to any lack of intelligence, he thought; they just didn't expect that kind of thing.

The class that concerned him most was the one that he had expected to be the easiest to handle—the twelfth grade calculus group. The work was easy enough and the students were well motivated but there were some obvious undercurrents or, perhaps, over-currents, due to the presence of Amanda Friedman and Jill Davis in the same small class. This was supposed to be an elective course, open only to students who were already fluent in algebra and trigonometry, but Amanda had wormed her way into it, presumably so that she could be with her beloved Miller, who must have turned a blind eye on her obvious difficulties. That had been at the beginning of the school year, and when Miller had switched his attentions to Jill (if that was actually the case) he had been stuck with Amanda in the class for the rest of the year. Jill looked like a cuddly little brunette but she was a very gifted student and felt free to express her contempt for Amanda's mental processes. "The dumb blonde strikes again", she would mutter when Amanda made an obvious mistake or asked to have a second or third repeat of something that everyone else had understood the first time around. Jill had a problem of her own, however; she was quite short-sighted and sometimes had trouble seeing the blackboard. Hume asked her why she didn't have glasses and she replied that she was waiting for a new prescription to come through.

Amanda was very polite to Hume whereas Jill would speak to him only in reply to a direct question, never volunteered in class and stalked straight out of the door at the end of every lesson. Other students often wanted to talk and ask questions and Amanda was usually the last to leave, giving Hume an awful feeling that she would soon ask him for some extra help. If that happened he'd have to ask Hamilton for some advice—he certainly didn't want to be alone in a room with Amanda. Meanwhile, if Jill didn't cease and desist pretty soon he'd certainly have to speak to her.

Hume's thoughts passed on to his new colleagues. Hamilton, who taught biological sciences and evidently functioned as the headmaster's right-hand man, seemed to be the complete professional as far as his dealings with students, teachers and parents were concerned, but Hume had seen that beneath this professionalism there was a private person with doubts and reservations. Hamilton's willingness to let various cats out of the bag at their first meeting had probably been uncharacteristic, as had Hume's almost overwhelming impulse to reveal his own guilty secret, but the Englishman sensed in his new colleague a carefully, perhaps painfully, concealed vulnerability that echoed his own. The feeling of trust and shared values reminded him of Colin Woodcock, his old headmaster at the Nave School. That had been a different situation but the idea was the same, always to do the right thing by the students, no matter what was going on in your own life. But Woodcock's ability to maintain that degree of rectitude had been connected to his sense of humor and his knack of not taking himself too seriously, and these were qualities in which Hamilton might be somewhat deficient.

For different reasons, Hume knew that he himself didn't belong in the Woodcock category either; he had let the course of his life be dictated by the enormous load of guilt that he expected to carry with him to the end of his days. At the Nave he had taught with concentrated efficiency, dry humor and total aloofness, and had been seen as a perennial bachelor, shy and asexual. Well, it was probably better not to think about the Nave—it led only to prolonged fits of painful introspection. What about his other new colleagues?

The junior member of the science department was a young physicist who had graduated from the Bronx High School of Science and CCNY. His name was Robert Fine and enthusiasm for his subject bubbled out of him with the strong accent of the neighborhood in which he had grown up and where he still lived, now in a one-and-a-half room apartment. For his physics classes with the eleventh grade he shared the lab with Hume, but apart from that he mostly taught math to the upper elementary school classes and had a desk in a corner of the faculty lounge in the smaller building. Most of the high school math was taught by Elsie Smith, who had her own room at the front of the building on the same floor as Hume's lab. Her door and Hume's faced each other across a wide space from which other doors led to another classroom, the elevator and the front and back stairs.

Elsie was the widow of an army officer who had been killed in Korea in 1952. Now in her early forties, she had accepted a modified version of widowhood, which she referred to as "singularity", as a way of life. Blessed with a fine crop of auburn hair that was still as genuine as her unwrinkled skin, she played tennis, worked out at the gym and dressed about twenty years younger than her actual age. She still liked men, but she told her friends that she enjoyed her independence and her creature comforts and felt quite contented. Not all of her friends were convinced of Elsie's contentment, however. Keen observers said that she liked rather a lot of men and that, having been fended off by the headmaster, she had set her sights on Hamilton with more success. Some of this may only have been gossip, but the fact remains that in spite of any attachment she might have had to the Head of Science, she immediately took a great interest in her new colleague. The result was that after a long chat with Elsie about the math curriculum, Hume found that he had a brunch date with her for the Sunday after next.

"I'd make it this Sunday", she said, "but I'm booked up for the day."

She didn't mention who had booked her.

Hume had had some amusing shop talk sessions with Bobbie Fine and had exchanged greetings with various English, history and language teachers, but everyone seemed very preoccupied and anxious to get from one place to another and, apart from Hamilton, Elsie and Bobby, none of them had been particularly forthcoming. Hume was happy with the situation—he was allergic to effusiveness and he would have been quite surprised if he had known what was going on in Elsie's mind.

And then, of course, there was Sally. She didn't have to get from one place to another, and if she wasn't on the phone or otherwise busy she was always ready to pass the time of day. She had a way of stirring up something in Hume that had been suppressed for twenty-five years. So far it was quite mild, not unpleasant and not too nervous-making.

When Thornbury had introduced Hume to the school at the weekly assembly on Monday morning, he had mentioned his new teacher's naval service. The assemblies were devoted to presentations on current events and matters of general interest, and Hume had reluctantly allowed himself to be persuaded to give a talk about his wartime experiences on the following Monday. There was a lot of buzz about the Vietnam War among the students, some of whom had heard Coretta Scott King speak at the great anti-war rally in Washington the previous November. Others had swallowed the domino theory and went around wearing "Bomb Hanoi" buttons, but the chief preoccupation among the older boys and their girlfriends was the draft. President Johnson had already increased the number of American troops in Vietnam to 400,000 and no one knew how much further the escalation would go or how long the war would go on. Continuous fulltime education would keep the boys safe for a few more years but maybe that wouldn't be enough. Hume, who had followed the events in south-east Asia ever since the defeat of the French at Dienbienphu in 1954, heartily disapproved of the attempts to re-colonize the area. Feeling pretty sure that any talk about war was likely to end up in a heated discussion of Vietnam, and assuming that it was against school policy for teachers to discuss their political views with the students, he decided that the best idea would be to stick to reminiscences that would give the most vivid possible impression of what it was like to be involved in the war in Europe and to disclaim any knowledge of the politics behind it. This would make it more plausible for him to claim ignorance of the Vietnam situation.

Turning his mind to next week's chemistry lessons, he thought it would be a good idea to do a thorough check of the storeroom behind the office. This was a small, locked space, about ten feet by eight, with shelves of all the standard chemicals occupying one short wall, glassware and electrical apparatus on the long wall opposite the door and a big steel cabinet, labeled "Poisons and Acids" and fitted with a very imposing padlock, on the other short wall below the one small window. Hume had done a quick reconnaissance soon after arriving but now he wanted to make sure that everything he needed for the rest of the year was available. Once again he was impressed with Miller's efficiency. Everything was very clean and in excellent order and there were no obvious deficiencies. There were, however, two things that didn't seem to belong, one of which was a row of dusty old books on a shelf in the dimmest corner of the room. Hume saw titles like *Alchemy and Chemistry* and *From Paracelsus to Newton* and, opening one of them, came upon the inscription, "A. Thornbury October 1932."

The other object that seemed out of place was a pair of rimless glasses standing unobtrusively in a 500ml. beaker on a low shelf opposite the door. Looking through them, Hume could see that they belonged to a short-sighted person. This he found very intriguing since he knew a short-sighted person who was missing a pair of glasses.

Hamilton wanted to talk to Thornbury before the headmaster disappeared for the weekend, which is why he had been in too much of a hurry to be able to spend time with Hume. Nothing had been said all week about the Friedman situation and Hamilton wanted to know if there had been any new developments. Also he had an ulterior motive—he wanted to take a good look at the headmaster and see if his condition had improved at all now that things seemed to have settled down. It was a few minutes after three and there were still a lot of students in the building. Sally was sitting at the reception desk and as Hamilton approached the headmaster's door, she said, "He's gone."

"Gone?" Hamilton echoed weakly. "Gone where?"

"He didn't say where. In fact he didn't say anything—he just up and left without even bothering to close his door."

Hamilton looked into the office. A strong breeze flowed in through the window but the cigar smoke was still heavy in the air. Opening the file cabinet, Hamilton saw that the scotch bottle was almost empty. He went back out to Sally but couldn't think of anything to say.

"I know", Sally said. "It's bad. I think it's the Friedman business. She wanted to see him at lunchtime and he wouldn't."

"Mrs. Friedman?"

"No, Amanda."

"That's very strange—why would she want to see him?"

It was, in fact, very unusual for a student to ask to see the headmaster, since there were proper channels for complaints, requests and suggestions. Amanda was in an exceptional situation, being the only student in the school who had ever claimed to have been sexually assaulted by a teacher, but the whole thing was supposed to have been settled, and if any further discussion was needed it would surely be with the parents.

"I don't know, but she had a mean look in her eye. There's something I think I ought to say to you officially—Mr. Hamilton—which is that he's drinking a lot and he's been coming on to me in a way I really don't appreciate. Well you know that on the whole I prefer older men and I do kind of like him, but . . ."

Hamilton sat down heavily on the chair next to Sally's desk. It was all getting to be too much but he couldn't help smiling.

"You mean you really *do* appreciate . . . You're a very naughty little girl, Sally."

"I know I am—aren't you glad?"

"I'm delighted", Hamilton said. "And, by the way, I'm thinking of looking for another job—somewhere away from the city."

This was more a question than a statement and Sally replied in the same tone.

"That's probably a good idea. It's a bit sudden but I might just do the same."

Sally looked at Hamilton. She was a very confident, outgoing young woman but there was a touch of shyness in the smile that spread over her face.

Hamilton smiled back.

"So you don't think I'm crazy?"

"Not in the least—unless we're both crazy."

"Maybe that's what it is."

The conversation might have gone on but a couple of students walked into the front hall at that moment.

"Come up to the lab at four o'clock—that is, if you want to", Hamilton said after the students had passed by.

"I want to."

"Oh, and er . . ."

"What?"

"Better not let Elsie see you."

"Mr. Hamilton—I believe you're as naughty as I am."

Hamilton smiled complacently.

"Don't worry—there's nothing much to it. It's just that she still thinks—well, you know."

"I wouldn't dream of worrying—what about Jean?"

"She doesn't know either."

"About me or about Elsie?"

"I hadn't thought of that. Now that you come to mention it . . ."

Hamilton was looking very thoughtful as he made for the elevator.

One of the facts of life at the Ben Thompson School was that no one checked the building for stray students until about five o'clock, when Luis Alvarez did his rounds and locked the building. Even then it was very easy for someone as inquisitive as Amanda Friedman to conceal herself and sneak around as long as she liked after extra-curricular activities were over. So it was always possible to keep an eye open for extra-extra-curricular activities and leave through the basement door. She had noted that Friday afternoon seemed to be the time when certain teachers tended to hang around for no real reason, and she had already made some interesting observations that might possibly have some cash potential. It was important to have a back-up plan in case Thornbury refused to cooperate, so on that Friday she didn't leave until well after four o'clock. What she had in mind would not be as lucrative, but it was certainly worth a shot.

7

Hamilton and his wife had bought their house on West 85th Street when that part of the Upper West Side was a depressed and fairly dangerous place, but in the course of building big public elementary and high schools on West 84th Street, the city had cleared away a big area of urban blight and the slow process of what became known later as "gentrification" had started. As Hamilton wryly observed, the public schools seemed to be very well run and the students better behaved and better dressed than some of Ben Thompson's flock.

Jean Hamilton, however, was a bit of a surprise to Hume. Whatever mental image he had of the impeccably stylish American hostess was dispelled on Saturday evening when she appeared at the front door wearing faded blue jeans and an old sweatshirt, and said, "Hi John, come in and have a drink. After a week in the madhouse you could probably use one."

Jean Stewart had been an English teacher at the Benjamin Thompson School when James Hamilton joined the faculty in 1948, but she had already written two fairly successful Scottish romances under the name of Hamish McGregor. After marrying James she had become a full-time writer and a string of McGregor stories had contributed generously to the financial stability of the Hamilton household. Hume, who knew nothing of this, followed the wiry, gray-haired authoress with the strong jaw and tired eyes and soon found himself sitting in an unpretentious living room with a glass of scotch in his hand.

"You can have half an hour", Jean said, "and then it's French bread, cold cuts, salad and ice cream, so it's ready whenever you are. I have a chapter to finish, but it shouldn't take that long."

Hume and Hamilton talked about students and curricula in a rather desultory way for ten minutes before Hamilton broke off and said abruptly, "Look John, you know as much about teaching as I do. If there's anything you need to know about the way we do things here you can always ask, but right now I don't feel like talking about that stuff. I'm more concerned with the whole picture and it looks pretty bad."

"More trouble with the Friedmans?"

"I don't know—maybe. Amanda wanted to talk to Thornbury yesterday afternoon and he'd already left. My impression is that either he's already an alcoholic or he's getting there pretty fast. There ought to be something we could do about him but I have no idea what it is."

"Have you tried to talk to him about it?"

"I've made a few pointed remarks and dropped a hint that I might not be around much longer. I'm serious about that, by the way, but I didn't get any change out of him—just a prolonged stare."

"How long has the drinking been going on?"

"It's not just the Friedman case", Hamilton said, following Hume's thought. "I'd say it started getting serious at the end of the last school year."

"Family troubles?"

"There's very little family to trouble him. His wife died fifteen years ago and there weren't any children. He shares an apartment with an unmarried sister whom I've never met, since she never shows up for any of the school functions and Thornbury never invites anyone to his home. I guess you could say it's an unusual set-up."

"Would it be worthwhile to try to talk to her?"

"I'm not totally convinced that she exists. I took it for granted for a long time that the situation was as described to me—not by him, incidentally, since he hardly ever mentions her. It seems Elsie tried him out for a while and he told her some things. Now I've begun to wonder if the sister is real, and if she is maybe she's not his sister. I have to say that he was always very good at his job in spite of the fact that he took to keeping a bottle of scotch in the file cabinet several years ago. He was quite open about it—with me, at any rate. He said that no one but an idiot would take on a headmastership and the occasional nip out of the bottle was necessary if he was to avoid murdering somebody. And the odd thing is that as far as I understand it, there's no need for him to work at all. His grandfather made a huge fortune manipulating real estate in the late nineteenth century and his father and uncles are or were all wealthy and influential landowners, lawyers and politicians. He's an only child but he has cousins all over the place, which can be helpful when the school needs special treatment of any sort."

"What was his subject—I mean at university?"

"Medieval and renaissance history. Why do you ask?"

"I found a row of old books on sixteenth century scientists in the storeroom and I was wondering if he was interested in chemistry."

"Well, his doctorate is in sixteenth century philosophy and he used to spend quite a bit of time in the lab with old Noakes—Miller's predecessor. I think he had the idea of repeating some of van Helmont's experiments, but that was a long time ago. He's probably forgotten that the books are there. And by the way, going back to the previous subject, you should probably be a bit cautious with Elsie."

"Why—has she tried you out, too?"

"Sort of, and you know what they say about the female of the species."

Hume was about to ask what "sort of" meant but Jean reappeared at that moment and cut him off.

"'More deadly than the male'—yes, Jim, Kipling got it right and you'd better remember it."

This was spoken lightly but there was a subtle edge to it and Hume was surprised to see that Hamilton looked quite shaken. It seemed that there might be an unexpected crack in the Hamilton façade, but the moment passed and for the rest of the evening Hamish McGregor and his works provided most of the conversation.

8

Hamilton's assessment of Amanda Friedman had been very accurate; she wanted what she wanted when she wanted it, and became very frustrated if she didn't get it. It was all well and good that her parents had received a big pay-off and that she now had such convenient leverage in the matter of grades and recommendations, but what she really wanted was some money of her own. At her meeting with the headmaster in the park she had told him exactly what her requirements were and what would happen if he didn't come through, but evidently he hadn't taken her seriously. She had spent the week waiting for some response, and when he left early on Friday afternoon she assumed it was to avoid seeing her. Her late afternoon reconnaissance had yielded some encouraging observations in other directions, but obviously some further action was needed in the matter of Aloysius Thornbury, so she called her friend Michael Schwartz at the *Galaxy.* So far she hadn't told any of her friends about the alleged rape because keeping quiet was part of the deal and any leakage would jeopardize her situation at school. But she couldn't put up with being ignored and she knew that Michael needed money too. The *Galaxy*, a tabloid that appeared in supermarkets every Tuesday, made a living out of dirt, and its circulation was such that it didn't have to worry about lawsuits. Michael could explain this very carefully to Thornbury and point out that the *Galaxy* was running a very popular series on assaulted and missing girls in New York City.

Thornbury might well agree that it was worth a significant sum to keep Amanda's story from becoming Manhattan's latest scandal. If her plan worked, she and Michael could split the proceeds and still keep it out of the papers as long as it was to her advantage to do so.

Talking it over on Friday evening, they agreed that if Amanda had made no progress with Thornbury by the following Thursday, Michael would call him at his home, explain who he was and suggest a meeting with Amanda on Sunday to discuss the situation.

Peter Miller had not left New York City. On Sunday morning, two days after Amanda and Michael Schwartz discussed their little plot, Miller was lying on his bed in his Brooklyn apartment, trying to figure out his next move. He had several things to worry about, but money wasn't one of them. The $100,000 check that he had deposited a few days ago was equivalent to about seven years' salary and although it wouldn't be of much use in the jungles of Vietnam, it might help him to avoid going there. He was fairly sure that he would be safe from the draft for several months but being single, healthy, twenty-five and unemployed, he felt very vulnerable. Amanda had been a pleasant diversion until he discovered the less desirable aspects of her personality, and even then she had had her uses. Jill, however, was the real thing. Unlike Amanda, who was physically attractive but intellectually challenged, possessive and emotionally chilly, Jill was mentally agile, warm and cuddly, and very responsive to his anxieties about the draft. It was frustrating that he had had to leave both G. E. and Ben Thompson because of sex scandals when he hadn't had the pleasure of undressing either of the women involved. Not that he thought of Amanda as a woman—just as a kid who had taken his fancy for a while. Jill was different. She was going to be seventeen next Sunday and they had already decided how they would celebrate her arrival at the age of consent.

Not this Sunday, though; today they had to perform another task, which involved sneaking into school and retrieving the pair of glasses that Jill had left behind in a moment of panic. She knew exactly where they were and Miller thought it would have been very easy to say that Jill had left her glasses somewhere and someone had picked them up and popped them into a beaker which someone else had returned to its rightful place on the shelf; but Jill was worried and it was a good excuse for them to spend some time together in a safe and secluded spot. This was possible because in the flurry of leaving the school he had forgotten to return his keys and no one had thought of asking for them. He thought that late on a Sunday afternoon it was highly unlikely that anyone else would be in the building.

Jean Hamilton had begun to wonder why her husband was finding it necessary to spend so many Sunday afternoons at school. This had been going on for several months, and an unpleasant association had formed in her mind between that observation and the fact that he was becoming increasingly distrait and inattentive to her. In spite of her anxieties she had managed to put on a fairly good show while Hume was visiting, but as soon as he had gone she tackled Hamilton on the subject. He was—or acted—very surprised and rambled on about pressure of work and worry about how the school would make it through the present crisis. He categorically denied being involved in an affair and cut the discussion short by claiming that he had school work to do.

"Why do you have to do it now?" Jean asked. "You have all day tomorrow."

"I have a meeting tomorrow and I may have to be in school for several hours."

"What kind of a meeting—not with the Smith woman by any chance? I've seen her eyeing you."

Hamilton's laugh was not altogether convincing.

"Elsie? That's ridiculous—where the hell do you get these ideas? I have twenty-four papers to correct and you'd better go to bed and sleep it off."

Apart from the lack of a Scottish accent, this was just what a character in one of Jean's novels might have said. She went to bed with an unpleasantly icy sensation in the pit of her stomach and a strong feeling that she had to know what was going on, no matter how distressing the process might be. Being a strong-minded person, she spent the next morning and early afternoon working on her new Hamish novel while waiting for her husband to leave. The time dragged on and when she finally went to see what was happening, she found that he had already left. Realizing that he must have done so with unusual stealth and might have been gone for hours, she grabbed her overcoat and a wool hat and followed as fast as possible in the direction in which she assumed he had gone. At the 90th Street entrance to Central Park she found a bench where she could keep an unobtrusive eye on the school, and it was only after she had been there for several minutes that it occurred to her that if her husband really was cheating on her it might well not be in his workplace. Elsie lived on her own just around the corner from the Hamiltons, so it would be much more convenient for them to do whatever they were doing there.

Jean stayed where she was however, and after a few more minutes she saw Hume crossing the street toward the park. He gave no sign of recognition but she was pretty sure that he had seen her. She thought she would wait another ten minutes and was just getting up to leave when Hamilton and Sally emerged from the front door of the school. Jean took evasive action and watched from a distance as they walked into the park and indulged in a long hug and a parting kiss. It might conceivably be harmless but she didn't believe it, and now she thought she understood why he had laughed at the idea of Elsie. It had seemed at first that Hamilton and Elsie somehow made sense whereas Hamilton and Sally were an unlikely couple; but the thing that really made sense was the basic principle that a middle-aged man was not likely to want to exchange one middle-aged woman for another middle-aged woman. It didn't occur to Jean that her husband might be exploring both possibilities at the same time, so she was consoled by the thought that Sally was probably just enjoying a pleasant dalliance with an older man, whereas with Elsie it might have been deadly serious. Sally wasn't such a hard case as Elsie and might be easier to deal with. She considered confronting her husband as he walked back toward Central Park West, but at this stage she didn't want him to know that she had been following him, so she waited until he was out of sight and then made her way home. She didn't hurry—it wouldn't do any harm for Jim to find that she was missing and wonder where she was. Next week it would be different. She had no keys to the school but that could be rectified—it wouldn't be so surprising if Jim mislaid his keys for a day.

For twenty-five years Hume had found in solitude a source of consolation. He had expected that the steel door at the foot of his private staircase would provide a barrier against any unwelcome incursions into his little world, but now, in this teeming city of eight million people, he was surprised to find that he was lonely and would rather be almost anywhere than in his new apartment. Blessing the wisdom that had dedicated hundreds of acres in the middle of Manhattan to grass, trees and ponds, he spent many hours walking or sitting in the park, where he began to feel some kinship with others who walked, sat or played there. No doubt there were people who had made messes of their lives and at any moment he might be looking at one of them. He was not tempted to speculate about their identities or misadventures. It was just a comfort to know that they were there. Much of the time he sat on a bench not far from the 90th Street entrance, letting his mind go blank and taking in the scene with no analysis and no judgement, but on this particular Sunday afternoon he was wondering why Jean Hamilton was sitting by herself in the park. A possible explanation presented itself when he saw Hamilton and Sally coming along, arm-in-arm, from the direction of the school. It was too late to hide and they would certainly have seen Hume if they had not been completely preoccupied with each other. They stopped almost opposite Hume's bench and after a hug and a kiss that didn't look like a mere friendly peck, Sally went on into the park and Hamilton walked back toward Central Park West. It took Hume some time to realize that the unaccustomed sensation that he was feeling was jealousy. He wondered if Jean Hamilton had seen them and was feeling the same thing.

As it gradually got dark, people left the park and Hume mechanically got up and went with them. The light over the main entrance of the school dimly illuminated a young couple standing just outside the door. The man was tall but he was standing one step lower than the girl and as Hume passed, on his way to No. 3, her face appeared over his shoulder. She had her eyes closed and Hume caught only a brief glimpse, but he was quite certain that it was Jill Davis.

9

Thornbury did three things after arriving at school on Monday morning. The first was to tell Sally that Amanda was not to be allowed anywhere near his office, and the second was to tell Hamilton to take charge of the morning assembly, at which Hume was to give his talk. The third was to retire to his office and shut the door.

Hume had made a good impression in his first week and with one notable exception the resentment felt by those who had been particularly attached to Miller had begun to fade. As he rose to begin his talk on Monday morning the students greeted him politely and he soon felt that he had their interest and attention. The centerpiece of his presentation was the experience of losing his ship late in 1940 to the torpedoes of a German submarine. This had happened several hundred miles off the coast of Ireland and most of his crew had been lost. As captain he had remained on the bridge until the last possible moment and was here to tell the tale only because his radio operator happened to be a strong swimmer. He bore no particular rancor toward the Germans. That was what war was about—he was doing his job and they were doing theirs. He didn't mention that being in the throes of an idiotic infatuation with a fifteen-year-old girl, he hadn't cared very much whether or not he survived and had thought it would make things easier for his wife if he didn't.

There was time for a few questions at the end and Jill Davis was the first to raise her hand. She was puzzled by the fact that Hume had spoken of war as if it were simply a natural process, something that just happened, like an earthquake or a volcanic eruption. Most of his crew had died when his ship went down, and yet it seemed that he had no feelings about the people who had made the war happen or whether what he was doing was morally justified.

Hume now found it impossible to stick to his resolution to avoid the politics of war.

"I wanted to avoid questions of morality because I knew that they would almost certainly take us into a discussion of Vietnam. It isn't that I don't think it ought to be discussed—just that I shouldn't be the one doing it. But I'll tell you this; there have been two major wars involving the whole of Europe, another one in the Pacific and countless wars going back throughout history. And it has usually been for the same reason that a common robbery takes place. Someone wants something that belongs to someone else. Only in the case of war it's the political and military leaders who want something, and often it's two nations squabbling over something that doesn't belong to either of them. But it's the ordinary people who have to die, very often having little or no idea what they're dying for. In my opinion the events leading to the Second World War are clear and horrible enough, but I was too deeply involved to feel able to talk about it objectively. And as for Vietnam, you may be able to deduce my opinion from what I've just said, but as a foreigner and a chemistry teacher I don't feel that it would be right for me to say any more."

Jill's hand went up again but Hamilton stood up and pointed at the clock.

"I'm sorry but we'll have to close at this point."

He thanked Hume and there was a respectful round of applause.

Hume's first class was ninth grade general science but when he got upstairs he met Jill Davis coming out of the lab.

"Hello, Jill. What are you doing here?"

Jill seemed confused for a moment but quickly pulled herself together.

"I just wanted to say I liked your talk and I'm sorry if I've been rude to you."

"Thank you, Jill. I appreciate it. I was going to say something about your habit of making comments about another student but now perhaps I don't need to."

"I won't do it any more."

"Good—and if you would look in for a moment at recess I think I have something that may belong to you."

Jill wanted to ask questions but the ninth-graders were coming in and Hume shook his head.

The question of Jill and her glasses had been bothering Hume. Maybe the pair that he had found belonged to someone else, but if they didn't—well, as far as he knew, only he and Bobby Fine had been in the storeroom since Miller's sudden departure. If Jill had somehow got in it would hardly have been just to drop a pair of glasses into a beaker on the bottom shelf. This indicated that Jill had been there while Miller was still around, which indicated that . . . Hume wasn't sure what it indicated, but whatever it was it didn't look good. At recess, having disposed of the ninth grade, he was sitting at the demonstration bench looking at the glasses and waiting for Jill to appear when David Klein, one of her classmates, poked his head around the door and asked if he could have a word.

"I was wondering if you could help me with this problem."

It was a fairly simple matter needing only a brief explanation, and as David was about to leave he said, "Oh, you found Jill's glasses." As he turned he almost bumped into Jill.

"Look, he found your glasses!"

Jill turned dead white and then brick red.

"When did you lose them?" Hume asked.

"Oh, ages ago."

David looked surprised and said, "But you had them . . ."

Jill interrupted him.

"This is an old pair—I still can't find the others."

Hume nodded toward the door and David left. He could be questioned later if necessary.

"Do you know where I found these?" he asked.

"No."

"Don't you want to know?"

"Not specially—does it matter?"

"Can you remember where you were the last time you had them?"

"No—why are you making such a deal of this?"

"Why didn't you tell me you had lost your glasses instead of making up that story about a new prescription?"

Jill's manner had gone from fearful to defensive to truculent.

"It wasn't a story. Can I have my glasses—I need to get to my next lesson."

"Maybe you shouldn't use them if they're such an old prescription."

Jill had no reply to this, so Hume gave her the glasses and went upstairs to the biology lab. Hamilton seemed very tired and on edge, but he listened to Hume's story and commented, "You think she was in the storeroom at the crucial time."

"Yes, I do. Obviously that story about an old pair of glasses was made up on the spur of the moment. It makes sense that way. I also doubt very much whether she really came to apologize this morning. She was already leaving when I got there."

"You think she was poking about in the back in the hope of finding her glasses. OK, let's try it out. Miller shifts his affections to Jill. She's with him in his office Friday afternoon. They're having a petting session and when they hear Amanda coming she picks up her glasses and slips into the storeroom."

"Maybe the two of them were already in the storeroom and Miller came out. The glasses were on the lowest shelf, not where she would have put them if she'd just gone in there to hide."

"So they were in there on the floor when Amanda arrived. They hear her and he comes out and pretends he was just putting something away, which I guess he may have been, in a manner of speaking. He sits with Amanda for a moment. She has her panties rolled up in her hand and slips them under the table. She does the kissing routine, and runs downstairs. It could have been that way. Sally and I arrive before Jill has the chance to leave and as soon as we've gone she makes herself scarce, forgetting her glasses. She's fairly shorted-sighted so she must have been in a hurry but that's quite plausible. The point is that one way or the other she knows Miller didn't try to rape Amanda."

"Exactly. So if we're right about this she could get Miller off the hook for rape, but she doesn't say anything because she doesn't want to get into trouble."

"Maybe he's being chivalrous—he knows he's going to be fired either way. Or maybe he just likes the money. We don't know that he went back to California, by the way, and I'll bet they've been seeing each other since it happened."

Hume thought they had seen each other the previous afternoon but at that moment the warning bell rang for the end of recess and all he said was, "Nothing much we can do about it, I suppose."

"Doesn't look like it."

But it struck Hume that if Jill had been in the school the previous afternoon it might well have been to look for her glasses. They hadn't been there, so today she had had another shot at finding them.

10

Hume's second week of teaching at the Benjamin Thompson School was an improvement on his first. The students were getting used to his dry sense of humor and were impressed by his mastery of whatever subject matter he happened to be dealing with. They had liked Miller's willingness to be drawn into moral or political issues connected with science, but they also appreciated Hume's business-like habit of sticking to the point and doing his best to ensure that they all got what they were supposed to get. He was surprised to find that Jill's apology and promise of better behavior actually meant something. Amanda was allowed to blunder along without comment and Jill sometimes smiled and said, "Thank you" at the end of the math lessons. The glasses she was wearing looked exactly like the ones Hume had found in the storeroom, and she could obviously see the blackboard much better.

Hume was also getting to know his colleagues better and finding the experience unexpectedly tolerable if not exactly pleasurable. The unexpectedness was part of the residue of a quarter of a century of solitary preoccupation with his load of guilt, and had nothing to do with any preconceptions about the qualities of American academics. Bobby Fine was an excellent physicist and an accomplished teller of tall stories, and Elsie Smith was a good listener with a well-known taste for male company, so the two of them adopted Hume as the third member of a kind of informal club that met at odd times when they all happened to be free, usually in Hume's office behind the lab, where he had a small refrigerator and coffee- and tea-making supplies. He took their incursions good-humoredly and generally breathed a sigh of relief when they departed. Apart from inviting Hume to brunch, the only thing that Elsie had done that might be connected to Hamilton's insinuations about her man-eating propensities, was to take an inch or two off the hems of her skirts; they still didn't match Sally's in brevity but somehow she still contrived to make the Englishman nervous.

Continuing his policy of invisibility, Thornbury was successful in his efforts to avoid Amanda, so on Thursday evening Michael Schwartz made his call. The headmaster put up a good fight but eventually felt compelled to agree to a meeting on Sunday afternoon. He then turned to his usual form of consolation.

At seven-fifteen the next morning, an hour and a quarter before classes were due to start, Thornbury telephoned Hamilton to say that he would be late arriving as he had some kind of food poisoning. This was not too much of a problem, as the business manager and the school secretary shared an office on the first floor and Sally was invariably punctual. Nevertheless, Hamilton called Sally to let her know what the situation was and Sally asked if he thought whiskey counted as a food.

Sally, who had chosen that day to wear a translucent silk blouse over a bare minimum of underwear, was at her desk by seven-forty-five. Shc was just removing her overcoat when Hamilton arrived and he had to struggle to maintain his equilibrium.

Sally smiled at him indulgently.

"What's the matter, don't you like the way I'm dressed? Careful, now, there'll be kids arriving at any moment."

Hamilton removed his hand from one of the points of maximum attraction and said, "OK—I have to go up and tell everybody what's up with the headmaster, but later on I'll show you how much I like it."

While this was going on, Hume, Bobby and Elsie were drinking coffee in the back room behind the chemistry lab. The two men were wearing their regulation suits, but Elsie had evidently decided that it was time to give Sally some even more serious competition, and the effect was by no means unpleasing. She was taller and a little more muscular than her rival, but she had kept her youthful figure and could show a few extra inches of well-shaped thigh below her dark green mini-dress without creating any feeling of incongruity. Hume observed this discreetly, but Bobby Fine made no attempt to disguise his appreciation.

The Miller-Friedman incident seemed to be drifting into the past with no publically known repercussions, and Bobby was holding forth about the eccentricities of a great physicist.

"So Heisenberg tried to make some conversation and asked Dirac if he had seen any good plays recently . . ."

At this moment Hamilton walked in. He was about to speak when he saw Elsie, who was on a tall lab stool, leaning back with her elbows propped on the edge of Hume's table, a position that showed her legs to maximum advantage.

Unlike Hume, he didn't avert his eyes—it just took him a few more seconds to find his voice.

"Just for your information", he said, "the headmaster won't be in this morning."

"What's the problem", Elsie asked.

"Food poisoning", Hamilton said, with just enough nuance in his tone to express his reservations about the accuracy of the diagnosis. "It won't affect your schedules."

He left, but not before giving Elsie another appreciative glance and a smile.

Bobby said, "And Dirac said, 'Why do you wish to know?'"

Thornbury was still missing on Friday afternoon, and calls to his home were not answered. Hamilton did a careful check of the headmaster's office, including his in and out trays, and found nothing that needed immediate attention, so he went up to his office, where he had arranged to meet Hume for their weekly conference.

Hume was already there, sitting at the desk and looking mournfully out of the window at nothing in particular.

"Anything wrong?" Hamilton asked.

"I think they call it the week-end drop", Hume said with a rueful smile. "As long as I have work to do . . . But you don't want to hear about this . . ."

"Maybe it would do you good to talk about it. I mean, being such a long way from home and everything familiar that goes with it."

"That's true but it isn't the real thing."

Well, perhaps if he talked about the real thing, Hamilton would understand—after all, Hamilton seemed to be going through something a bit like it himself.

"Forgive my asking, but are you and Sally . . ."

Hamilton didn't know whether he ought to be defensive or angry about such a personal question, but his real problem was confusion; he had already committed himself to Sally without un-committing himself to Elsie, and until a few days ago he had been finding it increasingly easy to forget that he was actually married to Jean. Now Jean was finding subtle and disturbing ways of reminding him. Best, he thought, to put a bold face on the matter.

"Yes, we are. Why, are you smitten, too?"

Hume smiled.

"Only a little bit. It's just that you might understand . . . I mean, it's very different because Sally is grown up but . . ."

And so it came out, bit by bit, reluctantly and with the acute self-loathing that Hume always experienced when he thought about Jessica, the young evacuee from London, who had stayed with him and his wife for a few days when he was on leave from his ship. Back on duty, he had obsessed about her for several months until his ship went down and he was sent home to recuperate. Once again he saw it all in slow motion—Jessica lying terrified on the bed, half naked, while he feverishly undressed in front of her, Susan's voice at the door, the rush to the stairs and the intolerable sounds of Jessica's head hitting the oak floor of the hall and Susan weeping.

"We buried her in father-in-law's back yard and then at the end of the war we had to move her. She was there, under my lab for twenty years until the fire. I thought somehow she knew I was there, but now she's in a proper grave and . . ."

"She doesn't know you any more?"

"Yes. She's gone now."

"And the police?"

"They know all about it and I often wish they had given me the punishment I deserve."

"But after all this time—I mean, doesn't it get any better?"

"I keep thinking maybe it does, but then something happens and I'm back in the same old place."

It was a long time before Hamilton could think of anything to say.

Finally, "It could have been me. I know Sally's older, but people just don't understand what it can do to you. And, by the way, I'd rather this wasn't known around the school. I hadn't realized that we were being so obvious."

"You aren't", Hume said. "I just happened to see you in the park."

On leaving Hamilton's office at about 3:20, Hume found Elsie sitting in the biology lab.

"Next on line", she said. "You guys love to talk, don't you?"

Shortly after four o'clock, when it seemed that all the students and most of the teachers had left, Sally went upstairs and found Hamilton sitting at his desk in the back room. He had a pile of reports in front of him but he didn't seem to be doing much with them. She pulled his chair back, took the red pencil from his hand and sat down on his lap.

"You're a funny guy, Jim", she said. "Middle-aged, not too much hair and a hint of a paunch, but I want you very much and I can't get you out of my mind. How do you do it?"

"Thanks for the compliments. I don't do it—it just happens and it's best not to think about it."

"In case it stops working, you mean. OK, I'm sorry—don't bother with diets and hair restorers. Elsie and I like you the way you are."

Hamilton stood up abruptly, and Sally would have been deposited on the floor if she hadn't clung on to him.

"Sorry again—I just can't help teasing you. Sit down and tell me what we're going to do? And are you sure Jean doesn't know?"

"I don't think she knows, but I'm afraid she's getting the idea."

"And what about Elsie", Sally asked, with a slightly malicious grin. "Did you see the way she was dressed today?"

Then, her natural honesty prevailing, she added, "I hope I look as good as that when I'm her age."

"For God's sake, will you stop about Elsie? I couldn't care less about her—she'll just have to lump it. Anyway, I thought it was settled. We try to behave ourselves until June and then . . ."

"And then we run away together. Any idea where?"

"Yes—probably Connecticut or upstate New York. I've put in a couple of applications."

"How about Thornbury?"

"He doesn't know about the applications, but I'll have to tell him pretty soon."

"Whereabouts?"

"One is a fairly posh day school in New Haven and the other's a boarding school in Pauling."

"How would I fit in?"

"That's easy—we live in sin until the divorce."

Sally chuckled.

"I'd love to live in sin, but would it be possible at a boarding school?"

"Not all the teachers live in and in any case we can find an apartment nearby."

"Or maybe a little cottage—the only thing is . . .

"What?"

"I don't think I can wait that long."

"Good—neither can I. Now, about the way you're dressed . . ."

They were in the middle of some serious explorations when Amanda Friedman walked into the room.

"Oh, I'm so sorry", she said and was gone before either of the adults could react. She had had time, however, to notice that Sally's blouse was open all the way down the front and both her breasts would have been visible if Hamilton hadn't had his hand on one of them.

It wasn't exactly what Amanda had been expecting, but now she might have the opportunity to kill three birds with one stone instead of only two.

11

Hume found Sunday brunch with Elsie rather difficult and unexpectedly late. "Brunch" sounded like a compromise between breakfast and lunch, so he was surprised to find that two o'clock in the afternoon was a typical New York brunch time. They had intended to meet at a restaurant but on Sunday morning she called and persuaded Hume that it would be much nicer if he came to her apartment on Riverside Drive, where they could eat at a window overlooking the Hudson River. Unlike Jean Hamilton, Elsie actually cooked and did so in large quantities. Steak and eggs was a combination that Hume had not previously encountered and, together with the standard hash browns and toast, provided a gastronomic challenge that he only just managed to meet. He had naively expected that Elsie would want to continue their mathematical discussion but found himself subjected to a sympathetic but quite insistent probing of his family background, education and experience of marriage.

"My marriage didn't last all that long", Elsie said. "Jack's parents had this big old apartment and we set up in military quarters, but then they moved to Florida and Jack went off to Korea and didn't come back. So I moved in here and got a job at Ben Thompson. All very boring really—you had a much more exciting time, but it must have been very difficult for you and your wife."

For all Elsie knew, Hume might never have been married. It was a subject that he much preferred to avoid but here it was in the form of a statement, not a question. He would have liked to say, "What makes you think I was married", but Hamilton and Thornbury already knew and it was bound to get around.

"My wife was a nurse and while the blitz was on her life was just as difficult and dangerous as mine."

"Did something happen to her?"

Yes, Hume thought, something happened to her. It was something called Jessica.

"No, she's still alive and well—as far as I know."

"Oh, I'm sorry. Have you been on your own very long?"

"To all intents and purposes I've been a bachelor for twenty-five years."

"Do you like it? I mean, don't you ever think of finding someone?"

"It's just the way it is and, if you don't mind, I'd really rather not talk about it."

This was said rather abruptly and put a damper on the conversation for several minutes. Eventually they got around to politics and the war and how Elsie had enjoyed Hume's Monday morning talk, but Hume couldn't match her enthusiasm and was relieved to make his way to the door. His excuse was that he had to spend an hour or two getting things ready in the lab, but Elsie was ready for this.

"Oh, I'll walk over with you—I have a couple of things to see to in my room."

As they passed No. 3, Elsie said, "Don't you find it lonely up there at night and on the weekends, with a whole empty building below you?"

Hume had been lost in his own thoughts and in an unguarded moment he said, "Yes, it is rather."

Elsie seemed to be about to make a suggestion so Hume quickly pulled himself together and added, "But it's a nice little apartment and it's very convenient."

Since the lab was on the same floor as the math room, Hume had to put in a token appearance even though there wasn't really anything for him to do there. He sat at his desk, mechanically rearranging a few papers, and was surprised to hear someone moving around on the floor above. Hamilton must be up there doing some preparation for the next day. Or maybe Sally was with him and there was no need to be surprised.

It got very quiet and half an hour later, at about four o'clock, he crept out of the lab and listened. Elsie was still pottering around in her room, so he tiptoed down the stairs to the front hall. Hearing loud voices, male and female, coming from the headmaster's office, he decided to go down another flight and let himself out through the basement door. Halfway down to the basement, he heard some more voices, and he paused at the foot of the stairs. It sounded as if there were people making love in the little infirmary opposite the elevator. Hume didn't want to know about it so he let himself out as quietly as possible, crossed Central Park West, went into the park and sat down on a bench. If people wanted to quarrel in the headmaster's office or tryst in the infirmary and the bio lab, they were welcome and it was none of his business. What really bothered him was his response to Elsie's questions, which had only confirmed what he had been saying to Hamilton. It was ridiculous to have let them upset him so much and it just showed how little progress he had made in dealing with his load of guilt. He sat for a long time and his only clear thought was that it had probably been a mistake to come to America; in fact it was a mistake to be anywhere. If he had received due punishment, he would have been hanged by the neck until he was dead and he wouldn't be worrying about anything now. The one odd little bright spot in his existence was that he felt slightly jealous of Hamilton. Maybe the attraction he felt toward Sally would push Jessica a little further into the background of his consciousness. But if Sally was going to mess about with a married man, why did it have to be the short, stocky science head? Why not the tall, ex-naval officer?

As if on cue, Hamilton and Sally came into view and Hume hastily got up and hid behind a tree, not because he wanted to spy but because it was always his instinct to hide when he saw anyone he knew. As before, they were walking away from the school, but this time they kept on walking. Hume waited until it was quite dark before returning. He didn't want to meet anyone else.

At about four-fifteen Elsie noticed that it was awfully quiet and began to wonder what Hume was doing, so she went to the lab to see. Finding it unoccupied, she sat on a stool and gave her tactics a critical once-over. She soon reached the conclusion that she had been much too obvious and that this had scared Hume away. It didn't necessarily mean that he didn't like her, but it did mean that she would have to review her *modus operandi*. At first it had seemed that it would be a good idea to work on him as a back-up in case things didn't go so well with Hamilton, but the Englishman was mysteriously attractive, and if she could find the right approach, he might be more than just a fail-safe alternative.

In the circumstances it was natural to take a more critical look at Hamilton, who had lit her fire and kept it stoked for several months. In addition to some risky and therefore extra-exciting sessions behind the biology lab, it had been very easy for him to walk home in the afternoon by a slightly circuitous route that took him to his brownstone on West 85th Street via her apartment on Riverside Drive. When that hadn't been sufficient, he had invented the occasional emergency faculty meeting that would take him out of the house for an hour or two on a Sunday afternoon. Although he wasn't much to look at, the sex and the conversation were both good, so she didn't want to let him go. But over the past couple of weeks, he had seemed rather distant and preoccupied, and there were a couple of disturbing possibilities; one was that his wife might have figured out what was going on and the other was that there was a potentially formidable rival sitting at the front desk. Elsie had no concrete evidence of any defection in the latter direction, but she had sniffed something in the air and the odor had been powerful enough to push her into some uncharitable remarks about Sally and Hamilton at her last little meeting with the headmaster.

She had just reached this point in her cogitations when she heard footsteps on the floor above her. It sounded as if someone was leaving the biology lab, so she ran to the elevator and pressed the button, thinking that she would be able to catch whoever it was. While the antique cab was on its way up from the first floor, she heard voices from the stairwell and was just in time to catch a glimpse of Hamilton and Sally on their way down. It took considerable restraint on her part to stop and realize that there was no point in chasing them.

Instead, she went to Hume's office and sat at his desk. So that really was the explanation for Hamilton's standoffishness—she had known it, but had been unable to admit it to herself. Her first thought was that it must be the end of her affair with him. She would have enjoyed being shared but she couldn't stand the thought of sharing. Then she thought about how Hamilton had looked at her on Friday morning and how cooperative he had been later in the day. She still had certain advantages over the younger woman, so maybe he wasn't a lost cause. The thing to do would be to launch a counter-attack in that direction, while seeing if she could get any further with Hume. Thinking there might be something to be found that would give her more of a clue about her new colleague, she investigated his desk very thoroughly, but Hume wasn't the sort to leave letters or photographs lying around, and the only intriguing thing she found was a matchbox—intriguing as, to the best of her knowledge, Hume didn't smoke and neither did his predecessor. Idly giving the box a shake, she realized that whatever was inside, it wasn't matches. She wasn't sure what she was hoping to find, and she was faintly excited when it turned out to be a Yale key. The prosaic explanation occurred to her almost immediately. It wasn't the key to some illicit romance, but only a spare for the storeroom. It had been tucked away at the back of the drawer, so Hume probably didn't even know it was there. She put the key back where she had found it and lapsed into a long daydream in which Hamilton and Hume both featured. It was a long time before her self-respect took over, something that happened quite often but never seemed to last very long. She was just getting up when she heard the elevator, so she ran quickly back to her room, where she could keep watch from her open doorway. She had the impression that it had stopped on the floor above, and assumed that Hamilton had returned. She waited for a few minutes to see if anything else happened, and had just decided to go up and confront him when the elevator started moving again.

12

At 8:25 on Monday morning Hamilton and Sally were having an anxious conversation at the reception desk. The assembly was due to start in five minutes and Thornbury was supposed to introduce an eminent scientist who would talk about nuclear power. But the headmaster was nowhere to be seen and his office was locked. Hamilton had pounded on his door and Sally had called his home several times but neither had been able to get any response.

"Keep trying his phone", Hamilton said, "and I'll start the assembly."

Professor Godovski gave a very dry exposition of the benefits and dangers of nuclear power. After talking for ten minutes beyond his allotted time he looked at his watch, exclaimed, "Oh dear!" and rushed from the room. Hamilton, who appeared to have something on his mind, said, "Well, I guess there won't be a question period this morning" and followed almost as quickly.

"I notice Amanda Friedman and Jill Davis are missing", Hume said as he and Hamilton almost collided in the doorway. Hamilton didn't reply but went to the reception desk while Hume went up to the lab.

Sally looked anxiously at Hamilton.

"The Friedmans just called. They said that Amanda went out yesterday afternoon and never came home. They think it's something to do with Peter Miller and they've called the police. They want to talk to the H. M."

"What did you tell them?"

"Well, they didn't sound much like worried parents—more like dissatisfied customers. I had the impression that somehow they think it's all his fault. I told them he was in the assembly and would call later."

"What about Jill Davis—have you heard anything?"

"Yes—she called to say she has a very bad cold and her mother had already left for work. You know the family situation."

"Yes, the father ran off with the baby sitter or some such thing."

As acting Deputy Headmaster, Hamilton had a key to the headmaster's office and he decided to use it, remarking that there might be some clue as to what was going on. What he found was a very large clue in the shape Aloysius Thornbury, who was slumped across his desk with a cognac bottle grasped firmly in his hand. This seemed odd because the office stank of scotch. The explanation seemed obvious, however, since the floor was covered with the fragments of a broken whiskey bottle, the neck of which was poking out from under the desk. Evidently Thornbury had dropped his scotch bottle and had to switch to brandy. He stirred and muttered, "What time is it?"

Hamilton could hear Sally talking on the phone and a moment later she came to the office door and said, "That was the police. They wanted . . . Oh, my God!"

"Come in and shut the door. Tell me about the police while I clean up this mess."

"They wanted to know if Amanda had shown up yet. They said someone would be around to talk to us later."

Hamilton had opened the window and was picking up the larger pieces of glass and putting them in Thornbury's waste paper basket. Fragments had skated all over the polished wooden floor and it wasn't a job that could be completed by hand.

"Bobby is free this period and I hope to God he's here. Find out if he's in the lounge and ask him to bring a cup of black coffee. After he's done that he can go up to the bio lab and sit with the tenth grade until I get there. Meanwhile go downstairs and get the vacuum cleaner. This door will remain locked and if anyone wants to know anything, the HM's in a private conference."

Sally left and Thornbury opened his eyes again.

"What the hell's going on? It's damn cold in here."

Hamilton grabbed him by the shoulders, sat him up straight and said, "You tell me."

"Just get the hell out of here and leave me alone."

There was a knock on the door and Sally wheeled in a large upright vacuum cleaner.

"Luis was there and he wanted to know what was going on. Then he wanted to come and help. I told him it was just a flowerpot but I don't think he believed me. We don't have any flowerpots here but it was the first thing that came into my head."

"Never mind—did anyone else see you?"

"Yes, Mrs. Schroeder was just going into the infirmary and said good morning. I don't think she thought there was anything unusual going on—I mean people do need vacuum cleaners sometimes."

"Any luck with Bobby?"

"Yes, he's bringing the coffee. I'd better go back and make sure he doesn't barge in here. And a private conference with a vacuum cleaner's going to be hard to explain."

Robert Fine arrived at Sally's desk with the coffee a minute later.

"What's up", he asked. "Has the old boy got a hangover?"

"Shut up, Bobby, and don't ask any questions, OK?"

"I guess I don't need to. You doing anything after school?"

Sally pointed to the elevator and said, "Do me a favor, Bobby. Get up there before they wreck the place."

Bobby was still inclined to linger but at that moment the vacuum cleaner started and Sally said, "Just for Pete's sake get lost!"

The young man did as he was told and Sally gazed after him with an indulgent smile on her face.

In the office, Thornbury was sitting up with his hands over his ears and rocking violently back and forth.

"Stop it, stop it", he screamed, but Hamilton didn't stop until he had traversed the whole floor twice. There might be a few tiny shards left, but he had done his best to ensure that nothing was visible to anyone who happened to look in. Sally came in with the coffee. Thornbury stopped rocking and looked at it suspiciously.

"Drink it, damn you", Hamilton ordered.

The headmaster took a sip, spluttered and nearly spilt the whole thing. He tried again with a little more success and the drink seemed to steady him.

"What's going on?" he asked.

He looked around and saw the brandy bottle, the vacuum cleaner and the anxious faces of Sally and Hamilton. He began to cry.

Sally shook her head and went back to her desk.

Hamilton said, "What the hell have you been doing?" but there was no reply. "Drink the rest of this and I'll be back in a couple of minutes."

He was pushing the vacuum cleaner back across the front hall when the doorbell rang.

"Just let me get this out of the way", he told Sally, so she waited until he had disappeared into the elevator before buzzing in the visitor.

"Sergeant Michelson", the big man in the khaki raincoat announced, showing his police credentials. "I understand there's a student missing and I'd like to speak to whoever's in charge here—the headmaster, I guess."

"I'm afraid the headmaster has been taken ill. But Mr. Hamilton, who is the Acting Deputy Headmaster, will be here any moment now."

"What's the matter with the headmaster?"

Sally took her cue from the excuse that Thornbury had given on Friday morning.

"We're not sure, but it looks like food poisoning."

Hamilton emerged from the elevator.

"This is Sergeant Michelson about Amanda", Sally said. "Mr. Thornbury is still feeling very sick and I think we should get him to a doctor."

Hamilton followed Sally's unspoken train of thought. The school had enough trouble already without the addition of gossip about an alcoholic headmaster.

"Yes, I think you're right. I'll take Sergeant Michelson up to my office and the best thing to do will be to ask Mrs. Schmidt to take the desk while you help the headmaster with a cab."

Lydia Schmidt, the school secretary, had been with the school for several decades and could be relied on to help keep this latest unfortunate episode under wraps.

13

Hamilton took Michelson up to his office on the fourth floor behind the biology lab, where Bobby was entertaining the sophomores with a riddle about a nun on a camel. Michelson seemed interested but Hamilton knew the answer and tactfully persuaded him to move along.

"We're taking this report very seriously since there has been a series of assaults on young women and this may be part of it", Michelson said. "Usually when teenage girls disappear they do it voluntarily and very often they're home again in a day or two, but there have been several rapes and a couple of stranglings, so in the circumstances we want to get on the job quickly. There are several things we'd really like to know, the first being whether Amanda has any particular friends who might have an idea where she is. Naturally we've talked to the parents, but parents often don't know what their children are up to."

"That's a difficult question—Amanda wasn't exactly the most popular kid in the school. She was a bit more self-centered than the average teenager and inclined to boast about her . . ."

Hamilton broke off and Michelson said, "Yes, Mr. Hamilton? What did she boast about?"

There was a long pause while Hamilton tried to make up his mind. Finally, bowing to the inevitable, he said, "Obviously I'm going to have to tell you the whole story. A little over two weeks ago, Amanda claimed that one of our teachers had tried to rape her."

Michelson listened in silence to a report in which Hamilton stuck closely to the facts as he had observed them and said nothing about Miller's reported affairs with Amanda and Jill. At the end the policeman said, "So there was a lot of money involved—right?"

"Yes—Miller never admitted anything and we had to pay him off as well."

"And you didn't believe Amanda's story?"

"No, I didn't."

"Why not?"

"Well, for a start, it's a funny place to try to rape someone—I mean, anyone could have walked in on them at any moment."

"Yes, Mr. Hamilton, but rapes do take place in funny places—doorways, staircases and elevators—it happens all the time. So you're saying she boasted about being raped?"

Hamilton sighed.

"I'm making a mess of this, I'm afraid. Obviously I'm very concerned about the school and its reputation. This business seems to have started last summer and all I know about it is the scuttlebutt that's been going around. Do you want to hear it?"

"Sure."

Hamilton told the whole story, including Amanda's displacement by Jill Davis and Hume's discovery of Jill's glasses in the supply room. Michelson listened with great interest but as he was leaving he reverted to Bobby Fine's riddle.

"By the way how *would* you describe a nun on a camel?"

Hamilton seemed to have his mind on other things, and Michelson had to repeat the question before he replied.

"Oh, virgin on the ridiculous."

With Mrs. Schmidt installed at the reception desk, Sally went back into the headmaster's office. Thornbury was sitting up and looking a little more normal.

"Please type this up for me, Sally, one copy for each Board member—I've forgotten how many that is. It's my resignation and I'd like it to go out today."

Sally looked at the headmaster with a mixture of frustration and sympathy. He was really quite an appealing old gentleman.

"Don't be silly", she said. "I'll get you a cab and you can go home and sleep it off. You'll feel much better tomorrow."

Thornbury looked at her in silent astonishment, so Sally went on talking.

"OK, you're the boss and I have to do as I'm told. But if you're really resigning, you're not my boss any more and I can say whatever I like."

"You don't know anything, Sally, not anything. But give me the letter and I'll think about it. Now I'd like to be left alone."

Sally thought that she knew more than Thornbury realized and that she probably ought to mention that there was a policeman in the building asking about Amanda, but she decided to leave the headmaster in peace a little longer. She had the door half-open when he said, "I'm sorry if I've been annoying you. It won't happen again."

She came back into the room and kissed him on the top of his head.

"Actually I kind of liked it. It's just that . . ."

"You had someone else on your mind?"

She kissed him again before leaving and closing the door gently behind her.

Thornbury had half-risen from his chair, but the effort was too much for him. Now he sat staring straight ahead, and what he saw was not the familiar door and oak-paneled wall.

Sergeant Michelson left the building with various possibilities buzzing around in his head. It seemed likely that Amanda's disappearance had something to do with Miller, and maybe they were off somewhere together, although why she would want to associate with someone who had tried to rape her he couldn't fathom. Well, maybe he didn't try to rape her—maybe she was just trying to get his attention. Or maybe—and this was a much more exciting idea—maybe the whole thing was a scheme to con the school. If that was the case, how did Jill Davis fit into the picture? Anyway, Miller had an apartment in Brooklyn, so it would probably be fairly easy to find him. Michelson tried Miller's listed phone number and didn't get a reply, so he called Inspector Williams, the senior officer in charge of the investigation, got the go-ahead and took the subway to Jay Street in the adjacent borough.

Miller's apartment was on the second floor in a four storey house on a quiet street. Getting no response to Miller's buzzer, Michelson looked at the names and tried all the other apartments. Eventually the elderly woman who occupied the first floor came to the door.

"Police", Michelson said, holding up his badge. "Mrs. Cohen?"

"Yes."

"I'm looking for Peter Miller. Have you seen him recently?"

"Not for a couple of days. Why, has he done something wrong?"

Michelson ignored the question.

"Would you know if he was here?"

"Well, he's usually very quiet, but I'm right below him and I can often hear him walking around."

"So when did you last hear him?"

"I think it was Saturday night but I can't be sure. At my age one day's pretty much like another. Not last night, anyway."

Michelson went upstairs, rang Miller's doorbell and banged with his fist. Still getting no response, he gave Mrs. Cohen a card and asked her to call him if she saw or heard anything. Miller was the only lead he had and now it seemed a little more likely that Amanda had absconded with him. Michelson took the rape accusation more seriously than Hamilton did, but he liked his con job theory too. Maybe there was some evidence in the apartment, so the obvious thing to do was to get a search warrant. Also it was just possible that he might find a dead girl or some evidence of a live one.

On that same Monday morning, while Sally and Hamilton were cleaning up Thornbury's office, Jean Hamilton was sitting up in bed and feeling more like throwing her coffee cup at the wall than drinking its contents. She was angry with her husband because he was indulging in an affair with a woman more than fifteen years younger than himself or, more to the point, nearly twenty years younger than herself; and she was angry with herself for setting out on a piece of smutty detective work and making a hash of it. Taking Jim's keys had been easy enough but then she had found that they weren't labeled and she had to get the whole lot copied. On Sunday she had guessed that Jim would leave around 2:30, which had become his usual time, and had gone out before him, giving no explanation and leaving him looking puzzled. It was a cold day so, muffled up to the point where her face was hardly visible, she had discreetly loitered near the corner of 90th Street and Central Park West opposite the school entrance. At first everything had worked according to plan and she had to wait only about fifteen minutes before Jim arrived. After another five minutes Sally came walking along and let herself into the school. It was a little after three o'clock and Jean decided to give them fifteen minutes to settle down to whatever they were doing. At 3:20 she thought maybe she could guess well enough and it might be better just to go home and confront her husband when he arrived. She wrestled with this idea for a few more minutes before getting hold of her bunch of keys and resolutely crossing the street. She was about to climb the steps to the front door when she looked along 90th street and saw Hume and Elsie coming along. She dodged around the corner and made it back to her vantage point without being seen. Now it seemed possible that nothing illicit was going on—it might just be some kind of teachers' meeting. She waited a little longer and was about to try again when a young couple, looking remarkably furtive, approached the school and went down the steps to the basement door. Just before they disappeared the man took off the scarf that had obscured the lower part of his face, and Jean was surprised to see that it was someone she knew. It was now 3:40 and whatever her husband and Sally were up to, they had been at it for over half an hour.

Jean crossed the street again and after several attempts found a key that worked. She had just made her way into the front hall and was standing irresolutely by the reception desk when the doorbell rang and she heard footsteps in the headmaster's office. She just had time to move back into the archway that led into the auditorium before Thornbury emerged and let his visitors in—a young couple that Jean didn't recognize. The school seemed to be alive with people and she really didn't want to be seen, so it seemed that her best policy would be to stay where she was until the coast was clear enough for her to make her escape. The result was that for the next hour or so she saw and heard everything that transpired in and around the area of the front hall.

It had been Jean's idea, a couple of years previously, that she should sleep in her study so that she could commune with Hamish into the small hours without disturbing Jim. After getting home around five o'clock that Sunday afternoon, she had been so tired and angry that she left a curt note for her husband and went straight to bed, although not to sleep—so when Jim arrived some time later, he found that his wife had a headache and he would have to get his own supper. He had an unpleasant feeling that Jean had found out what was going on and, in any case, he didn't feel like eating.

Jean got up around midnight and spent several hours bashing out her hostilities on the typewriter. She got back into bed around four in the morning, and was still there when her husband left for school. So among Hamilton's many worries on Monday was the fact that he didn't know what his wife was thinking. His guesses were not very reassuring.

14

Having made her peace with the headmaster, Sally returned to her desk, sent Mrs. Schmidt back to her normal duties, and left Thornbury to his cogitations for as long as she dared. When the Friedmans called again she told them that the headmaster was sick and Mr. Hamilton would return their call shortly. She called up to the biology lab but got no reply—Hamilton must be too involved in his lesson to answer the intercom—so she decided she'd have to break the bad news about Amanda to the headmaster. She knocked on his door, walked in and sat down on the visitor's chair in front of his desk.

"We have a difficult situation", she said. "Amanda Friedman is missing. She was out all night and isn't in school today. There was a policeman here some time ago and Mr. Hamilton talked to him. We told him you weren't available and I just told the Friedmans the same thing. Do you want to talk to them or shall I wait till Mr. Hamilton's free? It's only fifteen minutes to lunch time."

Thornbury was still staring straight ahead, and Sally wondered if he had heard her.

"Mr. Thornbury", she began again, but he silenced her with a gesture.

"Go and get Mr. Hamilton now. His class can have an early lunch."

The phone rang and Thornbury put his hand over it.

"Go", he said.

It was still ringing when she returned with Hamilton. Sally answered it at her desk.

"It was the policeman", she said. "He just wanted to know if Amanda had shown up."

"OK, Sally", Hamilton said. "Stay here while I talk to Mr. Thornbury, and if the Friedmans call again tell them I'll get right back to them."

There was nothing much to say, however. Hamilton thought he probably ought to mention the business of Jill and her glasses, but he doubted whether Thornbury was in a fit state to follow Hume's reasoning. The headmaster agreed that there was very little they could say to the Friedmans, apart from expressing sympathy and optimism.

"Ask Sally to come in for a minute", he said.

"I want to apologize for the mess I made and thank you both for cleaning it up. As Sally knows, I was on the verge of resigning this morning and thanks to her I had second thoughts. I'm more sober now than I have been for some time and I intend to keep it that way. I think I should tell you that Amanda has been blackmailing me—well, blackmailing the school, really. She knows a man who works for one of the tabloids and she's threatening to sell her story to him, with embellishments and a full account of her affair with Miller last summer. She's quite shameless about it and as far as the effect on the school is concerned it's like the original story—it doesn't make any difference whether it's true or not. She says her parents have taken charge of the payment we made and she wants some money for herself."

"When did you see her last?" Sally asked.

"Yesterday afternoon. She came here with her reporter friend and obviously I ought to tell the police about it."

"What happened?" Hamilton asked.

"They made demands and threatened to publish the whole story—her version of course—and I more or less told them to go to hell. So they left."

"And it's going to be a tabloid headline tomorrow? Which one?

"The Galaxy, but I think the whole thing may be just a bluff. She was confident that I'd go along, and when I told them there was nothing doing she was very surprised."

"What happened then?" Sally wanted to know.

"They left and I got drunk."

"I'd wait a bit before telling the police, if I were you", Hamilton said. "She'll probably show up as right as rain any moment now. Let's just give the Friedmans a sympathetic, noncommittal call."

Thornbury made the call.

Inspector Williams agreed with Michelson that a search of Miller's apartment was indicated, so at about four o'clock in the afternoon, Michelson obtained his search warrant and went over to Brooklyn again. There was no sign of Miller, no paper trail, no photograph, and no girl, dead or alive—not even a scrap of errant female underwear—but he did find a lot of anti-war literature. He also obtained some information about Miller's car, which was a blue, 1964 Dodge Dart, bought in his more affluent days as a GE scientist. Mrs. Cohen hadn't seen it recently, but then, as she said, Miller probably couldn't afford to garage it and it might be parked anywhere within half a mile or so.

A few minutes after four o'clock, just about the same time as Michelson was setting off for Brooklyn again, Hume was unlocking the door of the storeroom behind the lab. He switched the light on, took a step back, locked the door again and sat down at his desk. After a moment he called Hamilton on the intercom. Getting no reply, he tried the front desk and asked Sally if she knew where Hamilton was.

"He's with the headmaster and I'm not supposed to interrupt them."

"Well, you'll have to interrupt them. Tell them to come up to my office immediately."

"Why, what's the matter?"

"I've found Amanda."

There was a long pause before Sally asked, "Is she . . ."

"I'm afraid so. You'd better telephone the police."

15

Hume unlocked the storeroom door again. He had been quite certain that Amanda was dead and one touch confirmed that his diagnosis was correct—she was lying on her back in a perfectly natural position, just as Jessica had lain at the foot of a staircase in Gloucester, but Amanda was very cold and stiff, and someone had covered her body up to the shoulders with a brown raincoat. Nerving himself to take a more careful look, Hume raised the raincoat enough to see that she was wearing a short tan dress and long, leather boots. There were marks on her bare arms and there was a small patch of blood on the left shoulder of her dress. He heard footsteps behind him and let the raincoat drop.

"Poor kid", Hamilton said, as he knelt down by the body. "She wasn't a nice child but . . ."

"I know—only seventeen. It's amazing how people . . ."

"Change? Yes, she might have . . . Thornbury's talking to the police. Then he's going to call the Friedmans. They haven't seen Amanda since yesterday afternoon. Do you mind waiting here? I feel a bit . . ."

"That's all right. I'm sure it won't be long."

Hume was thinking that Hamilton probably had no experience of dead bodies. He hadn't seen his ship go down, leaving two hundred men struggling in the oily, U-boat-infested waters of the Atlantic, and he had never caused the death of a beautiful, outrageously talented girl of fifteen. Hume was thankful when his train of thought was derailed by the arrival of the headmaster and two uniformed policemen who took everybody's name and address and turned the back office into a crime scene. The police doctor arrived ten minutes later, accompanied by Inspector Williams and a couple of technicians. Williams, brown hair, brown eyes, medium height and medium everything else except for his very sharp brain, customarily worked with Michelson, who had phoned in and was on his way back from Brooklyn.

While the examination was going on, the civilians were herded back into the lab. Hume was the last to go and he clearly heard the doctor's preliminary verdict.

"Died sometime yesterday afternoon or evening. Probably not here, there ought to be a lot more blood. Severe trauma to the head, a nasty contusion on her left shoulder and bruises all over her body. Consistent with falling down a flight of stairs . . . Nice touch, covering her up with her raincoat—maybe he thought she might catch a cold."

The victim was Amanda, but the image of Jessica's broken body wouldn't go away. The doctor was right—there had been a lot of blood. Hume desperately wanted to be alone with his misery, but as the discoverer of the body, he was the first to be questioned. Like almost everyone else, Elsie had left for the day, so after an interminable wait, Williams took Hume to her room while Thornbury went down to his office to call the Friedmans, and Hamilton stayed in the lab. Michelson arrived just as the questions began.

Was the storeroom always locked? How often did he open the door and when had he last opened it? Was he sure it had been left locked on Friday? Who else had a key to it? Why had he gone in there on this occasion? Was Amanda in any of his classes? Had he ever seen her outside school hours? How did she seem on Friday? Apart from the information that Hume, Fine and Hamilton all had keys to the storeroom and that Hume had been told that there was a full set of keys in the safe in the headmaster's office, none of these questions yielded any particular insight.

Michelson joined in the questioning.

"Were you aware of any problem Amanda may have had with anyone in the school?"

"I have no direct knowledge but I know that she accused my predecessor here of trying to rape her."

"Do you believe the story?"

"I only know what I've been told, so I have no basis for an opinion."

"Who told you the story?" Williams wanted to know.

"Mr. Hamilton."

"Does he believe it?"

"It might be better if you asked him."

"Are you a British citizen, Mr. Hume?"

"Yes."

"How long have you been in this country?"

"Just over three weeks."

"Did you have this job lined up beforehand?"

"No."

"So why did you leave England?"

"My wife and I had a bad falling-out, ending in divorce. I wanted to get away."

"Are you in any trouble with the British police?"

Hume hesitated before truthfully answering, "No."

The detectives noted the hesitation but knowing that the British police would be very cooperative, they didn't say anything.

"I see you live in the school building next door", Williams said, "so if you would give us your last address and employment details in England, we'll be through for the moment. Please stay in this building for the time being."

Hume wondered whether he ought to have told the police about seeing Hamilton and Sally near the school the previous afternoon and Miller and Jill the Sunday before, but his desire to end the interview was paramount. Later on he would tell them everything, but if they wanted any more information now, they'd have to ask.

Obviously Bobby Fine would have to be interviewed, but he had been teaching in No. 3 and had left for the day, so leaving

Amanda's body in the care of an underling, the detectives accompanied Hamilton to the headmaster's office.

"I'm glad to see you're feeling better, Sir", Michelson said to Thornbury, who found the remark puzzling. Surely no one had told the detective that he had been drunk and incapable earlier in the day, so all he could think of to say was, "I beg your pardon?"

"I understood you were ill this morning, Sir."

"Oh. Oh, I see. Yes, I'm feeling much better, thank you."

Michelson glanced at Williams, who raised an eyebrow. Obviously there was something there, but he'd better confer with his superior before following it up.

So they started on the questioning. Having had a quick briefing on the alleged rape, Williams wanted to know how Thornbury viewed the matter, but first he asked whether the Friedmans knew about Amanda's death.

"I talked to Dr. Friedman. He's picking up his wife and should be here in a few minutes. As far as the supposed rape is concerned, I wasn't aware of anything until Mr. Hamilton reported the incident to me. I immediately called Dr. Friedman at his office and Mrs. Friedman at their home. They arrived separately about half an hour later and meanwhile I heard Amanda's account and interviewed Miller. It took a lot of negotiating but in the end, to put it very bluntly, the school purchased everybody's silence at a heavy price."

"You didn't think of calling in the police?"

"I didn't even consider it although, of course, the Friedmans did—that was their leverage."

"And how did Miller feel about the arrangement?"

"He never admitted anything, but he seemed glad to take the money."

"And run?"

"Exactly."

"So as far as you were concerned the thing was settled?"

"Yes—after a lot of discussion it was left in the hands of the lawyers. There was a written agreement, all properly signed and sealed. Miller admitted no guilt and the Friedmans agreed to take no further action."

There was a buzz on the intercom and Thornbury hesitated.

"Better pick it up, Sir", Williams said, but before he could do so the door opened and Sally walked in.

"I'm sorry", she said. "Jill Davis is missing. I got a little nervous after . . . you know. I called the home and no one answered, so I called Mrs. Davis at work and she thought Jill was at school. I think she thought Jill was playing truant, but then she got nervous and went home to check and Jill isn't there. I suppose she may be playing truant but . . ."

"Maybe she is", Michelson said, "And if she is I'm pretty sure I know who she's playing it with."

Williams said, "This wouldn't be so serious if we didn't already have a dead body on our hands. We'll need her address and a full description and we'll put out a call for her and Miller. Is her mother still on the line?"

"No—she's staying by the phone in case Jill calls."

"Does she know about Amanda?

"Not from me."

"Good. Is there an outside line from Mr. Hume's office upstairs?"

"Yes, just dial 9 first."

"OK, give me Mrs. Davis's number and we'll make our calls from there."

Turning to Thornbury, he added, "That floor has to be off limits for the time being, Sir. What are your plans for tomorrow?"

"School will be closed tomorrow. Sally has already informed the class representatives and they'll be working their telephone trees. Further than that I don't know. I'll get hold of as many of the trustees as I can for an emergency Board meeting this evening and when we do open again we may find that we don't have any students. You can't hush up a thing like this."

Williams grunted sympathetically.

"We'll have to interview all faculty and staff. If you can have everybody here at nine o'clock in the morning we'll get through it as quickly as possible."

"I'll see that they are informed. I'm sure Sally will be willing to make the calls, although it's outside her working hours."

"Maybe I should stay down here", Michelson said to Williams.

"OK. Try and get hold of Robert Fine while I talk to Mrs. Davis. And get a couple of scientists to make a complete examination of all the staircases and the elevator."

Turning back to Thornbury, Williams added, "I understand there's a full set of keys in the safe here and I'd like you to check that the chemistry storeroom key is there."

The headmaster removed a portrait of Benjamin Thompson from the wall behind his desk, revealing a door about twelve inches by eighteen. There was no lock on the door but behind it there was a steel safe with a combination lock which it took Thornbury several attempts to open. He pulled out a metal tray, fumbled in it for a few seconds and said, "It isn't here."

He handed the tray to Williams.

"It's a Yale key with a label attached."

"Better check the whole safe—it may have fallen out of the tray."

Thornbury did so and asked Williams to check for himself. There was no Yale key there.

"OK, Sir. Could someone have borrowed it—who else knows the combination of the safe?"

"Mr. Hamilton and Mr. Johnson, the business administrator—and, of course, Mr. Weinstock, the deputy headmaster, only he's been in the hospital for the past two weeks."

"OK, so when did you last see it?"

"Frankly, I've no idea. I've never needed to use it."

"How about you, Mr. Hamilton. Do you know anything about this key?"

"No—as the headmaster said, I have my own."

"Could you show it to us?"

Hamilton pulled out a key wallet and exhibited a Yale key in a compartment with the rest of his school keys.

"I see you don't label your keys", Williams said.

"No, they're all recognizable enough."

"Is this a complete set?"

"Yes."

"So you can open any door in the school?"

"Right."

Williams turned to the headmaster.

"I'd appreciate it if you would bring the Friedmans up to the third floor after you've finished with them. We'll have some more questions for you also, but that can probably wait until the morning. Oh, and would you please write down the combination for me?"

"That's easy", Thornbury said. "It's THOMPS."

"One more question—do all the teachers have complete sets of keys?"

"No—they all have front door keys and any keys they need for their work."

"So although anyone can get out through the basement door, most of them can't get in that way."

"That's correct."

Hamilton waited until the detectives were on their way back upstairs.

"Are you planning to tell them about Amanda's blackmailing activities?"

"I don't know. I'll have to think about it."

"Well, don't forget there's a journalist who knows all about it."

16

Hume had been aimlessly wandering around while he tried to figure out what had happened. Evidently Amanda had died some time on Sunday afternoon or evening, and there had been people all over the building during the afternoon. He had been there with Elsie at three thirty and he had heard voices in the headmaster's office as he left. Hamilton had been there with Sally. He hadn't seen the occupants of the infirmary, but he guessed that they were Jill and Miller. Another reasonable assumption was that one of Thornbury's guests had been Amanda—Hume had seen the two of them disagreeing rancorously in the park two weeks previously. Someone had killed Amanda and hidden her body, but why was she left in the storeroom? Or maybe her death was accidental—she had fallen down a flight of stairs and inexplicably someone had moved her and covered her with her raincoat. Hume didn't want it to be stairs, so he tried to think of some other possibility, like a fight with someone. It didn't seem very plausible. He went into one of the front classrooms on the fifth floor and looked down at the police cars double-parked on the street. He really ought to tell the police all he knew about the occupants of the school, but he was reluctant to do so without first conferring with Hamilton. If the detectives had finished with him he would probably be in his office. He started down the stairs and bumped into a policeman.

"Sorry, Sir, you can't come this way but you can take the elevator—we've finished with it."

The fourth floor was deserted, so Hume sat at Hamilton's desk and put his head down. Once before in his life he had suppressed the evidence of a murder and now he was doing it again, the difference being that this time it was somebody else's murder and he didn't know whose. He felt desperately tired and his mind began to wander. His last clear thought was that whereas everyone had liked Jessica, no one seemed to have liked Amanda.

Mrs. Davis was not very coherent. It took Williams some time to elicit the information that Jill had been out all afternoon the previous day and had returned home about six o'clock for a quiet birthday celebration. She hadn't wanted any guests, so they were just going to have some supper together and open some presents. Jill had seemed very strange, however. She didn't want to eat and went to bed without opening her presents. Later she had come out of her room and apologized to her mother and seemed to be feeling better, so Mrs. Davis hadn't worried too much.

"Did you see her this morning?"

"No—I have to leave at seven o'clock and she doesn't usually get up until after I've gone."

"So you don't actually know she was there. Could she have left in the night without waking you up?"

"Oh, my God, I don't know—I guess so."

"I'd like to see her room—there may be something there that will help us."

Mrs. Davis agreed that Williams could visit her apartment as soon as he'd finished up at school. He was about to try Bobby Fine's number when the intercom buzzed and Sally told him that the Friedmans had arrived and were talking to the headmaster. She had called Bobby and he was on his way back to school.

If Hume had been present at the interview between Williams and the Friedmans, he would have concluded that he was right about Amanda—even her parents didn't seem to have liked her very much. Dr. Friedman had identified the body without turning a hair, and whatever emotion his wife showed on hearing of her daughter's death was more like annoyance than grief. Their primary concern seemed to be to get the funeral arranged and over so that they could return to their normal lives, and they couldn't understand why there had to be a post mortem.

"Surely the cause of death was obvious", Dr. Friedman insisted. "How long are we going to have to wait?"

Williams, who had a lot of experience of dealing gently with grieving parents, spouses and lovers, found his patience wearing thin.

"All I can tell you is that the P. M. is mandatory and they'll be as quick as possible. As a doctor, you must know that the cause of death is not always the obvious one."

"I'm not that kind of doctor", Friedman snapped.

"He's a doctor of philosophy", his wife explained, with a note of pride in her voice, and immediately spoilt the effect by adding, "Although what digging up ancient graveyards has to do with philosophy I've never been able to figure."

"Pardon me", Williams said. "Do you have any idea what she would have been doing here? Could she have been meeting someone?"

Amanda's parents looked at each other and hesitated. Finally Dr. Friedman said he thought Miller was involved.

"You don't really believe that, do you, Dr. Friedman?" Williams said.

Getting only a glare in response, he went on.

"It doesn't seem likely that she would arrange to meet someone who had tried to rape her."

Still getting no response, Williams continued.

"I have been told that there was a love affair between Amanda and Peter Miller that went on for some months before the alleged sexual assault in this building. Mr. Thornbury has given me some information about a settlement involving a large sum of money. I'd like to know if you have any comments."

"What do you mean by 'alleged'?" Mrs. Friedman hooted. "Of course there was an assault. He tried to rape her. In our opinion the school got off lightly, and Miller ought to be in jail."

"Do you know of any evidence of that, apart from what your daughter said?"

"If you've heard the story", Dr. Friedman said, "you know that her panties were under Miller's table."

"Would you say that Amanda was always a very truthful girl?"

"Absolutely."

"So you don't think she might have put them there herself?"

Dr. Friedman stood up.

"I don't think we have any more to say. Come, Stella, we're leaving now."

"One more question, Dr. Friedman; did Amanda say anything about her plans for Sunday?"

But the Friedmans were already halfway to the door.

"Weird", Michelson said when they were out of sight.

"Very—obviously a background check is indicated. We'd better do a routine check of Amanda's room, but if there's anything to hide, they'll have hidden it by now."

By six o'clock the technicians had reported that there was blood on the landing where the basement stairs did a one-eighty halfway down, and that there were traces in the elevator. Bobby Fine had been no help at all. Yes, he did have a key to the storeroom, but he hadn't been near the school since Friday. He had spent Sunday morning in bed, and the afternoon and evening in the same place after being joined by a young lady whom he would prefer not to identify.

While Bobby was being interviewed, Thornbury arranged the Board Meeting for eight o'clock and went out for a meal. Sally was reluctant to leave, although she had finished making her phone calls and had been told that she could go home. Hamilton had called his wife and given her a fairly accurate account of what had happened, while leaving her with the impression that the police were still there and that he would be needed for another couple of hours.

There was only a small element of truth in this—Williams had told him and Sally that they wouldn't be needed until the morning. The inspector had then gone to see Mrs. Davis, leaving Michelson to do one more walk through the building before going home.

"Come on", Hamilton said to Sally, "we have to figure some things out." They went up to Hamilton's office, where it was almost pitch dark. Sally gave a little squawk when she switched on the light and saw Hume slumped over the desk.

"He isn't dead, is he?"

Hume sat up groggily as Sally put a hand on his shoulder.

"Hello—I was waiting for you and I must have fallen asleep."

He looked at Sally and then at Hamilton.

"Well, I guess you've found us out", she said, not knowing that she had already been the subject of a conversation between Hume and Hamilton.

Hume smile wanly.

"You seem to have been fairly discreet during school hours but a bit careless at weekends. I just tend to potter about on Sundays and sometimes I notice things, some of which I ought to tell the police about. That's really why I'm here—I wanted to talk to you first."

"You're not . . ." Sally began.

"No", Hamilton interrupted, "he isn't."

"Blackmailing you?" Hume asked in astonishment. "Of course not! Whatever put that into your head?"

"I'm sorry, John. If you want to know the truth, I like you very much and so does Jim—it's just that Amanda was . . ."

"Blackmailing Thornbury? I'm not surprised—I saw them in the park two weeks ago and I'm almost certain she was in his office yesterday."

"What were they doing in the park?" Hamilton asked.

"Having a very loud argument. The last thing she said was, 'I'm serious, you know' and I think he called her a stupid little bitch. It doesn't look good, does it?"

"No, it doesn't. And there's more that you don't know about. We really ought to talk to him, but he's gone out and when he comes back he'll be with the trustees."

Sally had another idea.

"If you want to talk, let's go over to Kelly's and have a drink together and try to figure it out. Maybe it wouldn't all seem so awful if we got a little bit drunk."

They trooped over to Amsterdam Avenue and found a table in the little Irish bar. Hamilton ordered a round of double scotches and said, "Sally and I have been in love for a long time . . ."

Sally smiled.

"You're such an old romantic, Jim. It's been about three weeks. And I'm not sure it's flattering if it seems like a long time. Now this is where you say, 'It seems like we've always been in love.'"

Hamilton didn't look particularly amused, but he went on.

"I think Jean has begun to get the idea—but I guess that's not what you want to talk about."

The drinks arrived and, remarking that she liked to keep up the continuity, Sally immediately ordered another round.

"I don't want to talk about anything", Hume said, "but the school was like a railway station yesterday. You were up behind the bio lab, I was down below, Elsie was in her room—I had brunch with her and we walked over together—Thornbury was having a heated argument with two people in his office, one of whom might have been Amanda, and there were people making love in the infirmary. That makes nine altogether and it seems fairly likely that at least one of them—or us, I suppose I should say—had something to do with Amanda's death. As far as I know, the police don't know any of this. As Jim knows, I've been involved in a murder case before and on that occasion I withheld evidence. Now that the shock of finding Amanda's body is beginning to wear off, I don't want to do it again. Obviously I ought to have told them that I was in the building, and they're going to wonder why I didn't."

"They're going to interview everybody tomorrow morning", Sally said, "and I don't suppose Elsie will think there's any reason why she shouldn't mention that she was there with you. And you can bet they'll ask the doormen across the street if they saw people going in and out. Like you said, we may have been a bit careless. I guess we have to tell them we were there. Maybe it's got to the point where Jean has to know anyway. What do you think, Jim"

Hamilton was silent. He had always known that at some point he would have to break the news to his wife, and as long as this unhappy event was scheduled for some unspecified future time he had been fairly calm about it. Now he was beginning to think that she had somehow found out already. When he talked to her on the phone she had been grumpy and monosyllabic, as if she didn't much care whether he came home or not. But the idea that he might have to talk openly to her about Sally, maybe on that very evening, still came as a great shock and left him in the grip of some powerful and unexpected emotions.

"I'm sorry", he said eventually. "I guess I'm really a complete coward. You know, after twenty years . . ."

Feeling very much out of place, Hume stood up and said, "I should leave."

Sally didn't agree.

"Sit down, John. This is about murder, not about marriage. I just learned something new about Jim, but I'll deal with that later. What's really bothering me at the moment is the idea that someone in the school is a murderer. I vote we tell the police everything and let the chips fall."

Hume had been thinking the same thing.

"Maybe we should tell them tonight—the longer we wait the more suspicious it's going to look."

"OK, but let's have another drink first. Come on, Jim—have some more Dutch courage. I still love you, but I don't want to marry a coward."

"I'm working on it—a couple more drinks and I'll tell anybody anything."

"Great—well you'd better keep working on it. Anyway, we should probably tell John what the headmaster told us. You know, about Amanda. And then I have an idea."

"You'd better tell us the idea first."

"OK, it's really simple. The three of us agree that none of us killed Amanda and then we figure out who did. What do you think, John?"

"I'll take the first bit as a working hypothesis", Hume said seriously. "But I'd really rather not be involved in a murder investigation."

Sally was taken aback.

"You really think one of us might have done it? Or both?"

"I know that neither of you would deliberately kill anyone. But people die in different ways, and when you're responsible for somebody's death you may see things from a different angle. I came over to America to get away from something for which I was responsible, and now I'm up to my neck in the same kind of thing, only this time I'm not responsible. I'll tell you everything I know and then we'll tell the police. And then I'd rather not have anything to do with it."

"And the fact that Amanda was blackmailing Mr. Thornbury doesn't alter that?"

"I don't see why it should."

"Because what we tell the police will make it look obvious that he killed Amanda and I don't think he did. What you don't know is that he spent all Sunday night in his office and he was still dead drunk this morning. And there was a scotch bottle smashed all over the floor? Obviously he got so angry he hit her over the head with the bottle and hid the body in the storeroom. That's what they'll think."

Hume had some information that he didn't want to contemplate, but now it was necessary to force the words out.

"She had a lot of bruises as well as the head wound. The doctor said she might have fallen down a flight of stairs. There would have been a lot of blood."

"That doesn't make sense", Sally said. "If you're right about hearing her in Mr. Thornbury's office, she was on the first floor already. I can't think of any reason why she'd go upstairs."

"Or down", Hume added.

Hamilton stirred restlessly. All this stuff with the police would be very difficult and probably take a long time. He ought to call Jean again but he knew he couldn't.

"So Thornbury hit her with the bottle, picked her up and threw her down a flight of stairs and then took the body upstairs and hid it in the storeroom. Drink up and let's go."

17

The Davis apartment was a fifth floor walk-up on East 83rd Street. Mrs. Davis was waiting at the door and pointed silently along a narrow passage that led to the living room. Inspector Williams hadn't seen Jill but he had noted her description and heard her described as a round and cuddly brunette, so he was surprised to find that her mother was a tall, willowy blonde. The explanation, however, was visible in the shape of a family photograph standing on a low table next to a sofa-bed under the room's only window. Jill, who looked about ten years old, was standing between her parents at Coney Island Beach and her mother looked sensational in a dark blue bikini, whereas her father, dark haired and a couple of inches shorter, seemed to have made up for his lack of vertical extension by growing a prominent beer belly.

Following Williams's gaze, Mrs. Davis picked up the photograph and finally spoke.

"I still can't think why I married him. He was a used car salesman."

"Was?"

"Well, maybe he still is—I was one of his customers and I guess I thought I was getting a bargain. He seemed to be in pretty good condition and I didn't find out until later how high his mileage was. Talk about used! I haven't seen or heard anything of him for six years, which is one reason why we're living in this cruddy apartment. I'm sorry—I don't suppose you're interested in that stuff. Have you heard anything?"

Actually, Williams was interested—missing fathers were sometimes linked to missing children—but he didn't want to get into that possibility yet.

"No, I'm afraid not—I take it you haven't either."

"Not a thing. I don't understand Jill doing this. We're pretty happy together—I mean as happy as a middle-aged mother and a teenage daughter are likely to be."

"You don't look middle-aged."

"Well, I try not to act it either—it just creeps up on you. This is my first year of being thirty-nine."

Williams smiled sympathetically.

"Are there any relatives she might have gone to?"

"Her father came from Long Island City and we never had much contact with his side of the family. My nearest and dearest are all in Ohio."

"What about boyfriends?"

"I don't have one at the moment—Oh hell, I'm sorry again. The fact is I'm worried out of my mind and a bit hysterical. She liked boys and there was all that talk about her and Peter Miller, but Jill said all they did was talk sometimes and I thought it was mostly put about by that nasty little—well, I shouldn't use that word . . . I mean Amanda Friedman."

No use putting it off, Williams was thinking. If she didn't hear it, plain and unvarnished, from him now, she'd get it sensationalized from the papers in the morning.

"I'm sorry to tell you that Amanda is dead—her body was found in the school this afternoon."

Mrs. Davis crumpled onto the sofa and Williams thought she had fainted.

"I'll be OK", she said after a moment. "How did it happen?"

"It's hard to say. It seems she fell down the basement stairs but her body was found in a closet upstairs. Are you OK?"

"It's a shock to hear about this when my own daughter has just disappeared. I've been stretched out all day and I guess I was just letting go. You look like a nice man—would you like a drink? I didn't start yet because I knew I wouldn't be able to stop and I wanted to be sober when you got here. I don't have much but there's scotch, rum and vodka in the cupboard and coke and beer in the fridge."

She patted the sofa beside her.

"Then you can sit down and talk to me. You can call me Chrissie. Are you married?"

"Not so you'd notice. I'll get you a drink and then I'd like to take a look at Jill's room. What would you like?"

"Rum and coke, but I'll get it myself since you're being so goddamn professional. I was just hoping you might help me take my mind off things. Jill's room is at the other end of the passage. We only have two rooms—I sleep on this damn sofa-bed."

Twenty minutes in Jill's room yielded very little except the information that she was deeply involved with the anti-war movement. The Beatles evidently took third place to Joan Baez and Pete Seeger. There were posters and fliers with information about protest marches, along with pamphlets from Students for a Democratic Society. One thing that Williams very much wanted to know was whether Jill had taken anything with her that suggested that when she left the apartment in the morning she wasn't expecting to come back. He returned to the living room. Mrs. Davis had pulled out the sofa-bed and was lying under a pink sheet with her bare shoulders and enough cleavage showing to suggest that she hadn't bothered with a night dress.

She held up an empty glass and said, "You really take your time, don't you—this is my third."

"'Was', you mean. Can you stand up?"

"Yes and there's no need to be insulting."

Williams smiled inwardly. Fornication might be immoral but it wasn't illegal, and as long as it wasn't illegal . . . Some other time maybe . . .

"OK then, Chrissie, put something on and come and tell me what's missing from Jill's room."

He went back to the bedroom, and when she joined him a moment later she appeared to be wearing just the sheet.

"I looked in the hall closet", she said, "and she's just taken her usual jacket. I don't know half of what she has so I can't tell by looking at her other clothing. Oh . . ."

"What?"

"I can't see her raccoon."

"Her what?"

"It's a stuffed animal I gave her when she was a baby—she never goes anywhere without it. It's quite big and she usually leaves it on her pillow."

They searched the whole room without success and finally Williams said, "You realize this is a good sign, don't you?"

"Yes—it means she left of her own accord."

"And you're sure you haven't quarreled?"

"Well, I'd know about it if we had, wouldn't I?"

"OK. Listen, this almost certainly has nothing to do with Amanda. Probably Jill is off with a boy somewhere, having a good time. I'd better be going. Here's my card—let me know if you hear anything."

"OK, Patrick, now I know your first name. I expect you're right, and I wouldn't mind having a good time too—are you sure you wouldn't like to . . ."

Williams wasn't at all sure. He looked at his watch. Chrissie grinned.

"I thought so", she said as she let the sheet drop.

18

When Williams got back to his office, he found Sally, Hume and Hamilton waiting for him.

"Sorry you've had to wait such a long time", Williams said, "I've been trying to clear up some loose ends. What can I do for you?"

Hamilton was silent and Sally looked at Hume, who reluctantly took the lead.

"I hope you won't arrest us for withholding information. We want to tell you some things that we ought to have mentioned earlier."

"It's a nuisance but it happens all the time. Go right ahead."

Hume nodded to Hamilton but nothing happened until Sally said, "Come on Jim, I hope you're not feeling embarrassed on my account."

Hamilton shook his head and there was another awkward pause before he started.

"All right, I suppose the first thing is that all three of us were in the school on Sunday afternoon. Miss Evans and I were in my office behind the biology lab from about three o'clock until four thirty or so."

"What was the purpose of your visit, Mr. Hamilton?"

"We were studying physiology, of course", Sally put in. "Is that clear enough?"

"Yes, thank you, Miss Evans. Did you see or hear anyone else in the building?"

"No, but that doesn't necessarily mean anything. We were in the back of the fourth floor and kind of preoccupied. But really there's never anybody there on a Sunday afternoon."

"Never? How long has your affair with Mr. Hamilton been going on?"

"Why do you want to know?" she asked, unconsciously echoing Dirac.

"They want to know everything, Sally", Hamilton said. "Since the middle of January, Inspector. And, for your information, my wife doesn't know about it. Although—I don't know—maybe she does."

Sally looked at Hamilton in surprise but Williams took it in his stride. After twenty years of police work he was no longer surprised at the things that spouses did and didn't know about each other.

"Did either of you notice anything unusual in the elevator?"

"We didn't use it", Sally said. "I know I said there's never anybody there, but the elevator makes so much noise and I'm always afraid the door will open and someone will be there. It just seems safer on the stairs? Why, was there something?"

"We'll come to that later—maybe. Now, Mr. Hume, what's your story?"

Hume was silent for a moment. Hamilton and Sally had been intending to tell the inspector everything they knew, but Williams had cut them off at the pass by asking questions instead of just letting Hamilton get on with it. So nothing about blackmail and the state of Thornbury's office and the fact that he had been there overnight had emerged. Well, that wasn't Hume's business—Hamilton and Sally would have to decide if they wanted to say any more.

"Yes, Mr. Hume?"

Once he got started, Hume talked fast in the hope of not being interrupted.

"I had brunch with Mrs. Smith and we walked over to the school together. We got there at about half past three and went to our rooms on the third floor. I heard someone moving about on the floor above me. I did a few odd jobs and went downstairs at about four o'clock, intending to leave through the main entrance. There were voices coming from the headmaster's office. I had the impression that he had two visitors, one of them female. It sounded like a rather heated discussion, so instead of using the main entrance, which would have taken me right past the office door, I went downstairs and out through the basement door. When I reached the foot of the stairs I heard soft voices and giggles coming from the infirmary."

"Infirmary?"

"It's a small room used by the school nurse, opposite the elevator door in the basement."

"Does it contain a bed?"

"I believe so—I've never been in there."

"It does contain a bed", Hamilton said.

"But we weren't using it at the time", Sally added.

Williams, who greatly appreciated her habit of not mincing matters, smiled and shook his head at her.

"Sorry", she said.

Hume continued.

"I went into the park and saw Mr. Hamilton and Miss Evans walking away from the school about half an hour later, although I don't think they saw me."

"I saw you", Sally said. "You were hiding behind a tree."

"Is that correct, Mr. Hume?"

"Yes."

"Why were you hiding?"

"I . . . It's hard to explain."

Sally came to the rescue.

"John is a perfect English gentleman and he's very shy. He's also one of the nicest people I've ever met and he didn't want to embarrass us."

"I see. Go on, Mr. Hume."

"I stayed in the park until it got dark and then I went back to my apartment."

"Can anybody confirm that?"

"Not that I know of—I didn't see anyone."

"What time did you get back?"

"About five thirty."

"OK, now I have an account of your movements yesterday—is there anything else you'd like to tell me?"

"Yes", Hume said. "The first Sunday I was here, which was two weeks ago yesterday, I saw Mr. Thornbury talking to Amanda in the park. It was not a friendly conversation."

Hamilton was intently studying the floor but Hume caught Sally's eye.

"OK", she said. "We were going to tell the whole story, so here it is."

And there it was. Williams sat in silence as he heard about the state of the headmaster's office, the fact that he had spent Sunday night there and his admission that Amanda had been blackmailing him. One thing that Sally didn't mention was that Amanda had walked in on her and Hamilton on the previous Friday afternoon.

19

Sharing a cab uptown, the three reluctant witnesses found very little to say to one another. After dropping Sally off on the East Side, Hume and Hamilton crossed Central Park at 86th Street, where Hume was happy to get out and walk the rest of the way. Hamilton arrived home around eleven o'clock and found that the situation was the same as it had been on the previous evening except that there was no note. Jean didn't appear in the morning, so by the time he arrived at school on Tuesday, he hadn't seen his wife for almost two days.

Sally was right—Aloysius Thornbury had become Williams's number one suspect, although the detective still didn't know exactly where or how Amanda had died, why there was blood on the basement stairs, and why the girl had been taken up to the storeroom. It would be a good idea to talk to the headmaster before anyone else did—meaning Hamilton, Sally or Hume—and before he had the chance to get rid of his bloody clothes.

After his conference with Hume, Hamilton and Sally, Williams called Thornbury at home and then at school and got no response in either case. He looked at his watch—9:45. Maybe the meeting with the trustees was still going on and they weren't picking up. Better go and see. Fifteen minutes later he and Michelson were standing at the corner of 90th and Central Park West, where a large limousine was waiting. There was a light on in Thornbury's office and they were about to ring the bell when the door opened and a middle-aged woman appeared. She was wearing a bright red beret from which strands of grey hair protruded randomly, and her angular face was innocent of make-up. Williams thought he had seen her somewhere before.

"Who are you?" she snapped. "Police, I suppose. Are you going to arrest Thornbury?"

She stood back and as they entered, Williams said, "Thank you, Ma'am. What makes you think that?"

"Well, look at the time. Obviously this isn't a social call and somebody had to get rid of that girl."

"Why was that?"

"She was a liar and a blackmailer—well, he's in his office. You might as well go in and get it over—only you can take my word for it, he didn't do it."

"How do you know?"

"Too much of a coward."

"Are you one of the trustees, Ma'am?"

"Yes, I am. Mrs. George M. Picard the Third. You may have heard of me."

Michelson was wondering if this meant that she was the third Mrs. George M. Picard, but the penny had already dropped for the inspector.

"Victoria Picard?" Williams asked.

"Only in public. My husband was very old-fashioned."

Victoria Picard was the queen of *haute couture*, who notoriously never wore any of her company's clothing or used any of their beauty products. "Vicky Picky" to her employees, she was well known for her sharp tongue but was rumored to have a kind heart. She was definitely not the kind of person the police would want to keep waiting around while they interviewed someone else.

"Well, go on. I can't wait here all night."

"Actually, Mrs. Picard, there's no need for you to wait at all. We may need to talk to you again, but it doesn't have to be now. And I'm not expecting to arrest anyone tonight. Have all the other trustees left?"

"Yes. They're all the yes-Sir-no-Sir-three-bags-full kind and I wanted to find out what was really going on, so I made him tell me."

Thornbury appeared at his office door and said, "Oh."

"I'll leave now", Mrs. Picard said. "Tell them everything, Aloysius. They know you didn't do it. I told them."

Thornbury retreated into his office. Williams and Michelson followed him, but Mrs. George M. Picard III muttered, "Silly old fool", just loud enough to be heard, and marched out of the building.

The first thing the policemen noticed about Thornbury was that he was wearing a different suit.

"Do you keep some spare clothing in the school, Sir?" Williams asked.

"No, I'd been wearing the same clothes for a day and a half, so I slipped home and changed before the trustees arrived."

Williams swallowed this silently. Could he conceivably arrest Thornbury as a material witness and get a search warrant for his apartment? Probably not, Williams thought. Ben Thompson might not be anything to write home about, but its headmaster was an independently wealthy man with influential connections. If Williams had known earlier what he knew now, he would have told the scientists to make a serious examination of the headmaster's office. Meanwhile, someone might already have disposed of some bloodstained shoes and clothing.

The ensuing interview was very difficult. It had been a very long day, Thornbury said; he had been ill in the morning and he needed to go home and go to bed.

"What was the nature of your illness", Williams asked, while Michelson began a minute examination of the floor.

"Hangover. What's he doing?"

"Just looking", Michelson said, holding up a couple of slivers of glass. "What would you say these are?"

"Evidence that I'm telling the truth—I dropped my whiskey bottle last night."

Williams said, "I think, if you don't mind, Sir, we'll move out to the receptionist's desk. I want to seal this room and have it thoroughly examined in the morning."

"I gather that you spent the night in your office", Williams continued after getting the headmaster settled in Sally's chair.

"Yes."

"Is that a frequent occurrence?"

"No."

"When did you last see Amanda Friedman?"

"Yesterday afternoon."

"What did she want?"

"Money."

"Was anyone else present?"

"Yes."

"Who?"

"A reporter from the *Galaxy.*"

"Do you know his name?"

"Yes."

"What is it?"

Williams could keep this up all night but Thornbury couldn't. His eyes were drooping as he replied, "Michael Schwartz."

"What did you talk about?"

There was no reply; Thornbury had fallen asleep.

"Go up to the third floor", Williams told his sergeant. "There's an electric kettle and a jar of instant coffee on Hume's desk. We'll give him ten minutes and then give it to him hot and strong."

So for the second time that day, Thornbury was given the black coffee treatment, but this time it seemed to wake up a streak of obstinacy in him.

"Look, I've already told you", he said when the questioning started again. "They wanted money. I told them there was nothing doing and they left. That's all. Now I want to go home."

"So they left the building and the last time you saw Amanda she was alive and well?"

"I didn't see them leave the building. I just stayed in my office and they left—and unless you're planning to arrest me, that's what I'm going to do now."

Michelson took the Manhattan phone book from the shelf next to Sally's desk and discovered that fourteen Michael Schwartzes were listed as well as several M. Schwartzes. Williams pointed out that the name might equally well be Schwarz, since the pronunciation would be the same, and this brought the number up to two dozen. There were people working at the *Galaxy* offices, but no one admitted knowing where Michael was. When Williams finally managed to convince one of the senior editors that this was a police enquiry he was met with a barrage of questions. "What was the enquiry about? How was Michael involved? Inspector Williams—aren't you the officer in charge of the serial rapist investigation? Are you making any progress? Can you give us a line?"

It took several minutes and the threat of a police investigation of the Galaxy's methods and sources before Williams could get the information that it was Schwartz with a "t" and an address on West 89th Street. He tried the phone number that went with the address and almost dropped the phone in surprise when Schwartz answered. Williams told Schwartz that his name had come up in connection with an investigation and didn't mention the fact that he and his sergeant were just around the corner at the school. It was his opinion that a good look at the enemy's headquarters was always potentially helpful, and at this point he regarded Schwartz as the enemy.

Michael Schwartz had the whole third floor of a brownstone between Columbus Avenue and Central Park West. Williams, who harbored a stereotypical image of a bachelor apartment, was surprised to find himself in an immaculately kept living room talking to a personable young man with a taste for delicate china ornaments, dried flowers and watercolor landscapes. Michelson, bulky and not gifted with the art of graceful movement, stood by the door, feeling exactly like a bull in a china shop. He had had a lot of experience of reporters, and Schwartz's apparent inoffensiveness only made him more deeply suspicious.

Williams was aware that Schwartz almost certainly knew the rules, but he thought he would try him out anyway.

"We'd like you to tell us how you spent your Sunday afternoon, Mr. Schwartz."

Schwartz smiled and asked, "On what grounds?"

Williams was ready for this.

"Attempted blackmail."

From his vantage point by the door, Michelson thought he saw a momentary look of relief on Schwartz's face.

"You'll have to be more specific—I don't remember trying to blackmail anybody."

"Then you'll be surprised to hear that we have received a complaint from the headmaster of the Benjamin Thompson School?"

"Not in the least—you know he's an alcoholic and has no idea what's going on half the time?"

"No, I didn't know that—and I'm wondering how you do."

"I have friends in the school."

"Is one of them called Amanda Friedman?"

There was no reply, so Williams continued:

"We have information that you and Amanda tried to extort money from Mr. Thornbury on Sunday afternoon. There were several other people in the school at that time who were aware of your presence, so it's not just a matter of your word against his."

"Who are these other people?"

"That's our business, Mr. Schwartz. Blackmail is a very serious offence, so if you won't cooperate we'll have to take you in for questioning."

Schwartz hesitated and Williams thought that he was probably calculating the advantages of being arrested. For a tabloid reporter, a night in jail might create a lot of useful copy, but it seemed that the idea didn't appeal.

"OK—I was at the school with Amanda yesterday afternoon. Amanda feels that she was badly treated over an incident that happened a couple of weeks ago and that she ought to be compensated. He refused and we left."

"What kind of response did you get from Mr. Thornbury?"

"He was contemptuous—told Amanda that the thing was settled and she'd better talk to her parents before doing anything stupid."

"Did he seem angry or likely to become violent?"

"Obviously he was angry—I don't know about violence."

"Did you see a whiskey bottle in the room?"

"Yes, there was a bottle on the floor by his chair—I think he thought it was out of sight."

"Did you and Amanda leave together?"

"No—she wanted to talk to him on her own so I left and she stayed."

"Did you see her again later?"

"No—I had some work to do, so I came home."

"What time was that?"

"I don't know—around four thirty, I guess."

"Exactly where was Amanda when you left her?"

"In Thornbury's office. I'm not stupid, Inspector. What's happened to Amanda?"

"First I'd like to know what your relationship was with Amanda."

"We were acquaintances. I met her at a party and we exchanged phone numbers. After that I bumped into her on the street a couple of times and that was about it. I was surprised when she called me about the incident but . . ."

"You thought there might be a story?"

"That's what I do for a living—finding stories. Now, tell me about Amanda."

Williams could see no point in delaying it any further, even though it might result in a lurid story in next week's *Galaxy.* He was pretty sure that the work that Schwartz was doing after his session with Amanda and Thornbury was the hasty concoction a story for Tuesday's edition, which was probably being printed at that very moment.

"Amanda died on Sunday afternoon, probably as a result of falling down a flight of stairs."

There was no perceptible reaction for several seconds. Finally Schwartz said, "And you think Thornbury might have pushed her?"

"We're treating Amanda's death as an accident, but we have to investigate all the possibilities. We'd like to know more about what was said in your interview with Thornbury and why you left before Amanda. It may jog your memory a bit if I tell you that your conversation in the headmaster's office was loud enough to be heard quite clearly outside the door."

"It's like I told you. Amanda's parents had done very well out of the deal, but she wanted some money for herself. Thornbury more or less told her to get lost and she got very upset and started yelling at him. He started yelling back and got out of his chair. Look, Inspector, it would have made a lovely scene if he'd attacked her and I'd been there to report it, but I didn't want that kind of trouble, so I pushed him back and tried to get Amanda to come away. She wouldn't, so I left on my own."

"And came home to write up your story?"

"Yes, and you can read all about it tomorrow."

"It already is tomorrow", Michelson muttered, thinking regretfully about the meal that he had been about to start several hours previously.

20

On Tuesday morning, Williams and Michelson sat in Elsie Smith's room for two hours interviewing people. Amanda's teachers were quite willing to talk about her character failings, but when they had last seen her she had been her usual difficult self and no one had any knowledge of her plans for the weekend. Elsie's evidence was of great interest as she had been in her room opposite the chemistry lab for some time after Hume left, and might have been aware of any goings on, such as people dragging bodies around. All she would say, however, was that she had gone to have a word with Hume at about 4:15 and, finding that he had already left, had gone back to her room and got on with her correcting. She was rather vague about what time she left, but she thought it might have been about 5:20.

Thornbury stuck to his story, one item of which disagreed with Schwartz's account. Williams asked the headmaster about it.

"Did you say that Schwartz and Amanda left together?"

"Yes. He didn't want to leave—in fact he seemed to be egging her on—and she practically had to drag him out through the door."

"What time did they leave?"

"I can't tell you exactly, but my guess is that it was a few minutes after four."

Hamilton and Sally had nothing to add to what they had already told the police, but Hume did have two more items to contribute. One was his recollection of seeing Jill Davis with a young man outside the school on the previous Sunday afternoon. The other was the episode with Jill's glasses, with the implication that she had been in the storeroom when the rape incident took place.

"So if the rape was a set-up, all of them were involved", Michelson said to his superior after Hume had left.

"Not necessarily", Williams replied. "I can think of several possible combinations of those three and we don't know whether it had anything to do with Amanda's death. In any case, Jill must have believed it was a setup—unless she's weird enough to elope with her boyfriend after watching him try to rape another girl. But I don't see how we can get any further with it until we find Miller and Jill. Now I'm going downstairs to have a quick word with Sally, and I want you to find Hamilton and ask him where he went after leaving school on Sunday and what time he got home."

"Miss Evans", he asked, "where did you and Mr. Hamilton go after leaving here on Sunday?"

"We went into the park. Mr. Hume saw us there."

"And then?"

"Jim walked a little way with me and then he went home."

"Where were you when you parted company?"

"About half way across—not far from the Delacorte."

"Where did you go then?"

"I crossed over to East 79th Street and he went back to the West Side—probably at 81st. Why? Does it matter?"

"Probably not—we just like to know where everybody was."

Michelson found Hamilton in his fourth floor office, where he was deep in conversation with Elsie. He seemed very distracted, but his answers agreed perfectly with Sally's, as the sergeant found when he compared notes with his boss.

"He said he got home some time after five and his wife had gone to bed with a headache so there's no confirmation. I can't see any reason why he would be involved."

"Neither can I."

By lunch time everyone who wasn't needed had been allowed to leave. Sally was at the front desk, Thornbury was in his office, Hume and Hamilton were talking over sandwiches on the fourth floor and Williams and Michelson were sitting in Hume's office.

Williams was looking at the report on the examination of the headmaster's office.

"Well, she wasn't killed in Thornbury's room", he said gloomily. "The way head wounds bleed they couldn't possibly have cleaned it up without leaving a trace. I suppose he could have taken a swing at her with the bottle and got her on the shoulder. There wasn't much blood there and her clothing might have absorbed it."

"Yes", Michelson replied without much enthusiasm. "He hits her, she runs out of the office and through the door to the basement stairs. He chases her, she falls down the stairs and he goes back up for the key to the storeroom, goes back down and totes her along the passage and into the elevator, takes her upstairs and hides her. Young Michael Schwartz wouldn't have left the building while there was still something juicy happening, so he looks on and applauds. I think the old lady's right—Thornbury didn't do it."

"I agree, except for one thing."

"The key?"

"Right—if he did it, it would explain why the key wasn't there."

"But it still doesn't make much sense—he'd have had to go back upstairs for it. It would have meant a lot of running up and down."

"I know—why not just leave her where she was? Anyway, we'd better get hold of Schwartz again. Either he's lying or Thornbury is. And like I said before, we need to find Miller and the girl—that is, assuming it was Miller and the girl in the infirmary. No one actually saw them, but we know from Hume that they were there the previous week."

"Probably", Michelson said.

"OK, probably, but it would also fit in with Jill's disappearance. Something I meant to ask Mrs. Davis last night only I got distracted—does Jill have any money?"

Michelson knew about Williams's tendency to get distracted, and Williams knew that he knew, so no comment was necessary.

"Want me to call her?"

"Yeah, maybe that would be better—I don't think she'll be at work today."

Michelson located Chrissie Davis at home and learned that Jill had several hundred dollars in a savings account. After a long pause she reported that she couldn't find Jill's passbook. All she knew was that the account was at the local branch of the Manhattan Bank for Savings.

"So it's possible she withdrew her money and went off on her own", Michelson said. "But I don't think so—I think she's with Miller."

"Right. What's intriguing me is what difference it makes whether Amanda and Schwartz left together or separately. Thornbury might think that if they left together it gets him off the hook and Schwartz thinks if he left and went home while Amanda was alive and well it does the same for him. Not very good logic on their part but from our point of view it's very suggestive. Apart from that, just suppose for the moment that everyone we've seen is telling more or less the truth . . ."

Michelson snorted derisively, drawing a grimace from Williams.

"OK, I know, but just suppose it. If Amanda fell down the stairs on her own, who had anything to gain by hiding the body? Supposing it was Thornbury who hit her on the shoulder—obviously he wouldn't admit that, but maybe it was only incidental anyway. That would mean Schwartz had already left, like he said. He hit her and she ran but he stayed in his office. She fell down the stairs and killed herself and someone found the body and for some reason decided to hide it in the storeroom, presumably to delay its discovery. And who would have been most likely to find it on Sunday afternoon?"

"Miller and the girl."

"Yes, and don't forget that Miller apparently still had his school keys and would have been very likely to think of the storeroom. And, if it wasn't them they may know who it was since they were right next to the elevator. The trouble is I can't think of a plausible reason for anyone to move the body. If whoever it was had left it where it was, it wouldn't have been discovered until the next morning. Now here's something else—from what I saw in Jill's room, she's very preoccupied with Vietnam."

"And Miller is very draft-eligible and has a roomful of anti-war stuff in his apartment."

"It gives you something to think about, doesn't it? OK, it won't do any good but we'd better go down and talk to the business manager."

Andrew Johnson was a lanky, dark-haired Scot in his late thirties, one of the many Caledonians who continually proclaim the superiority of their native land while greatly preferring to live somewhere else. Fifteen years in Manhattan had modified his accent to the point where he was able to speak intelligibly and reassuringly to parents, teachers and board members, but he had very little to say on this occasion. The school was generally in good financial shape, but the Friedman affair had had a devastating effect on the accounts for the current year and it had been necessary to draw on the rainy day fund. The only item that appeared to have any possible bearing on the investigation was the fact that the Friedmans were in considerable arrears with their tuition payments.

One thing that didn't crop up in the conversation was that Johnson was a great fan of Hamish McGregor and had been amazed and delighted to discover that his favorite author was actually the wife of one of his colleagues. The result had been a number of long, enthusiastic and perfectly innocuous conversations about a highly romanticized version of the Land of the Mountain and the Flood. It also meant that when Jean was in trouble, Andrew was the person she naturally turned to.

"It must have been Miller", Hamilton said as he finished his last bite of sandwich and dropped the wrappings in his garbage can. "She had the drop on him over the fake rape and was probably trying to get some of his money."

Hume didn't reply. The conversation up to that point had been about nothing in particular, but now it was on a subject that he didn't want to think about.

"OK, I know you want to stay out of it. Could you tell me about your divorce or don't you want to talk about that, either?"

Hume still didn't respond, so Hamilton plunged on.

"I'd really like to know—I'm thinking about a divorce and it's scaring the hell out of me."

On the previous Friday, when he had encouraged Hume to talk about his troubles, Hamilton had been very tactful in his approach; now this insistence on probing a painful area seemed so foreign to his usual conversational style that Hume looked up in surprise.

"Was your divorce very difficult?" Hamilton asked.

Finally Hume spoke.

"You're not so sure about it, are you? Is that what the real problem is?"

"I guess so. Do you mind if I talk? You don't have to say anything."

"Go ahead", Hume said. Listening was almost as bad as talking, but it might be possible to switch off and think about something else.

"Well, the real problem is that I've realized that it's Sally's physical body that I'm in love with. I've seen it happen with other middle-aged men. Most people don't think of the skin as an organ, but it's really the sexiest organ we have and when you get older something happens to it and it stops being sexy."

This was something that Hume had never thought about, but he supposed it might be true—at least for some people. In his own case it had been the face and not the skin. The face had a way of proclaiming the personality, and if the face wasn't right, no amount of gorgeous skin could make up for it. When his personal disaster had struck, Susan had been twenty-seven and physically irreproachable. At fifty-two her intelligence and humor still shone out of her eyes, and she would still be his wife but for one small detail.

"Sally has a beautiful mind, too, in a way", Hamilton went on, "but it's not really my kind of mind and when I'm with her I have to be somebody different. And I keep doing it because I want her physically so much and I can't stand the thought of anyone else having her."

Hume was getting impatient. Jessica's combination of mind and body had been perfect too, except for the same small detail that had made life so difficult for Susan, but she was only fifteen and now he was wondering what she would have been like at Sally's age and whether, if things had been different, he would have got over his obsession quickly enough to have stayed with Susan. Well, that wouldn't have worked either; Susan and Jessica were infatuated with each other. He really didn't want to listen to Hamilton any more but he couldn't think of any way of stopping him without being rude. In any case, Hamilton had listened patiently to Hume's painful account of past history, so it seemed only right and proper that Hume should endure the details of Hamilton's current dilemma.

"She thinks it's all settled. I'm getting a divorce and taking a job somewhere else and we'll settle down and live happily ever after. And that's what I want but it's beginning to make me very nervous. And I can't face telling Jean—she hasn't done anything wrong."

Hume's impatience finally got the better of him. This man, with all his "ifs", "ands" and "buts" obviously had no idea what total infatuation really meant.

"Then don't tell her. You sound like the average adolescent who thinks he's really in love for the first time and nobody else has ever experienced anything like it before. Only for him it's normal, whereas at your age it's just temporary insanity. To be quite honest I can't imagine what makes you so attractive to Sally now, and just think what it's going to be like in ten years, when you're over fifty and she's still in her thirties."

Hamilton flushed deep red and half stood, but at that moment the telephone rang.

It was Sally.

"Hello, nothing special. I just wanted to say, 'Hi'."

"Oh, Hi Sally."

Hamilton sounded very awkward. Hume decided it was time to go for another walk.

An hour later Hume was sitting on his usual bench, muffled up against a cold wind and wondering what had happened to make Hamilton so unlike his usual self. He had a strong feeling that his colleague's problem was more complicated or deep-seated than merely being worried about his questionable romance, and anyway, it was none of his business, even though Hamilton had tried to make it so. It was also possible that Hamilton had never been the person that Hume had taken him for. He decided to think about something else and it was at that exact moment that Sally appeared in front of him.

"Hi John, I thought I might find you here."

Without asking permission she sat down beside him.

"I just split up with Jim", she said.

Hume started to speak, but Sally overrode him.

"I'm not saying it's your fault. I wormed it out of him. You didn't want to talk but he made you and then he didn't like what you said. Everything you told him was true but the thing is, as far as I'm concerned it doesn't make two cents worth of difference. That's what being in love means and maybe it never happened to you. The trouble is it made a difference to him. He was very nervous about the whole thing, but if I could have got him away I'd have made everything OK. But now you've scared him and he'll never get away."

"I was in love once", Hume said, "and it killed one person and ruined the lives of two others. He was scared already, you know."

"Yes, but only of telling Jean. Now he's scared of me—he says I'm bound to meet someone younger and then I'll ditch him."

"Well, isn't it possible that he's right?"

"It's possible. You never know—I mean you can't always expect things like that to last forever, no matter what the age-groups are, and I wasn't counting on it. I just thought we would have a wonderful time together and if it didn't last, well, it didn't last."

Hume was thinking that Hamilton's expectations for the future had almost certainly been quite different from Sally's, but she went on again before he had the chance to say anything.

"Anyway, it's also possible I might meet someone older. Since you've messed things up for me there's one thing you can do to make up for it."

"What's that?"

"Kiss me."

Hume hesitated. It had been a quarter of a century since he had kissed anyone under the age of fifty, and he was still feeling slightly shocked at the revelation of Sally's hedonistically unscrupulous attitude; but now Sally was sitting on his lap and he was having unaccustomed sensations around the lower part of his abdomen. All he needed was a little more encouragement.

"Come on—I'm not totally unattractive."

Hume kissed her briefly and then she kissed him longer and stronger and then he kissed her for a very long time. Being the man that he was, even in these moments of peak enjoyment, he couldn't switch off the contemplative part of his mind, and he was struck by the thought that when the proportions are perfect the actual size is apt to go unnoticed. He had never realized how small Sally was. It was almost like having a child on his lap. What Hamilton had said was true up to a point; her body was divine even though her mind was imperfect and, in any case, Hume had his own imperfections to worry about, so why bother with hers. He tried to stop thinking and concentrate on what he was doing.

It was, perhaps, unfortunate that Elsie Smith happened to walk by while this was going on.

21

The *Galaxy* hit the supermarkets in the early afternoon. Events at a small private school in upper Manhattan were not important enough for the front page, but anyone who looked inside would see a picture of the façade of the Benjamin Thompson School, with the headlines "Scandal erupts at Ben Thompson" and "Sex crime suppressed." The story described the attempted rape and didn't bother to use the word "alleged." Amanda had given Schwartz all the details of her parents' part of the deal and there was speculation that Miller had been paid off too. Amanda had felt that she was not being treated fairly and had asked to see the headmaster, taking Schwartz along as a witness. There had been an acrimonious discussion in which Thornbury had become abusive and Amanda had asked Schwartz to leave. That was all for the moment, but readers could look forward to further revelations next week.

Further revelations had already taken place, however. The Friedmans had not been quiet and the news that the school would be closed for the day because of an "accident" had created quite a stir. The morning papers didn't have anything, but "Girl Killed at Ben Thompson" appeared quite prominently in the *Post* and the *News*. So anyone who read both the supermarket and the evening tabloids was able to get some serious entertainment out of a deplorable event. "School had a Dead Girl in the Closet" made a very compelling headline.

O-O-O-O

The headmaster and the trustees had decided that there would be a faculty meeting on Wednesday morning and that school would reopen on Thursday in the hope of getting back to some appearance of normality as soon as possible. When Thornbury saw the *Galaxy* and realized that the story of an attempted rape had escaped into the school's constituency with no qualifications such as "alleged", he changed his mind. There was a rape that probably wasn't a rape and an accident that might have been a murder, but rape and murder were indissolubly linked in people's minds, and he felt that he and his colleagues couldn't face the students and their parents with no coherent or convincing story that might persuade them that Ben Thompson was a safe and healthy place. An immediate decision was required, so he decided to bypass the Board, postpone the faculty meeting until Friday and reopen the following Monday. Maybe by then the police would have finished their investigation, one way or another. He was pretty sure that by that time a lot of parents would already have made new arrangements for their children, but there was nothing he could do about it.

Sally had returned from her late lunch and started on the large number of phone calls necessitated by Thornbury's decision. She was still at it half an hour later when Elsie Smith walked in, gave her an icy look and made for the headmaster's office.

O-O-O-O

When Williams returned to his office he found several news items waiting for him, some of them rather surprising. One was a preliminary post mortem report which indicated, among other things, that there was no evidence of any sexual activity and that Amanda had, in fact, been a virgin. Also, assuming that she actually had fallen downstairs, some of the marks on her arms might have been caused by a struggle before that happened. The contusion on her shoulder might have been caused by a blow with a heavy, blunt object or by being thrown against a wall.

"So much for all that sex on the back seat of Miller's car", Michelson observed sourly.

The second item was a message from Chrissie Davis; Jill had called to say that she was OK, but she had refused to give any information about where she was, who she was with and where they were going. She would call her mother again when things had settled down.

Most surprising was the information that Miller's car had been found in Manhattan, illegally parked on West 97th Street. The inspector and his sergeant had assumed without question that Miller, his car and Jill would be together, maybe at this point somewhere in the Midwest on their way to California, where Miller presumably had friends. Now it seemed that the couple might be holed up in Manhattan. Williams pondered the idea and thought that it didn't make sense. Hiding in Manhattan might not be too difficult, but it would be very inconvenient and not something that a sensible person with any alternative would want to keep up for very long. Miller, trying to avoid the draft, and with a wad of Ben Thompson's money in his pocket and a seventeen-year-old girl-friend, would find it much easier to be inconspicuous on the other side of the continent.

So why was the car in Manhattan? Answer: because Miller assumed that the police would be looking for it and it would be too easily spotted. How did they travel? Answer: the car was left just around the corner from two car rental offices on West 96th Street, which might have been a mistake on Miller's part if that really was his plan. Williams reached for the directory and dialed All-America Rentals. After identifying himself he got the information that the office opened at seven o'clock every morning but that no young man answering Miller's description had been there any time on the previous day. The inspector had better luck with Empire State Car Rentals. The description was not needed. Miller had rented a compact sedan at 7:30 on Monday morning. He had shown his New York State driver's license, paid the necessary deposit and rented the car for a day to visit relatives upstate. Furthermore he ought to have been back by now and there was no sign of him. No, he didn't have anyone with him. The car was a dark green Chevy Nova, about as inconspicuous as you could get, but at least there was a known registration that the police could look out for.

After setting the wheels in motion, Williams called Gloucester Central Police Station, on the off chance that at eight o'clock in the evening there would be someone on the premises who had some information about John Hume. The duty officer, Sergeant Bunn, told him that Inspector Phelps would be the person to speak to and he was sure that all the required information would be forthcoming in the morning. It took some time for Williams to convince the phlegmatic Bunn that this was a murder investigation and speed was essential, but eventually the American was able to get through to Phelps, who was very helpful and very concerned. Officially, Hume had a clean record, but he had admitted being responsible for the death of a young girl in 1941. Yes, there had certainly been sexual implications, but Hume had led an exemplary life for the past twenty-five years and Phelps found it hard to imagine that he would get involved with any more young women. Williams hadn't had any reason to suspect that Hume was involved in Amanda's death, but it was as well to know these things and it was certainly worth thinking about.

22

Wednesday was a long day for everyone. There was no particular reason for any of the teachers to show up at school and most of them didn't. Thornbury arrived fairly early with the mental set of a captain who was going down with his ship, and Hamilton got there a little later with the attitude of one who is in an unpleasant place because the alternative is an even more unpleasant one. He was pretty sure that Jean had found out about his affair with Sally and that the punishment would be that she would stay in her room or go around indefinitely with a stony face and refuse to talk; or she would leave, taking Hamish McGregor and a considerable slice of their joint income with her. He hadn't seen her before leaving for school, but he had heard her moving around in her room and it had sounded like someone packing.

Sally, dressed as provocatively as usual, was sitting at her desk when Hamilton arrived. Instead of her customary tight sweater or the see-through blouse that she had worn on Friday, she was wearing a shirt with a scooped out neckline that frankly invited scrutiny. Hamilton thought the best idea would be to pretend that he hadn't seen her. It seemed to be working, but Sally waited until he had gone a couple of steps past her desk and then called out, "Hey mister, don't you know a pretty face when you see one?"

Hamilton experienced such conflicting emotions that he almost fell down on the spot. He paused, turned, took a couple of steps toward her, paused and turned again before almost running to the elevator. Sally chuckled, but very quietly. She thought it was probably much worse for him than it was for her and, in any case, she had already sought consolation elsewhere.

On the fourth floor, the little room behind the biology lab and Hamilton's office had been converted into a tiny conservatory with windows let into the two outside walls. The back of the building faced more or less north, so the room didn't receive much direct sunlight and was populated by cool-weather plants that produced many shades of green. Hamilton sat on a stool and gazed between two hanging ivies at the wall of the adjacent building, where all the windows were fitted with Venetian blinds, not to keep out the sun but to defeat the idle curiosity of Ben Thompson's flock of teenagers. He ought to go down and see Thornbury or at least call him on the intercom and find out if he wanted to talk about the state of the school. At that moment, however, he felt that the school could and would make its own way to hell without his assistance. The sane and calculating part of his mind had persuaded him that breaking things off with Sally had been the best policy, but the rest of his mind and the whole of his body didn't agree and now tried to convince him that when she called out to him as he passed her desk it was because she still wanted him. Sanity and calculation prevailed but left him feeling so twisted up inside that for a few moments it was hard to breathe. Soon, he thought, there would be no Sally, no job and probably no Jean. It was hard to imagine how he could have made a more thorough mess of things and thinking about it only made it worse. He began to fantasize and after a while, almost without conscious volition, he started on the way to the front hall where he might find Sally alone.

He had only taken a couple of steps when the intercom rang in his office.

Thornbury, who had kept his resolution to remain sober, viewed himself and the general situation with unaccustomed clarity. Before the Amanda debacle, his private life was already a source of considerable anxiety, but at least he still had the public persona of the highly respectable head of a highly respectable institution. The cheroots had been part of this image of the successful man of the world, but now he thought of them with distaste, and his cigar box had become a receptacle for Camels. Unfortunately, the common cigarette didn't give him the feeling of satisfaction that the cheroots had generated. The sight of Sally, already at her desk when he arrived and looking even sexier than usual, had made him feel very old. The easiest thing to do would be to resign on the spot and go into retirement. Financially it wouldn't be a problem, but although he no longer trailed clouds of glory, there were still shreds of nobility in his make-up and a genuine concern for the school and his colleagues. Besides, if he left now, Vicky would never forgive him.

Well, that was another story—much too complicated to think about at this juncture. The only fixed item on his agenda was Friday's faculty meeting. There really wasn't much to discuss, but it would probably be a good idea to talk to Hamilton about it. He picked up his phone.

Hamilton put down the phone and continued on his way but the call from Thornbury had brought him back to reality. He wanted to talk to Sally but the most likely thing was that she would brush him off with a wisecrack or a sarcastic remark. It would be possible for him to reach Thornbury's office without having to acknowledge Sally's presence or endure her comments, and maybe that would be the best thing to do. He could take the elevator down to the basement, leave by the basement door and re-enter the school by the front door. That way he could arrive at his destination without passing directly in front of her desk. She would see him, of course, but it would be much easier to ignore her. Feeling annoyed at his own cowardice, he did this and was illogically disappointed when Sally ignored him. Annoyance prevailed and he walked up to her and said, "I want to talk to you."

"OK, go ahead."

"Not now—call me at home, later."

"Do I have to?"

"Yes, and stop treating me like a buffoon."

"OK, if you insist."

⚯⚯

"Listen, Jim", the headmaster said, "I hope you realize that we might as well all start looking for other jobs."

"I was already doing that", Hamilton said and, having arrived at a what-the-hell kind of mental attitude, went on, "I was planning to leave Jean and go away with Sally."

Thornbury, who had been under the impression that the Hamilton-Sally affair was not much more than a pleasant dalliance, found this amusing.

"Tell me, did Sally know about this?"

This was too much for Hamilton, who had already suffered one humiliation that morning. He would have punched Thornbury's grinning face if he could have reached it across the broad desk, but he got some satisfaction out of sweeping all the headmaster's papers, his in and out trays, his telephone, his cigar box and his glass of water on to the floor. Once more there were fragments of glass everywhere, but this time Hamilton had no intention of helping with the clean-up.

Sally heard the crash and came to the door as Hamilton was leaving.

"Don't bother", Hamilton said. "He can clean up his own mess."

"Well", Sally said to his retreating back, "you're a better man than I thought you were."

Hamilton hesitated momentarily and then kept going.

Sally added, under her breath, "But not much."

She turned to the headmaster, who was still sitting at his desk, and asked, "What brought that on?"

Thornbury shook his head and asked her to see if she could find Luis.

⚯⚯

Hume would have liked to stay in his room at No. 3 until someone asked for him. People knew where to find him if he was needed for anything and, like Hamilton, he preferred not to see Sally, only for a somewhat different reason, namely that he was developing a severe crush on her and if he didn't get it under control he would end up getting hurt. He thought that she had regarded their kissing session yesterday as merely therapeutic, but for him it had awakened the whole zoo. Like Hamilton, he couldn't get her out of his mind, but there was a lot more to it than skin.

Hume had another problem, however; he had had a very bad night that consisted of long spells of wakefulness interrupted by a recurrent dream in which he knew that someone injured and dying was locked in the storeroom. At first he thought it was Jessica and then he thought it was Sally and finally it seemed that the two had somehow merged. He was afraid to open the door because of what he might see, and then, when he tried, it was jammed and the key wouldn't work. Having been awake most of the night, he fell into a heavy sleep at dawn and didn't wake up again until eleven o'clock.

His first thought was that he must go and check the storeroom. It was absurd but he had to do it. It took him quite a while to make himself look respectable, and after entering the main building he practically sprinted past Sally's desk and took the elevator to the third floor. This was piling absurdity on absurdity—Sally was sitting at her desk, looking perfectly healthy, so she couldn't very well be lying dead in the storeroom. It couldn't be Jessica, either. Her remains had been reburied twenty years ago. Feeling like an absolute fool and with his heart beating about fifty percent faster than usual, he opened the door of the little room, switched the light on and saw that everything looked perfectly normal. He wasn't going to endure another night like that, however. Among the miscellaneous supplies there were nails, a few odd pieces of wood and a hammer, so he took a small, thin piece of wood and nailed it to the inside of the jamb just above one of the hinges. It was now impossible to shut the door completely, and he hoped this would head off any further nightmares.

He was putting the hammer away when he heard Elsie's voice.

Elsie Smith always liked to know what was going on, so she would have gone to school early if her room hadn't been on the same floor as Hume's lab. She had had a strong feeling that she might be able to get something going in that direction and that it might not have been one of her usual transient affairs, but, having seen him and Sally in the park, she felt irrationally angry with the two of them and thought avoidance would be the best policy. By lunchtime, however, she was tired of hanging around home, doing nothing in particular while imagining that Hume and Sally were having it off somewhere on the back stairs, so she went over to school ostensibly to work on a pile of papers that had been left behind in the previous day's turmoil. Soon after she got there she heard someone hammering and went to investigate. Seeing Hume in the storeroom, putting something away, she stood at the door and said, "Rough carpentry but effective—I gather you'd prefer not to find any more bodies."

Hume had nothing to say and Elsie didn't move, so there was an awkward moment. Finally Elsie took a step back and Hume edged past her, still without a word. He went back to his apartment via the basement and lay down on his bed.

Elsie returned to her classroom and cursed continuously and repetitiously for about a minute and a half. She knew in her gut that if Sally and Hume weren't already lovers, they soon would be, and that Hume's apartment would be extremely convenient for the purpose. The idea created an unpleasant churning sensation inside her, but she was a long way past the point where she could have taken a step back, let go and gone out for a drink. She had to know, so it wasn't merely her usual curiosity that drove her to take her overcoat and go downstairs a few minutes before four o'clock.

When Elsie appeared in the front hall, Sally was sitting at her desk with a dreamy smile on her face and a pleasant fantasy running through her mind. Emerging from her daydream, she looked at the clock and said, "Hi Elsie, another day gone!"

"Maybe it's just beginning."

Elsie thought she was saying this in a normal tone of voice, but some inkling of the thought behind the words got through to Sally. She didn't understand it, but it made her very uneasy. She quickly put on her coat, picked up her bag and made for the door, unaware that she was being followed.

Inspector Williams received another surprise on Wednesday afternoon. The green Chevy Nova had been found in the parking lot of a Howard Johnson's near Akron, Ohio. Nothing belonging to either of the runaways had been found, and no one knew how long it had been there. He called in Michelson and said, "Look, he's done it once that we know of and now it looks as if he's done it again."

"You mean he abandons one car and picks up another. Can the girl drive?"

"Yes, I asked her mother. She took drivers' ed and has a license."

"So they find a car rental, he gets another car, they drive both cars back to the parking lot, leave the Chevy and go on with the new one. Very smart. He's really scared, isn't he?"

Williams agreed but his phone rang before he could say so. He listened for a long time before asking any questions and Michelson had never seen him look so unhappy.

Eventually Williams cradled the phone and said, "It's the girl—she tried to commit suicide. Jumped off an overpass in front of a truck. The driver managed to swerve and hit her a glancing blow that spun her off the road. She's in the hospital with massive injuries and they think she probably won't make it. Mrs. Davis has been informed and she's on her way to Akron."

"Any note?"

"Nothing so far, but there's no doubt about it—two people saw her go."

At four o'clock Hume was still in his apartment. He had tidied up a little and put his sofa-bed away, but apart from that he had done nothing but sit and let his mind wander all over the place. Seeing the time, he got up in a hurry and started down the stairs. It was totally illogical and against his better judgement, but Sally had been involved in a lot of his roving thoughts and now he wanted to see her. He thought he might just catch her before she left for the day, but halfway down his private staircase he met her coming up.

"I've never been up here before", she said. "I just wanted to see where you live."

It was a lame excuse but good enough for Hume. He turned and led her up to the apartment.

"No, I don't want any tea. Can we just sit together for a little while?"

They sat on the sofa-bed and Sally kept on talking.

"I'm not a bad person really—I just like people and I like sex."

"You and Elsie", Hume commented before he had time to stop himself.

"Well, why shouldn't we? Everybody else does. It's not only Jim. Thornbury, Bobby, Peter, they all wanted a piece of the action."

"Your action?"

"Yes, if they could get it. Only . . ."

"They couldn't?"

"Well, Bobby's a pet and a lot of fun, only then he got to be a bit of a nuisance. I mean I still like him but . . ."

"You had other fish to fry?"

"Well, there was Peter, only he seemed to want me to share him with a couple of schoolgirls, and Thornbury's a dear old man but . . ."

"Too old for you?"

"Well, it wasn't his age", Sally said quickly. "He always smells of stale tobacco—it's very off-putting."

"So you settled on Hamilton."

"Well, I really do like him. He's very smart and very kind and surprisingly good for someone that age. Oh . . ."

Sally put her hand to her mouth and Hume smiled.

"Sally, dear, I do believe you're putting on an act."

She returned his smile.

"You're too smart for me, John. OK, the truth is that he settled on me. I mean I really do like him, but it wouldn't have occurred to me to go after him. I mean, I do have a life outside school as well. When he started giving signals I was just very curious at first, but he seemed genuine and straightforward and, like I told you, I thought it would be fun for as long as it lasted. But I guess I ought to have realized how explosive it might get."

"Well, it wasn't your fault—I mean, he ditched you. Anyway, I suppose this means you don't want to get involved with another old man."

"It depends what you mean by 'involved.' I think it's OK for two people to make love, if that's what they want to do. They don't necessarily have to be *in* love."

Hume smiled at this simple, unassailable logic.

"So you're going after me, but you don't want me to have any illusions?"

Sally returned his smile and didn't say anything. His private zoo was waking up again and the animals were howling; maybe getting over the crush would be easier than he had expected and Sally might help him put the ghost of Jessica to rest. Her miniskirt left a large expanse of thigh uncovered, and when he stroked her soft skin she didn't object.

"Don't worry about my illusions—I'll take care of them myself."

The sofa-bed pulled out easily.

Some time later Hume was lying on his back feeling remarkably happy. He'd been a bit clumsy at first, but Sally had made things easy for him. He had taken a little nap and now he was just dozing off again when Sally said, "I'd better go now, but there's something I wanted to tell you. It's about Amanda and the police don't know." Hume woke up a little and Sally started to talk; but his hand was already in a place where she couldn't ignore it, so she said, "Oh, what the hell—I'll tell you tomorrow."

Another half-hour elapsed before Sally said again, "I really ought to go—it's nearly seven-thirty and I promised Jim I'd call him around seven."

Hume sat up.

"I thought that was over."

"It is, really, but he seems to have something on his mind—like changing it, maybe. Listen, John, I had a wonderful time and I wouldn't mind doing it again, but I'm not in love with you. I just don't want any misunderstandings."

"I know", Hume said, with a smile, "As I said to your former lover, you need somebody younger. Don't worry—I'm not in love with you, either, and anyway I think being in love is a grossly overrated condition. But I do like you very much. Maybe we could keep each other happy until someone else turns up."

"You're a man after my own heart", Sally said. She finished dressing and blew him a kiss as she disappeared through the door.

"Perhaps I am", Hume said to himself, "but not in the sense that you mean."

23

Sally went back to the main building and was surprised to see Elsie sitting at the reception desk. If Elsie was surprised to see Sally, she didn't show it—she just went on calmly taking things out of the drawers, one by one.

"I was wondering what kind of things a person like you would keep in her desk", she said.

Sally found this behavior very disturbing, but all she said was, "Help yourself—you won't find anything."

She had intended to make her call from Hamilton's office but now the idea of being in Hume's domain gave her a reassuring feeling of warmth and fuzziness, so she got off the elevator on the third floor, went to the chemistry lab, switched on the lights and took off her overcoat. She had a pretty good idea what Hamilton wanted and was standing there trying to decide how she would respond when Elsie walked in and said, "Well, have you made up your mind?"

Sally had never seen Elsie in this aggressive mood before and for once she was confused and slightly intimidated.

"Made up my mind about what?" she said. "I don't know what you mean."

"Of course you do. Only you don't have to decide, do you? Just let 'em all come. Do you take them one at a time or in twos and threes? And do you know what's weird? They're all intelligent people and there's nothing whatever inside that pretty little head of yours. Well, maybe if it weren't so pretty . . ."

Elsie took a step forward and Sally fled into the back room, closing the door behind her. It didn't lock, but maybe it would give Elsie a moment to calm down. Sally picked up the phone and dialed Hamilton's number. It was what she was there for, but now half her motivation was to have someone there to deal with Elsie, and the moment he picked up she wished she had called Hume instead and couldn't understand why she hadn't. Elsie was very strange and scary and soon it was the same with Hamilton. It started calmly enough—how was she, and where was she, and he was sorry about what had happened—but as he went on his speech became so fast and incoherent that for several minutes she couldn't get a word in. He was still crazy about her and the school was obviously going bust and they could go away together now and get some kind of work until the new school year started. When he finally ran out of breath she said, "No, Jim, it won't work. It's over. Goodbye." As she put the phone down she heard him shouting, "Sally, stay there—I'm coming over." Now she was really frightened. She tried Hume's number but got no reply. She waited for a couple of minutes and tried again, still without success. Obviously the thing to do would be to get out of there before Hamilton arrived. She crept along the passage from the office to the lab and found that the door was open. Elsie, who had been listening to Sally's end of the conversation, retreated to the outer doorway, stationing herself there with her arms folded and barring Sally's way.

"So your precious Jim doesn't want me and now that you've seduced Hume you don't want him. Well, I've got you now and I may be old in your eyes, but I'm bigger and stronger than you are, so what are you going to do about it?"

This was so much like something out of a bad B movie that Sally almost forgot to be scared.

"Don't be silly, Elsie. Just go home and have a couple of drinks."

Elsie took a step forward and picked up a clamp stand from a nearby bench, but at that moment they heard the bang of the elevator door and Hamilton appeared in the doorway. He was panting and looked as if he had run all the way from 85th Street.

"Elsie", he half gasped and half shouted, "what the hell are you doing here?"

Elsie gestured toward Sally with the clamp stand.

"I've caught this little mantrap and I'm just trying to decide what to do with her."

"Jim, I want to go home—can't you get her out of here?"

"Oh", Elsie said sarcastically, "the little white knight is reinstated and rides to the rescue."

Hamilton shoved Elsie aside and confronted Sally, making a great effort to speak calmly.

"Come on Sally, she has a nasty tongue but she's really harmless. Let's go in the back and talk things over."

"There's nothing to talk about—I told you. Just let me go."

"See what I mean?" Elsie crowed. "Now she's had Hume she's realized she prefers tall and skinny."

Hamilton grabbed Sally by the wrists.

"What does she mean, 'had Hume'?"

"If you let go and ask her nicely, she might tell you what they were doing for three hours in his apartment."

Hamilton had no intention of letting go, but in his fury he half turned toward Elsie and relaxed his grip slightly. As Sally struggled and managed to get one hand free, Hamilton turned back to her.

"OK, little girl, I'm going to enjoy ripping that fancy shirt off you."

Sally slapped him across the face and turned to run into the back room, hoping against hope that she might be able to get to the telephone, but Hamilton still had her left hand. Something hit her on the head and she fell with a crash against the corner of one of the workbenches.

The apartment felt bare and empty after Sally left, so Hume put on his overcoat and went downstairs. It was cold outside with a hint of snow in the air. The park was not supposed to be a safe place to walk in in the dark, but he was past caring about such things as personal safety. He went in at 90th Street and took the path that slanted to the right and linked up with the wide southward drive that seemed to act as a racetrack for taxis. He walked as far as 81st Street and came out on Central Park West opposite the Natural History Museum. Feeling a bit like a museum piece himself, he went a little further south and stood for a minute in front of the statue of Theodore Roosevelt. Although it was possible, theoretically, for any American-born citizen to become president, it was obviously a long shot; and, thinking of long shots, pursuing a woman was even more hazardous than pursuing the presidency. However much he wished to deny the fact, Hume was in love with Sally and plainly there was no future in it. The funny thing was that it didn't bother him all that much, maybe because there was a chance that this new form of torture might displace the old one that still seemed as if it would never go away. He walked back up to 90th Street and, for no real reason, took out his keys and went into the main school building. It was after eight o'clock and he expected the place to be deserted; but the lights were on in the front hall and Elsie Smith was sitting Sally's desk. He thought she was looking sheepish, as if she had just been caught out in a piece of embarrassingly reprehensible behavior, and then he thought maybe it wasn't sheepishness. There was a touch of slyness or calculation about the way she was looking at him.

After they had looked at each other for a few seconds, Elsie said, "Hello, John. What are you doing here?"

"Nothing in particular", he answered truthfully. "I just want to check a few things in the lab now the police have finished with it."

"Oh, I thought maybe you were looking for your young woman."

"My young woman?" Hume echoed.

"You know—the one you were kissing in the park yesterday and entertaining in your apartment today. She's upstairs waiting for you unless she crept out through the basement."

"And meanwhile you've been searching her drawers", Hume said, putting two and two together and acutely conscious of the unintended double meaning of his question—at least to an old-fashioned Englishman who had just been doing the same thing in another sense of the phrase. At the same time something inside him was rotating rapidly as he imagined Sally upstairs giving a repeat performance with Hamilton as the male lead. He took the stairs two at a time while Elsie continued her search. She had already examined everything twice, but she was still obsessively trying to find something that would confirm her opinion of Sally. She wasn't expecting a shoebox full of old love letters, but she thought that in a dark corner there might be a note from one of her lovers or a supply of contraceptives.

Hume found no sign of anyone in the biology lab or the office behind it, so he went down to his office on the third floor and sat at his desk in the dark. Sally had been intending to call Hamilton and presumably she had come back into the school to do so. Elsie had seen her and assumed she was still there, but now it seemed that she had made the call upstairs and let herself out through the basement. It was simple enough and Hume felt foolish for having let himself get so het up about it. He switched on the light and looked at the storeroom door. It was still closed as far as his improvised doorstop would allow, but something was sticking out through the small opening. It looked like a shoe—one of Sally's shoes. He ran to the door. Sally was lying on her back and there was a terrible gash on the side of her forehead, but she was still warm and breathing. Hume needed a doctor and an ambulance as quickly as possible, but the only number he knew was the police emergency number that he had seen on the side of the patrol cars. He called 440-1234, reported a serious accident at the Benjamin Thompson School and was told that a patrol car and an ambulance would be there very shortly. Elsie Smith was still sitting at Sally's desk, almost as if she was waiting for something to happen, and when the intercom rang she picked it up without a moment's hesitation.

"The police and an ambulance will be here any minute now", Hume said. "Please stay by the door to let them in and send them up to the third floor."

"All right", Elsie said, and Hume would have been surprised by her lack of curiosity if he hadn't been so anxious to get back to Sally. He went back to the storeroom, knelt and kissed her very gently, just as Susan had kissed the dying Jessica all those years ago.

24

The night of Wednesday, February 17th seemed even longer than the day had been. Sally was still unconscious when the ambulance took her to Mount Sinai Hospital just the other side of the park. Hume had been interrogated briefly by the officers from the patrol car and now he was in the headmaster's office, being grilled by Williams and Michelson, who were both very grouchy at being hauled out again after a full day's work. There was a strong implication that there was something deeply suspicious about Hume's habit of finding bodies in the storeroom, and they wanted a minute by minute account of his activities throughout the day. This was pretty easy up to about four o'clock when he had met Sally on the staircase, since the only thing he had done before then was his bit of woodwork, which he didn't want to mention. Asked when and where he had last seen her, he gave an edited version of her visit with him in the late afternoon and mentioned that she had said that she was going to call Hamilton.

"Did she say what it was about?" Williams asked.

"No—only that Hamilton had said he wanted to talk to her. She also mentioned that there was something about Amanda Friedman that she hadn't told the police and she was going to tell me but . . ."

"But what, Mr. Hume?"

"Something interrupted us."

"How long was Sally with you?"

"About three hours."

"What did you talk about all that time?"

"We didn't talk all the time."

"OK, Mr. Hume—Sally comes to see you, spends three hours in your tiny apartment during which you only talk part of the time. What am I supposed to conclude?"

"All right—she came to me on the rebound and we spent several hours in bed together. But she made it very clear that this was probably one performance only. I felt differently about it, but I didn't say so. After she left I couldn't tolerate being in the apartment, so I went out and walked down as far as the Natural History Museum. Then I came back here and Mrs. Smith told me Sally was upstairs, so I went upstairs to look for her. I thought she might be with Hamilton. There was nobody on the fourth floor so I went to my office."

"What was this rebound you mentioned?"

"You know about her and Hamilton—well, they split up yesterday."

"How do you know?"

"She told me. She said it was because of something I said to Hamilton."

"You'd better tell me all about it."

Hume repeated what he could remember of his conversations with Hamilton and Sally.

"So her version is that Hamilton ditched her and your impression is that she was disappointed but not totally broken-hearted. And are you guessing that Hamilton asked her to call him because he wanted her back?"

"Yes, but it's pure speculation."

"So you went rushing up the stairs because you thought she might be with Hamilton. Did you have any reason to suppose that he would be here?"

"No—just the usual jealous lover's suspicions."

"Did Sally say anything?"

"No. I didn't either—I thought at first she was dead."

"And you didn't touch or disturb anything?"

"I touched her face and she was still warm and then I felt her pulse. Apart from that, no."

He didn't mention that he had kissed Sally.

"And you have no idea what it was that she was going to tell you about Amanda."

"I'm afraid not."

Williams called Hamilton and told him that there had been another incident at the school and that in view of the urgency of the situation a patrol car would pick him up immediately. Like Elsie, Hamilton didn't ask any questions—he just said, "OK", and hung up. The next call was to Thornbury, and Williams was not surprised when no one answered. Just for the hell of it, he called Schwartz and was quite gratified to find him at home. The call didn't seem to be about anything and Williams said it was just a routine check, which left Schwartz feeling very nervous.

"What the hell's going on?" he asked, but the inspector had already hung up.

Meanwhile, Michelson was talking to Elsie downstairs and learning that the only people she had seen while sitting at Sally's desk had been Sally and Hume.

"Why were you here?" the sergeant asked.

"I was searching her desk."

"What for?"

"Any evidence I could find of her nymphomaniacal activities."

"And did you find anything?"

"Only this—it's from Hamilton."

"I see you've opened it—what does it say?"

"It was open already and I don't know what it says—I don't believe in reading other people's correspondence."

Michelson almost laughed.

"But it's OK to search their belongings?"

"In a good cause—but one has to draw the line somewhere. Anyway, if you'd left me sitting here much longer I probably would have read it."

"Why are Miss Evans's activities so important to you?"

"That's none of your business."

Michelson didn't press her on this because he thought he knew the answer already.

"What time did you get here?"

"I was in my classroom all afternoon, correcting papers. I came down here around seven. Sally came in soon after that."

"Wasn't she surprised to see you at her desk?"

"She didn't seem very surprised. She just said, 'You won't find anything', and went upstairs. Hume got here about half an hour later."

"Did you notice anything unusual about him?"

"Yes—the moment I told him Sally was here he went bounding up the stairs like a young man in love."

"And then?"

"It couldn't have been more than about two minutes later, he called me on the intercom to say that the police and the ambulance were on the way."

"OK, let me make sure I've got this straight. You've been at this desk continuously from before Sally's arrival until after Hume got here—is that right?"

"Yes."

"And you're absolutely sure that no one else came in while you were here?"

"Absolutely. You do realize, by the way, that apart from the fact that something has happened to Sally, I have no idea what's going on."

"I was wondering when you would ask. We'll tell you about it shortly. I'll take the letter, but I can assure you we won't read it without permission."

Thinking that if Elsie believed that, she'd believe anything, Michelson left her in the company of an officer from the patrol car and went back up to the lab.

The amount of blood found on the floor in Hume's lab left no doubt as to where the assault on Sally had taken place. It also seemed that the weapon had been found, a small clamp stand consisting of a rectangular metal base, about six inches by four, and a two foot long, cylindrical steel rod that screwed into it. It was standing in one of the sinks, looking as if someone had washed it. Everything else in the lab was bone dry, but the stand and the sink were still wet. It didn't seem to make much sense, as Michelson remarked.

"If he dragged the girl into the storeroom, leaving bloodstains all over the place, why bother to wash the murder weapon?"

"It isn't murder yet", Williams pointed out, "but I agree—unless he was trying to do a complete clean-up, heard somebody coming and had to bolt. And it looks as if he thought the girl was dead."

"OK, well who is he?"

"How about 'she'?"

"You mean Mrs. Smith? I guess it's possible—she's not big but she's well built, and Sally can't weigh much more than about ninety pounds."

"Well, we were wondering why it was washed."

Michelson thought for a moment.

"That's pretty convoluted", he said. "That is, if I'm thinking what you're thinking."

"What are you thinking?"

"Some kind of double bluff, maybe, based on the idea that a woman would be more likely to . . ."

"OK, I agree it's pretty unlikely, but there's something about this whole scene that doesn't make sense."

"Several things, I'd say."

"Yes. We'll have a chat with Hamilton and then take all of them in and get statements."

25

A uniformed officer sat in the auditorium with Elsie and Hume while Williams and Michelson talked to Hamilton at the front desk. From where Michelson was sitting a band-aid was visible on Hamilton's left temple, but he decided not to ask about it until the inspector had finished. As usual, Williams tried to get as much as possible out of his victim before giving any indication of what the questioning was about.

"I went home about midday since there wasn't anything for me to do here. I was there until you called me."

"How did you spend the afternoon?"

"Well, for one thing, I took a long nap. I haven't been sleeping well. Apart from that I just pottered around, doing a few household chores."

"Did you see anyone after you left school?"

"Not anyone I know. I walked down Central Park West and across on 85th Street. We don't have a doorman."

"How about your wife?"

"My wife is away for the day."

"So there's no one who can vouch for your whereabouts between the time you left school and the time I called you."

"As far as I know that's correct."

"How long does it take you to walk home from school?"

"About ten minutes, I guess. I've never timed it."

"Did Sally Evans telephone you this evening?"

"Yes."

"What time was that?"

"About seven-fifteen."

"What did you talk about?"

"Our future."

"Can you be more specific?"

"Not unless you give me some idea why you want to know."

"So you have no idea why I'm here and why I'm asking you all these questions?"

"No."

"You don't seem very curious."

"I assume that something bad has happened and this is your way of finding out if I have anything to do with it. Presumably you'll tell me in your own sweet time."

"Very well", Williams replied, choosing his words very carefully. "In view of your feelings about Miss Evans I'm afraid you'll be very shocked to hear that she has been the victim of a vicious assault."

"Of course I'm shocked. Are you going to tell me what happened?"

"We're keeping the details to ourselves at the moment. I'd like you to tell me again about your relationship with Miss Evans, and I should warn you that it will be in your own interest to tell the truth."

Hamilton was silent for a moment.

"Well then, I guess I'd better tell you that the situation has changed over the past couple of days. In fact we broke it off yesterday."

"Why was that?"

"Because I realized that I was being rather stupid."

"So it was you who broke it off. What was her reaction?"

"She was very upset."

"And her phone-call today?"

"She wanted us to get back together."

"So you weren't expecting a call from her?"

"No—I thought it was all decided and that was what I told her. We only talked for a minute or two.

"You said that your wife was away for the day. Are you expecting her back this evening?"

"No."

Williams let this hang in the air for a long moment.

"OK", Hamilton said. "I'm not expecting her back. Period."

"In spite of the fact that you had broken things off with Sally? Are you sure it wasn't the other way around? That would have made you very angry with her."

"It was the way I told you and she was upset, but if you want to know, she wasn't as upset as she ought to have been, and it made things a little easier for me."

"In other words she might have just been playing you along?"

"That's an ugly way of saying it—she was genuinely fond of me and I was very much in love with her."

"But in spite of that you broke up with her. Did you know at that time that your wife was leaving?"

Hamilton's confusion showed on his face. Eventually he decided on the truth.

"No, I didn't, although I was afraid she might."

"When did you find out about your wife?"

"Today. I went home in the early afternoon and there was a note."

"What did it say?"

Hamilton pulled a screwed up piece of typewriter paper from his pocket and handed it to Williams. The note was very brief.

"Goodbye, Jim. Don't expect me back."

"She didn't even sign it", Williams said. "Maybe when you got this you changed your mind about Sally."

"No—I just thought my timing was terrible and I'd made a complete hash of everything."

"But you were still in love with her."

"Yes."

"So you'll be pleased to know that the doctors at Mount Sinai think there's a fair chance that she'll recover."

Hamilton's mouth dropped open and the color drained from his face.

"I thought you said . . ."

"Yes, I thought that was what you thought."

"And what happened to your face, Mr. Hamilton", Michelson asked.

"My face? Oh, that . . . I tripped over something."

"Really? What did you trip over?"

"My God, does it matter? I think it was a shoe somebody left on the floor."

Williams stood up and inspected the injured area.

"I'd like to see under that band-aid", he said.

"That's ridiculous."

"Of course, you can refuse, but that fact will be duly noted. And I'm sure we can get you another band-aid. The school is bound to have a first aid kit."

Hamilton didn't say anything, so while Michelson looked on, Williams carefully removed the band-aid and found a bruise and an abrasion.

"What did you hit your head on, Mr. Hamilton?"

"A piece of furniture. Is that all?"

"For the time being."

"He said he was shocked", Michelson said as he and Williams drove down to homicide headquarters, following the patrol car that carried Elsie, Hume and Hamilton. "But he didn't act shocked until he found out that the girl is still alive."

"No—he was trying to give the impression that he had no idea what had happened, but I'm sure that he's up to his neck in it—he already knew something had happened to Sally and he thought she was dead."

"If he knew something had happened, it's probably because he did it himself."

"But why did he drag her into the storeroom?"

"Beats me. What did you think of that thing on his head? I guess you wanted to see if she scratched him."

"Right, and it wasn't a scratch, but I don't believe his story—there was a ragged abrasion as well as a bruise, as if whatever hit him had scraped along a bit, and it was very fresh—not more than a few hours old, I'd say. And there was a big lump on the back of his head. The problem is, if he did it, surely he'd have known she wasn't dead."

"And we have no evidence that he was in the building at the material time."

"True, but don't forget the basement door. He could have been there, and the base of that clamp-stand has rough edges and could easily have made the injury on the side of his head."

"So he bashes Sally and then somebody bashes him? That could have been Hume."

"And then Hume moves her into his own storeroom, so he can find her there a little later? Meanwhile, Hamilton just gets up and leaves? Talk sense, Sergeant."

"OK, so maybe Hamilton is telling the truth and Hume is lying. He might have been there earlier. He assaults Sally, hides her in the store room, leaves through the basement and comes back in through the front door. He knows she's not dead and he can come back for her later."

"Why did he assault her?"

"Search me—but he was involved in something like this before."

"Yes—it makes you think, doesn't it?"

Michelson pulled in behind the patrol car as Hamilton, Hume and Elsie were getting out. Williams noticed that Elsie stumbled and had to grab Hume's arm to avoid falling, but the possible significance of the incident didn't occur to him until much later.

Shortly before midnight, while the three suspects were on their way back uptown in a police car, Williams was still discussing the case with Michelson. "Not a single goddamn thing. Nothing new and the only contradiction is that Hamilton says he wasn't expecting Sally to call him and Hume says she said Hamilton asked her to. The only trace of blood on any of them was on Hume's shoes and we already knew he walked through the lab. After all this, all we know is that someone bashed her, maybe with the clamp-stand, and dragged her into the back room and left. Either Smith is protecting somebody or whoever it was came in through the basement, went upstairs, did it and left the way he came."

"Or Smith did it herself."

"Yes, specially if she's got her eye on Hamilton or Hume . . ."

"Or both . . ."

"Right, and Evans gets in her way in both cases. As I say, it's possible, but I just can't see her getting out of control enough to swing that clamp stand."

"So what about Hume? There's no proof that he went for one of his walks in the park."

"Officially he doesn't have a key to the basement door of the main building but as we were saying before, that probably doesn't mean anything. He might easily have borrowed Hamilton's and had a copy made."

"Yes—he's admitted having this mania for secrecy—hiding behind trees when he sees someone he knows. He probably preferred to be able to come and go without being seen. He has sex with this girl for three hours, which is pretty good for an old man like him, she goes off to talk to Hamilton, he follows her and . . ."

"And what. He hears her say something he doesn't like and has a fit of jealous rage?"

"Well, we can check on the phone call. Assuming it was made at the time Hamilton said, if he followed her he could have heard her end of it. Hamilton says she wanted him back."

"Yes, but Hamilton may be lying. Either that or Hume is."

"Right—Hume says she told him Hamilton asked her to call. Hamilton says—Oh, shit! I almost forgot."

Michelson produced the envelope that he had obtained from Elsie.

"Mrs. Smith found this in Sally's desk. I thought it might be from Hamilton asking her to call him."

Williams noted that the envelope was addressed simply to Sally and the initials JH were in the top left corner.

"JH could just as well be John Hume."

"Yeah, but Smith seemed to be sure it was Hamilton—she probably knows his writing. We can probably tell from what the note says."

Unfortunately the envelope was empty.

Michelson summed up the situation in a few highly communicative words before asking, "Do we go after her now? Maybe she still has it on her."

"Or maybe she never had it. Sally probably read it and threw it away. Or maybe Smith tore it up and threw it away. Anyway, she's home by now. We can check the garbage can in the morning. One other thing—do you know why we're still on the Amanda Friedman case?"

"No, but I've been wondering. It doesn't seem to have anything to do with any of the other rapes and disappearances."

"Right. The real reason is that Thornbury has a lot of expensive and influential friends and relations and nobody wants a screw-up here. One of the Assistant Commissioners is a Ben Thompson alumnus and I've had several calls from higher up the food chain, asking about progress and hinting that it would be nice if nothing bad happened to this precious school and its headmaster."

"What did you tell them?"

"Same as I tell the damn reporters—we're following several leads and expect a resolution fairly soon."

"What makes them think we won't screw up?"

"Your guess is as good as mine."

26

When Thornbury arrived at school the next morning, he found Williams sitting at Sally's desk and Michelson kneeling on the floor, replacing items one at a time in Sally's garbage can.

Ignoring the conventional greeting he demanded, "Where's Sally?"

"Miss Evans is in Mount Sinai Hospital with a very severe head wound. Purely as a matter of routine I'd like an account of your movements yesterday afternoon and evening."

"What happened to her and what's the prognosis?"

Williams noted that unlike two of his other witnesses, Thornbury actually showed some concern about the victim.

"At this point we don't know exactly where, when or how it happened. The last I heard she was still unconscious and the doctors are very cagey about the prospects of a recovery."

Thornbury slumped down on the chair next to Sally's desk with his head in his hands and muttered, "I left soon after Sally did, just after four o'clock. I went home, rested for a while and went out to dinner with a friend. We went back to my apartment some time between nine and ten. Does that cover it?"

"What time did you meet your friend for dinner?"

"Seven o'clock."

"And where was that?"

"At a Brazilian restaurant on West Fifty-Sixth Street—she has rather odd tastes."

"Now, if you will just give me the name of your friend, I'll be able to leave you in peace for a while."

"Is this absolutely necessary?"

"Bearing in mind that this may become a murder investigation at any moment, I'd say it is."

"A minute ago you said the doctors were cagey—now you're saying Sally might die. For God's sake, can't you be more explicit?"

"Sally is in critical condition and they don't yet know the extent of the damage. Somebody attacked her and left her for dead, and we'd like to know who it was. The more people we can eliminate, the better our chance of finding out."

Thornbury groaned.

"OK. You met her on Monday—it's Vicky Picky, and if this becomes public I'll be the next murder victim."

"Really? Is there some reason why you shouldn't have dinner with Vicky—with Mrs. Picard?"

"It's not just a matter of dinner."

"Oh, I see—I think. But how can you possibly keep this secret?"

"It's easy. When she's with me she dresses smartly with clothes from her own company, wears a very expensive blonde wig and enough war-paint to round out the corners and make her look like a fairly convincing twenty-nine-year-old. You might not think it, the way she usually shambles around, but she has a very good figure. She lives with me a lot of the time, and since I own my house I don't have to bother with inquisitive doormen and so on."

"How long has this been going on?"

"Is this still part of your investigation?"

"Er—probably not."

"Well, I'll tell you anyway. She had a daughter in the school who graduated five years ago. That's how Vicky came to be a trustee, but we have a lot of trustees and most of them don't bother much with meetings. Well, George M. Picard the Third died when the kid was a junior, and shortly after she graduated, Vicky showed up at school in her disguise and nobody recognized her. She told me she was writing a history of private education in New York and asked if we could have dinner together. Well, she took me in completely and one thing led to another. When she let the cat out of the bag later on I didn't believe her at first—she had to take her wig off. When I got to know her better, I realized that it's the other look that's really the disguise. It's an act that she enjoys putting on—you know, the acid-tongued old lady who doesn't give a damn about anyone."

"I gathered from what she said on Monday that she knew all about Amanda's blackmailing activities."

"Yes, but the way she talked about it was part of the Vicky Picky character. Sometimes she just can't stop, and frankly I'm getting tired of it. It makes me feel like a bigamist."

It flashed through Williams's mind that it would be interesting to find out where Vicky Picky had been on the previous Sunday afternoon. After all, she had said that someone had to get rid of that girl. But this was much too fanciful, he told himself; with all those people milling around in the building, someone would surely have seen her. Thornbury was still talking.

"I don't suppose you want to tell me anything, but I'd really like to know how this happened and whether you have any suspects or any idea why. I mean, I'm still supposed to be in charge of whatever's left of this school. And I have to find someone to answer the damn phone. It was ringing its head off all day yesterday with parents wanting to know what the hell's going on."

"OK, let's take those things one at a time. I was intending to leave an officer in charge here, but from your point of view it would obviously be better to have someone the parents know, who could represent the school. Only it has to be someone we can be fairly sure has no connection with Amanda's death or the assault on Sally."

"Thanks—I'll get Andy Johnson to take over, at least for the time being. You can take it from me that he'd rather be dead than involved in anything criminal."

Williams was thinking that he had already taken a lot from Thornbury and wasn't at all sure how much of it was true.

"I guess you'll want to have your officer on hand anyway", the headmaster continued, "and you can tell Andy what to say about Sally—and I'll tell him what to say for the school, if I can think of anything sensible. Right now, 'Closed until further notice' is the only thing that comes to mind."

"I already spoke to Mr. Johnson", Williams said. "I gave him a bare minimum of information and he had the same reaction. OK, we'll set that up and then I want to talk to you in your office. And, by the way, the whole building is now off limits except for the administrative offices on this floor and the immediate reception area."

After putting Johnson and Michelson in charge of reception, Williams followed Thornbury into his office.

"First I have to remind you that we are still investigating the death of Amanda Friedman, and you are still on our list of suspects."

"That's OK, Inspector. May I take it that you have been receiving delicate hints from some of my friends and relations?"

"Well, as a matter of fact . . ."

"And alumni?"

"Yes, but . . ."

"Don't take any notice. Thanks to the good sense of my forbears I'm not dependent on any of them. I'd like the investigation to be wrapped up as soon as possible, so don't bother to pull any punches."

"OK, thanks and here goes. We don't know whether there's any connection between that and the assault on Sally Evans and at this point we're not taking anything for granted. I want you to tell me everything you know about Sally, since it's possible that we can get some clue about why she was attacked."

"Sally's parents died when she was nineteen. They were fairly well off and left her enough money so that she could get by without working, but without a whole lot to spare. She was in secretarial school at the time, and after she got her diploma she took the job here. She lives in a fifth floor walk-up on East 83rd Street."

"Isn't she over-qualified for a receptionist's job?"

"Yes, but she likes being around people and, as I say, the income from the job is really icing on the cake. Anyway, that was four years ago and she's so good at the job that she can get away with dressing like a tart and having affairs with anything that seems to have male physiology."

"Have you been involved?"

"No. OK, I did make an effort in that direction but I was gently repulsed. She was very sweet about it and I admit it was inappropriate for a man in my position. I hadn't realized how far it had gone with Hamilton—well, I probably still don't realize, but I've been getting the idea. And, of course, there was Fine and probably Miller. And, by the way, I like the way she dresses and I've ignored requests from the dowdier members of the community to talk to her about it."

"Where do you get your information?"

"If you're thinking that the headmaster is the least likely person to know what's going on among his faculty members, you're right, but I do have eyes and ears and a rather dirty mind, and for some reason one of my teachers has taken it upon herself to act as my personal pipeline."

"Mrs. Smith?"

"Exactly—how did you guess? No, don't tell me. I kind of understand Elsie. I'm a good headmaster, as one of my colleagues told me the other day, but I have my weaknesses and so does Elsie. She's a very good math teacher and a very respectable citizen except that the older she gets the more man-crazy she becomes. It's not like Sally, who's just doing what a young, unattached girl normally does. Elsie puts a lot of effort into disguising the fact that she's fifteen years older, and it makes it very hard for her when she can't get what she wants. She had a go at me last year . . ."

Williams interrupted: "You mean last school year?"

"Yes—in the spring. Anyway, when that didn't work she took to dropping in every so often, ostensibly to talk about school matters but always ending up with complaints about the way her colleagues were behaving. Reading between the lines I gathered that she had tried it on with Miller, who's about the same age as Sally. He was evidently quite cruel to her, so she switched to Hamilton, who was probably quite cooperative—at least until he got interested in Sally. Elsie didn't say any of this in so many words but it was pretty obvious from the way she talked. She had always spoken very highly of Hamilton, but all of a sudden, some time last week, she started delicately hinting that there might be problems in that direction—nothing that she had seen herself, but she had heard . . . well, you know how it goes. Kids were complaining about his teaching, there was favoritism and he was showing an unsavory interest in some of the girls. Of course, she didn't know whether any of this was true, but it was what people were saying, and she couldn't or wouldn't say which people. Then she started on Sally, and she didn't hold back. She called her everything she could think of without actually calling her a whore. So obviously she thought Hamilton was getting interested in Sally, and then Hume came along and the same thing happened."

"How do you know?"

"Elsie told me on Tuesday afternoon—not explicitly, but I'd never seen her so upset before. She asked me if I thought it was proper for school personnel to conduct their love affairs in full public view during school hours. She was obviously itching to tell me all about it, and it soon came out that she had seen Sally and Hume having a kind of cinematographic necking session in the park. Her attitude to Hume was deeply reproachful, but she was venomous about Sally, who had clearly been leading him on. In her usual oblique but unmistakable way, Elsie made it plain enough that Sally was a scheming hussy and responsible for all the problems in the school and had to go."

"And what do you think?"

"I think it's mostly nonsense. Elsie's frustrated and she gets worked up, but she lets off steam and calms down again. Sally is really very kind-hearted—probably too kind-hearted . . ."

There was a knock at the door and Michelson came in.

"Sorry to interrupt, Sir, but some reports came through that you probably want to hear."

"OK, I'll be with you in a moment."

Michelson left and Williams turned back to Thornbury.

"All this stuff may or may not be important and I'll have to talk to you again as soon as possible. I'll need everything you can remember about your conversation with Mrs. Smith. Please don't go anywhere or discuss this with anyone."

27

"From the Akron police—it's about Jill Davis", Michelson said when Williams joined him at Sally's desk. "She died early this morning. Never regained consciousness and there's still no sign of a note. They've contacted every car rental within a twenty mile radius and nobody under the name of Miller has rented anything in the past seventy-two hours. There were a lot of rentals by young men in their twenties and four of them sound plausible and are being followed up. It looks as if either he has a fake driver's license or he's on a Greyhound bus or a train somewhere. And Sally Evans is still unconscious. There was a blow to the back of the head as well as the wound on the left side. They wouldn't say much but I thought they sounded a bit more optimistic."

Williams was thinking about Jill's mother. When he had seen her before, it had been a case of a runaway teenager, anxiety-making but probably not very serious. Now it was suicide and she would be required to give evidence of her daughter's state of mind and how much she knew about Jill's relationship with Miller. The trouble was that Williams had qualms about seeing Chrissie Davis again. She had asked him to comfort her and he had done so with considerable satisfaction; but comforting anxious mothers was not part of his official duties, and although he felt no remorse about the episode, he thought that in the changed circumstances she might regret it and reproach him for taking advantage of the situation.

"Anything about Mrs. Davis?" he asked. "Is she bringing the body back to New York?"

"All they could tell me was that there's a cremation scheduled for tomorrow afternoon in Akron. In the circumstances they couldn't see any reason for delaying it, but they'd like some input from you. I asked them to stay on the line, but something else came in that had to be dealt with."

"OK, as far as I'm concerned they can get on with it. I guess I'll have to talk to Mrs. Davis—I want to talk to Thornbury again now, so just find out if they know when she's coming back to New York. I take it there was nothing in the garbage can."

"No torn up notes from Hamilton or Hume—just a lot of advertising rubbish."

Michelson picked up the phone and Williams went back to the headmaster's office.

Thornbury, who hadn't been told anything about Jill since her disappearance on Monday, took the news stoically but was clearly very distressed.

"From what I knew of Jill I would never have expected her to take her own life. She was self-possessed, outgoing, popular, and probably would have been able to choose between several excellent colleges. Have you caught up with Miller yet? He's obviously responsible for this."

"There's a lot that Miller may be responsible for and Jill might have been able to tell us, and between them they might have got you off the hook—you never know. We haven't found him yet but we will—and you must keep this information about Jill to yourself until I say otherwise. Now I want to go over everything that you heard from Mrs. Smith about Sally Evans and her love affairs or anything else that you can remember—even if it means repeating things you've already said. Start with Bobby Fine."

Thornbury wearily did as he was told. Fine had had his little fling with Sally in September. Hamilton had laughed about it and Elsie had been quite sympathetic toward the young man. Apparently she had never set her sights on him, but Miller was a different matter and she had been delighted when, after the fuss about his earlier goings on with Amanda had died down, he went after Sally and she told him his fortune.

"And all this information comes from Mrs. Smith?"

"Mostly—do you remember what it was like in High School? Everybody knew who was going with whom, why x and y had split up and who was to blame. It's just like that in the faculty, only it's a lot smaller and the only way you can avoid it is by keeping your personal life separate from the school. Nobody knows anything about Vicky and me, but it's probably common knowledge that I took a shot at Sally. Word gets around about things like that and although it rarely comes directly to me, Elsie sucks it all in like a vacuum cleaner and I get it anyway—well, her version. My impression is that she was furious with Hamilton for taking up with Sally and even more furious with Sally for making it happen. Now she's beside herself with rage because Sally has moved in on Hume just when she had him in her cross-hairs. What she thinks about Hume now I really don't know. She sounded more sorrowful than angry but she was plainly very upset."

"OK—now I'd like to hear your assessment of Hamilton."

"You mean, do I think he would murder someone?"

"Not necessarily—just anything that strikes you as possibly relevant."

"Well, he usually comes across as calm, quiet and well organized, and I'm not going to give you the old chestnut about still waters. If you want to know the truth, I have no idea how deep he is. The only time I've ever seen him thoroughly lose his temper was yesterday when I said something untoward about his expectations with Sally."

Thornbury had just finished describing the incident that had left another mess on the floor of his office when Michelson looked in again.

"Bobby Fine is here, Sir. He thinks he has something important to tell you."

"What's it about?"

Michelson shook his head and looked at the door. Williams got the idea.

"OK, I'll come and talk to him."

"He doesn't know about last night", Michelson muttered as they left the headmaster's office.

"Are you absolutely sure of that?"

28

After the round of interviews on Tuesday morning, Bobby Fine had been completely ignored by the police. They had insisted on knowing the name of the young woman with whom he claimed to have spent his Sunday afternoon and had discreetly checked his alibi. Discretion was highly necessary as the woman in question was not so young and was married to Andrew Johnson. She had reluctantly confirmed Bobby's story while maintaining that they were just good friends, and had promptly informed Bobby that she would not be making any more journeys to the Bronx and was withdrawing her offer to set him up in a nice apartment on the Upper West Side. Bobby wasn't heartbroken about this. Delia had given great satisfaction, but she had been showing signs of possessiveness and dropping alarming hints about leaving her husband, so it was really a relief.

It did leave him at a loose end, however. By Thursday he was tired of hanging around his little apartment, so he thought he might as well go to school and see if anything was happening. As he was locking his door, something on his key ring rang an alarm bell in the back of his mind. A certain episode a few months ago with the headmaster's safe had really started as harmless prank, but if the police found out that he had all these keys they might start asking awkward questions. Then again, the best thing to do might be to tell them about it.

Hume had got home very late the previous evening. He hadn't bothered to put his bed away after the session with Sally so, without removing even his outer clothing, he threw himself across it and immediately fell into a state of unconsciousness that was more like a drug-induced coma than a deep, healthy sleep. It lasted for several hours and this time there were no dreams of Jessica or Sally. When he half woke around four o'clock in the morning he knew that something was wrong but couldn't remember what it was. Drifting in and out of his stupor he puzzled over this for several hours, hardly able to move and completely unable to think of any point in doing so.

Gradually he put the pieces together. It wasn't just that he felt more exhausted now than when he had gone to bed. The real problem was that something had happened to Sally. She was lying in a doorway and her blood was spreading over the floor and he was kissing her pale face. Now he couldn't get it out of his mind that he was responsible. Because of something he had done, someone had tried to kill her. Logically it didn't add up, but his mental processes were all feeling and image—logic was not part them. Sally, extrovert and aggressively heterosexual, was the complete opposite of Jessica and yet, in his zombie-like state of mind, he kept confusing them. His intense guilt feelings about Jessica had spread out and enveloped his image of Sally, so that now he couldn't think of Sally without seeing Jessica—Jessica running away from him, running to the safety of Susan's arms, tripping on the green nightgown and hurtling down the stairs. Once again the picture came into focus—the long journey home after the loss of his ship and his near death in the Atlantic, Susan away, on duty in Portsmouth, and Jessica alone in the double bed. She was wearing Susan's nightgown—the special one that he and Susan had kept as a memento. He wouldn't have understood what had been going on if Jessica hadn't started explaining. He could still hear her. "I'm sorry, John—it's just that we love each other so much." It had taken a few seconds for the penny to drop, but when it did so it was with a noise like a thunderclap. While he had spent months on his destroyer, guarding convoys and struggling with his obsession,

Susan had been having what he wanted; so now he was going to take his share. The nightgown was too big for Jessica and it slipped from her shoulders very easily. He might have had his way with her, but at the crucial moment the front door opened and Jessica screamed for Susan. In that one second of hesitation she slipped out of his grasp and ran for the stairs. Then came the disaster, the terrifying sound of Jessica's head on the hardwood floor and Susan's inconsolable weeping that still haunted his dreams.

He had allowed the whole subsequent shape of his life to be dictated by this incident—his further years of service in the navy while he did everything in his power to get himself killed, his twenty years at the Nave School, where Jessica's remains had been buried in the foundations of a new science building immediately after the war, and his retreat to America after the discovery of her skeleton. Hume had no religious convictions and was not given to sentimentality, but he had stayed at the Nave because he felt that somehow he was taking care of Jessica and giving her some companionship in her loneliness, anonymously interred beneath a building where children received the beautiful wisdom of modern science, without being given the necessary caution that it could never come within light years of an explanation of the human condition.

Waking up a little, Hume puzzled over his confusion between Jessica and Sally and thought of a possible explanation. He had thought that he understood Sally, that Hamilton's analysis had been correct—an irresistible body and a narrow-gauge mind. His attraction to her had been primarily zoological, but that was probably more a sign of his condition than of hers. Maybe if he really knew her he would find that she was more like Jessica than he had thought. Maybe, however, he would never get the chance. He got up in a hurry and, without pausing for a change of clothing, set off down the stairs in search of news.

Elsie had slept badly, too, but unlike Hume she had been fully conscious in her wakefulness. She had kept telling herself that she was not really a bad person, that she was doing her best with the bad hand that life had dealt her; but other people had lost their husbands and undoubtedly some of them had indulged in streams of unfulfilling love affairs without eventually going out of their minds. And out of her mind was what she had been. She had been teetering on the edge for weeks, and the sight of Hume and Sally, passionately kissing in the park, had given her the final push. Now she wanted someone who would understand her troubles and her motivations, and the only person she could think of was Hume, who had secrets of his own and was kind and thoughtful as long as you stayed away from his sore spots. Elsie knew in her heart that this was wishful thinking, that what she really wanted was something that wasn't going to happen. The best she could possibly hope for was that he would greet her politely, ask her how she was and make some inane remark about the weather. When she tried to imagine him taking her in his arms the picture wouldn't gel; but she went to look for him anyway.

After learning from Andrew Johnson that there was no further news about Sally and that Hume hadn't been seen that morning, Elsie went to No. 3 and took the elevator to the fourth floor. She started up the final staircase just as Hume was leaving his apartment. They met at the midpoint and Elsie could only get as far as, "John, I . . ." before Hume said, "Sorry, I'm in a rush", and brushed past her. He disappeared and Elsie, hearing his echoing progress down four flights, sat on the stairs and tried to hold herself together. It didn't work and it didn't matter very much because after Hume had let the street door close behind him there was no one left in the building to hear the sounds of her torment.

When Hume entered the main building he saw Williams, Michelson and Fine standing by Sally's desk, where Andrew Johnson was still in charge. Williams saw the look on Hume's face and said, "Sergeant, please take Mr. Fine into the auditorium and I'll join you in a minute."

As soon as Fine was out of earshot he added, "I'm sorry, Mr. Hume, there isn't any good news about Sally Evans. All they'll tell us is that she is still unconscious and her condition is unchanged.

We're going to talk to Mr. Fine, and then I'd like to have a few more words with you, if you wouldn't mind waiting here for a few minutes."

After Williams had followed Michelson and Fine into the auditorium, Johnson said gruffly, "I can see that you don't feel like talking, Mr. Hume, so I'll not bother you with conversation."

"Thank you very much."

Meanwhile, Bobby Fine was trying to explain why he had felt compelled to experiment with the headmaster's safe.

"He told us at the beginning of the year that the trustees had insisted that the school needed greater security for sensitive items, including the spare keys that used to hang on a board where everybody could see them. He told them that all the paperwork was in Andy Johnson's office, but they said that he had to have a safe of his own and they arranged with a contractor to do the job on the wall and install the latest burglar-proof model. It turned out later that one of the trustees is a friend of the contractor, but that's another story. Thornbury thought the whole thing was a joke, and for some reason I decided to show them just how burglar-proof the thing was as soon as I had the chance. Sally has a key to Thornbury's office hidden in her desk, so I borrowed it and had a copy made. Where's Sally?"

"We'll come to that in a minute. Did she know you borrowed the key?"

"No."

Fine didn't seem to be embarrassed.

"I only had it for a few hours. Later that day, after everyone else had left, I went to the office and had a go at the safe."

"And?"

"They were right in a way."

"Meaning?"

"Well, I had overrated my talent as a safe-cracker—I got it open but only with guesswork. I thought Thornbury would have chosen something that would be easy to remember and I tried various bits and pieces of 'Benjamin Thompson'."

"OK, so what did you take from the safe?"

"Nothing—I didn't even take much of a look inside—I just wanted to prove I could do it."

"So why are you telling us this?"

"About a month ago I stayed late to get some apparatus ready in the lab upstairs and discovered that I had lost my key to the storeroom. There wasn't anybody about, so I went down to the headmaster's office and took the spare key out of the safe."

Michelson groaned.

"And", Fine continued, "I never remembered to put it back. Here it is."

"Thank you", Williams said. "It would have been helpful if you had told us this sooner."

"I'm sorry—it just didn't occur to me."

An undercurrent of nervousness in Fine's narrative prompted Williams to push his questioning a little further.

"Now, to go back a bit. Did you tell anyone about your first experiment with the safe?"

"No."

"And you're sure you didn't take anything else from the safe at any time?"

"Yes."

"And you didn't get copies of any other keys?"

"No, I didn't."

"Can you tell us where you were yesterday evening from about six until ten?"

"Yes, I was at home, killing time. What's this about?"

"Is there anyone who can verify your whereabouts?"

"No, I didn't see a soul."

"So if anyone says they saw you in the vicinity of the school around seven o'clock, they would be lying."

"Yes. I've told you, I was at home."

"And while you were messing about with the headmaster's safe, you didn't by any chance get yourself a copy of the key to the basement door?"

Professionally speaking, it was a pleasure for Williams to watch the blush spread over Bobby Fine's face and the tiny drops of perspiration appear on his forehead. The trouble was that this just complicated matters more than ever.

"It was really very useful", Fine muttered. "There were four of them, so I didn't think one would be missed."

Seeing that Fine was getting rattled, Williams decided to push his luck a little further.

"I guess Miller found it useful, too."

"How did you know that? I suppose Sally told you."

"Nobody told me, Mr. Fine. Did he borrow yours, or did you make an extra copy?"

"He saw me coming in one day and asked me how I got the key, and like a fool I told him."

"And he said that he'd keep quiet about it if you let him have a copy?"

"How do you know all this?"

"Not from Miss Evans—but you told her about it didn't you?"

"Yes—after I told Miller. She thought I was really stupid. I guess she was right."

"Yes, Mr. Fine—or maybe just a little naïve. Did you have an affair with Miss Evans?"

"Yes."

"When did it end?"

"In September, soon after it began. Why isn't Sally here?"

Williams looked at Michelson and nodded.

"Sally Evans was attacked yesterday evening and is still unconscious."

Fine looked at the sergeant, expecting him to say more, and when nothing else was forthcoming he asked, "Here? In this building?"

"Yes, in this building", Williams said, "but we're not releasing any further information at the moment, except to say that Miss Evans is in Mount Sinai Hospital in critical condition. You were still friends, I gather."

"Yes—we kid around a lot and I still ask her for a date several times a week and she always has some reason for saying 'no'. I guess she just prefers older men. She's not going to die, is she?"

"The last time we talked to the doctor he sounded just a little more optimistic, but he wouldn't commit himself. And you prefer older women?"

"Not really. Delia's very attractive, of course, and she's not that much older than I am. I think she thought she was just doing a bit of slumming with a social inferior but then it got kind of serious.

It was just after Sally gave me the push and I couldn't see any reason why not. Anyway, that's over now, since she had her little conversation with the police. I guess it's not possible to see Sally."

"I'm afraid not. I'm sorry about Delia."

"Don't be. It's really a relief."

"Good. Why did Sally give you the push?"

"She never told me in so many words but I guess it was because of Hamilton."

"Wasn't that rather humiliating—I mean . . ."

"You mean Hamilton is nearly double my age and he's not exactly your average matinée idol? Yeah, I was upset but it was more surprising than humiliating. I mean Sally could have anyone she wanted around here . . ."

"But you still like her."

"Yes, and I don't want to talk about it any more."

"OK, but let me tell you something off the record. Did you know that Sally broke up with Hamilton?"

"No—when?"

"Never mind about that—the point is this. I have a gut feeling that Sally's going to recover and when she does, she probably won't be interested in dating a schoolboy. Get it?"

"Got it—I think."

Michelson escorted Fine from the room and came back a minute later with Hume.

Williams was very brief and to the point.

"Do you have a key to the basement door of this building?"

"No."

"Why is that?"

"I wasn't given one."

"Did you try to get one?"

"No."

"Why not?"

"I didn't need one."

"But what about your habit of coming and going without being seen? I thought you liked secrecy."

"I certainly prefer to remain anonymous as far as possible, but I had all the keys that I needed. I have a habit of respecting institutional rules and regulations."

"Your habit didn't prevent you from having sex with a school receptionist thirty years your junior."

"Sally isn't an institution and I wasn't aware that I was breaking any rules."

Williams swallowed that, thought fleetingly about Chrissie Davis, and went on.

"Did you know that Bobby Fine has a key to the basement door?"

"No. You ought to realize, Inspector, that I've been in this school less than three weeks. What I don't know about it would fill volumes."

"OK, but you've been teaching on the same floor as Mrs. Smith all that time, so perhaps you can tell me what kind of shoes she wears in the classroom."

"Yes. She usually wears boots to school and changes into something more comfortable when she gets here."

"Have you ever seen her in high heels?"

"Occasionally—I think she keeps a pair here in case she has an appointment after school. I noticed them when she stumbled, getting out of the police car last night."

"So she comes to school in boots, has a pair of flatties for teaching and heels in case she's going out for the evening."

"That seems to be her system."

Williams nodded to Michelson, who got up and left the room quietly.

"She came to see me this morning", Hume said, "but I didn't want to talk to her."

"Why not?"

"Two reasons—the main one was that I was on my way here to ask about Sally."

Hume hesitated and Williams momentarily regretted the advice he had given to Fine. He probably ought to have stayed out of it and let the schoolboy and the old gentleman fight it out for themselves. Hume remained silent.

"Yes, Mr. Hume? What was the other reason?"

"Apart from yesterday evening, the last time I spoke with Mrs. Smith she was in a very strange mood. Well, to be strictly honest, so was I. I suppose I'll have to tell you about it."

"I can't wait", Williams said resignedly. This was the goshdarnedest, weirdest case with the oddest set of people he had ever encountered. It probably all arose from the constant interaction of adolescent and adult minds and people forgetting which was which. It wasn't just Bobby Fine—all these teachers seemed to be in state of arrested adolescence, including Hume, who had obviously gone dotty over a kid who could almost be his granddaughter. Pulling himself together, Williams added, "Go on, Mr. Hume."

"It started with a nightmare", Hume began.

Williams groaned inwardly.

Ten minutes later, when Hume passed though the front hall on his way to his usual bench in the park, Bobby Fine was entertaining a very puzzled-looking Andrew Johnson with a story about two hippopotami having a conversation in the Limpopo River. In spite of his preoccupations, Hume couldn't help smiling.

"You can't tell that story today", he said to Bobby.

"Why not?"

"Well, this *is* Thursday."

"Oh, yeah, you're right. OK, Andy, I'll tell you the rest tomorrow."

Meanwhile, the two policemen were sitting at the table in Hume's office behind the lab, examining a pair of leather boots, while Williams told Michelson about Hume's dream.

"She wore these to school", Michelson remarked, "but she wanted to change into something more comfortable, and when she was taking them off, this zipper jammed. She must have had a hell of a time getting it off. Then she puts on these . . ."

"Espadrilles, Sergeant—very comfortable and reasonably elegant, with very little heel and nice bloodstains on the soles. Why didn't she take them with her? If she'd had any sense she'd have been out of the building and home long before Sally was found."

"She could have just worn them home."

"They're pretty flimsy."

"Yeah, you'd have thought she'd be in a panic, but instead she goes down and calmly sorts through Sally's belongings. She seemed very self-possessed when I talked to her—not like someone who'd just tried to kill somebody."

"I think she forgot about the zipper. After finishing with Sally she knows she must have blood on her shoes. She's smart enough to realize that she doesn't want to track it all over the school, so she takes them off before leaving the lab, and then finds she can't get the boots on. She knows she's going to search Sally's desk and she's afraid of being found with the shoes in her possession, so she stuffs them down behind a row of textbooks and puts on her heels. Her problem was that once Hume arrived it didn't seem possible for her to go back and retrieve the shoes. Or if not that, something else . . ."

"Yeah, it doesn't really add up. Maybe she just wasn't thinking, or maybe she'll tell us if we ask her nicely."

"OK, we'll try it. Now, what about that door?"

"It's just like Hume said. A little bit of wood nailed inside the jamb."

"And Smith saw him doing it. Well, that solves one problem and points another finger straight at her."

"You mean she wouldn't have dragged the body all that way if she hadn't known she could get this door open? The way keys are flying around in this building we can't be sure of that."

"True, but either way she knew she'd be able to open it. What do you think about Hume's nightmare?"

Michelson rolled his eyes skyward.

"Nuts", he said. "The whole thing is nuts. He has a bad dream, so he comes and nails a bit of wood on a door so he won't have another one. The problem is I can't think of any sane reason for doing it, so maybe the nutty one is true."

"OK, so do we actually have anything against him at this point, apart from the fact that he has no alibi for either incident?"

"Not that I can think of. But we have plenty against Smith. Do we bring her in again?"

"Yes. Let's see—she came to see Hume and he wouldn't talk to her. That must have been an hour ago, so we can try her apartment—but my guess is she's still wandering around somewhere. I think I know where to look."

"So do I."

"OK, but I'll go and get her. I have an idea, and while I'm trying it I want you to bring Hamilton in. Tell him we have further information that we want to discuss with him, and keep him sitting here at the desk for an hour or so."

29

On the previous evening, the police car had first delivered Elsie to her home on Riverside Drive and then crossed over to the corner of Central Park West and 90th Street, where Hume got out. Hamilton could have been taken all the way home too, but he insisted on getting out at 85th and Central Park West, although he wasn't quite sure why. It had something to do with the anticipated sensation of opening the door and walking into an empty house. That was the thing about women—there was all that stereotyped nonsense about men being unwilling to wash dishes and unable to boil an egg or launder a shirt, but that wasn't the real thing. Sex was important, but the real thing was that a woman did something to the space you lived in and the air you breathed. When he got home, everything would look exactly the same, except for the missing typewriter, but the air would be dead. It would feel like living in a coffin.

These were unpleasant thoughts, but they served for a few moments to postpone consideration of his more urgent problems. That night Hamilton didn't struggle with sleep. Instead he drank two thirds of a bottle of whiskey and didn't emerge from his alcoholic stupor until early on the next afternoon. He had the vague impression that the telephone and the doorbell had been ringing on and off for several hours, but now the knocking was so loud that he couldn't ignore it. The open whiskey bottle was standing on his bedside table, so he took a generous swig before painfully making his way to the front door. It had seemed dark in the house and there was nothing but darkness in his thoughts, so he was surprised to see that the sun was shining and a strong breeze was blowing fluffy clouds across a bright sky.

The breeze ruffled Hume's grey hair as he wrestled with the same problem as Williams and Michelson, but with less information. He couldn't believe that Elsie had attacked Sally, but he couldn't see who else could have done it. He didn't know about the blood on Elsie's shoes and the possibility that she had seen a note from Hamilton to Sally, but he did have one advantage over the police—he knew he hadn't done it himself. When he had seen Elsie after doing his bit of woodwork on the storeroom door, there had been a barely controlled fury behind the few words she had spoken. Later on she had still been in a very strange mood and evidently obsessed with Sally. But Elsie as a murderer, even in a moment of blind rage? He leaned against the curved wooden back of his bench, closed his eyes and gained a little comfort from the play of the wind on his face. When he sat up and opened his eyes, Elsie was standing in front of him.

"John? I just want to say I'm sorry."

No, surely not this woman, whose anguish was in her voice and imprinted on her face. The impact of her distress took him back over the years to the little church next to the Nave School, where he and his wife and brother-in-law had gone to the morning service after reburying Jessica's remains. The liturgy had had very little resonance for him until they came to the General Confession; *We acknowledge and bewail our manifold sins and wickedness which we, from time to time, most grievously have committed* . . . This had driven a spear into the part of him that the believer would have called his soul, and now he thought perhaps that Elsie was undergoing the same kind of torture.

"Sit down, Elsie", he said. "What are you sorry for?"

Elsie sat but she didn't speak. When Inspector Williams found them some time later she still hadn't spoken.

Williams sat down next to Elsie.

"Listen, Mrs. Smith, it's time for you to start telling the truth."

Hume made as if to leave, but Williams said, "No, Mr. Hume, I want you to stay and listen. Now, Mrs. Smith, you told us you were in your room until about seven o'clock and then you went down to the reception area, where you went through the contents of Miss Evans's desk. You stayed there continuously until the police arrived, and the only people you saw in this time were Miss Evans and Mr. Hume. I'm sure I don't need to tell you that it would be better for everybody if you told the truth, so do you want to add anything at this point?"

"No, I don't."

Realizing that he had phrased his question poorly, Williams tried again.

"Is there anything you can tell us even if you don't want to?"

Elsie shook her head.

"All right—then let me inform you that we know you were in the lab after the assault on Miss Evans and there's nothing to show that you didn't commit the assault yourself."

"I suppose you found my shoes. Well, I thought you would."

Williams took this as some kind of admission and turned his attention to Hume.

"Now, Mr. Hume, about this sudden affair of yours with Miss Evans. We've heard that you were kissing her in the park on Tuesday afternoon, that you spent three hours in bed with her yesterday and that you arrived at school around eight o'clock and found her in the storeroom. Is that all correct?"

"Yes, it is."

"What corroboration do you have for any of these statements?"

Hume was surprised by the turn the questioning had taken, but he answered in his usual measured fashion.

"I have no idea who saw me in the park with Sally and no one saw us yesterday. Mrs. Smith saw me entering the school last night."

"It was Mrs. Smith who reported seeing you in the park with Sally, Mrs. Smith who saw Sally going up to your apartment yesterday, and Mrs. Smith who saw you enter the school. At this point there is no evidence that anyone apart from the two of you and Miss Evans was in the school at the time of the assault. To put it more clearly, there is no evidence that you and Mrs. Smith aren't jointly responsible for the assault and that the two of you cooked up a flimsy story to cover your tracks. That being the case, I shall have to place you both under arrest and take you downtown for further questioning."

Elsie stood up and faced Williams.

"You're right, Inspector—it's time for me to tell the truth. I was very angry with Sally. I followed her up the stairs and into the lab, and when I tried to talk to her she mocked me. When she turned away to go into the back room I picked up the nearest object and hit her with it."

"What was the object?"

"It was a clamp stand."

"Where did you hit her?"

"On the side of the head, just above the ear."

"What did you do then?"

"I dragged her into the storeroom."

"Did you think Sally was dead?"

"No—I was very shocked when I heard she might die. I didn't realize I had hit her so hard."

"Is there anything else you want to tell me?"

"No."

"Will you be prepared to make a written statement of what you have just told me?"

"Yes."

"Then I want you both to come back to the school with me before I take you downtown."

Hamilton was sitting at the front desk with Michelson and Johnson when Williams returned with Elsie and Hume. The inspector signed to Michelson to follow but nobody said anything as he conducted his charges into the elevator and up to the lab, where he handed Elsie a clamp stand similar to the one that had been found in the sink. Holding his rolled up overcoat head high against an open area of wall, and risking severe injury to his hand, he said, "Take a swing at that."

Elsie didn't hesitate. She picked up the stand by the end of its upright and swung it viciously against the overcoat.

"Thank you. Mr. Hume, do you wish to change anything in the sworn statement you gave last night?"

"No, I don't."

"Nothing to add?"

"No."

"Then for the moment you're free to go. Sergeant, pick up Mr. Hamilton downstairs and take him downtown. I doubt whether he'll object. I'll bring Mrs. Smith separately."

Andrew Johnson saw what was happening and dialed the number that Jean Hamilton had given him.

30

Hamilton sat alone in an interview room for three-quarters of an hour. He had thought of protesting, of demanding either to be charged with something or to be allowed to leave, and he might have done so if he hadn't felt so sick and if he had had a better idea of what the rules were.

After giving her statement, Elsie had been formally charged with the attempted murder of Sally Evans. Williams and Michelson were still talking things over.

"It's very neat", Michelson was saying. "She knew how it was done and she easily could have done it."

"But you don't think she did. Why not?"

"Well, it's kind of obvious, really. In fact, I'm surprised she doesn't see it."

"OK—maybe she does."

"Convoluted", Michelson said again—it was one of his favorite words. "And for another thing, you've got Hamilton here."

"OK, point taken—anything else?"

"From what you told me I have the impression that she thinks Hume did it. She wasn't going to say anything until you started on him, and then she suddenly makes a full confession."

"That could be true, but it might apply just the same if she did it herself."

"OK, I wasn't there but it sounds more as if she was trying to arrange things somehow . . . It's hard to explain. But if she didn't do it, she knows who did."

"Yes, she must have seen it happen."

"Which means it was Hume, unless . . ."

"Unless someone else was in the building."

"Someone Sally telephoned from Hume's office . . ."

"And who lives a few minutes walk from the school . . ."

"And has a key to the basement door. It's possible."

"Why would he try to kill her?"

"He wanted her back and she told him to get lost."

"So he went over to the school to try to persuade her."

"She sassed him and he slugged her. Probably didn't mean to kill her."

"But why drag her into the storeroom?"

"It doesn't make sense any way you slice it. I mean, I still don't understand why you didn't bring Hume in as well."

"Maybe I still will, but the reason is that I don't think he did it—it makes even less sense. We'd better go and talk to Hamilton."

Hamilton still sat at the table in the interview room, where a street lamp now shone through the one small window. His hangover had been so acute that nausea and headache had shielded him from all but the most primitive thought processes. For hours he had been conscious of nothing beyond severe, generalized fear and misery, but the sight of Williams and Michelson walking into the room produced an unwelcome focusing effect. He still didn't have the strength to protest about the way he was being treated, but he became alert enough to realize that his best policy was to say as little as possible.

"Sorry to keep you waiting, Mr. Hamilton."

This piece of blatant insincerity aroused an atom of fighting spirit.

"Liar!" Hamilton muttered. "I have nothing to add to what I told you before, so you might as well shut up."

"As it happens", Williams said, "we have something to add—two things, in fact. One is that whereas you told us that you weren't expecting a call from Miss Evans yesterday, we have evidence that you asked her to call you."

Hamilton gazed silently into the space over Williams's left shoulder, so the inspector grunted and continued.

"Mr. Hamilton, we have a sworn statement by one witness, and there is also the matter of the note you left for Miss Evans yesterday."

This produced a reaction.

"What the hell are you talking about? I didn't leave her a note yesterday."

"OK, so when was the last time you left a note for Miss Evans?"

"I don't know—some time last week, I guess."

"Can you describe the envelope the note was in?"

"Just a small, plain envelope with her name in the middle and my initials at the top left corner."

"And what did the note say?"

Silence.

"Mr. Hamilton?"

"Nothing in particular. Didn't you ever write a note to a girlfriend?"

"Did you often leave notes for Miss Evans?"

"Yes."

"Do you know if she was in the habit of keeping them?"

"I doubt it—she wasn't the sentimental type."

"Don't you mean 'isn't', Mr. Hamilton? Why do you keep thinking she's dead?"

"I just meant while we were . . ."

"Lovers? And you still deny asking her to call you?"

"Yes and I can't see what the hell it matters anyway. She called me and I talked to her."

There was a knock at the door and a uniformed officer entered.

"Sorry to interrupt, Sir. There's something . . ."

Williams wasn't sorry to be interrupted.

"OK, Mr. Hamilton, we'll be back shortly."

"I can't wait."

"Mrs. Hamilton is here", the officer said when they were outside. "And she's brought the family lawyer."

Jean Hamilton and Conrad Grossmann were standing a few paces along the corridor. When Williams and Michelson emerged from the interview room, Jean marched over and asked, "Why have you arrested my husband?"

"We haven't arrested him", Williams replied. "I am Inspector Williams and this is Sergeant Michelson. We were merely asking him a few questions."

Grossmann, elderly, thin and totally bald, but still able to move with a cat-like tread, joined the group.

"We understand that Mr. Hamilton has been in your custody for several hours. May I suggest that if you haven't charged him with anything, it's time to release him?"

"Mr. Hamilton is not in custody. He is here at our request and is free to go at any time."

"But he doesn't know that, does he?"

"I have no idea what he does or doesn't know."

Williams could have added, "That's what I'm trying to find out", but he didn't.

"Then I wish to see him and inform him of his rights", the lawyer continued.

"By all means. Help yourself."

Williams pointed to the door of the interview room and turned to Jean Hamilton.

"I understood that you had left your husband, Mrs. Hamilton."

"Oh, did you? Well, he's still my husband whether I left him or not."

"May I ask how you knew where to find him?"

"You can ask but I don't see why I should tell you. He's here and I intend to take him home now."

"You're going home with him?"

"It's none of your business where I'm going with him."

"Actually, Mrs. Hamilton, it is my business. Mr. Hamilton is under suspicion in one case of homicide and another case of attempted murder. And I'm sure you will see that it would be helpful for us to know how to get in touch with you."

"Homicide? You mean the Friedman girl? But . . ."

"But what, Mrs. Hamilton?"

Grossmann reappeared with Hamilton before Jean could answer the question. She was shocked at the sight of her husband.

"What have you been doing to him? He looks awful."

"It's not their fault", Hamilton said. "Just a common or garden hangover. Anyway, what are you doing here? I thought I wasn't going to see you again."

"I changed my mind. Come on, we're going home."

As Hamilton was leaving the building, flanked by his wife and his lawyer, Jean looked over her shoulder and told Williams, "If you can't get me at home, try Andrew Johnson."

Williams said to Michelson, "Too many unsupported statements in this case and the business of the note was a screw-up. The fact is we don't know anything for sure about any of these people's movements last night. Hamilton could have been anywhere and Smith and Hume might have been wandering around all over the place. The only confirmation of Hume's time of arrival comes from Smith and she's obviously in love with him. There's something fishy about Smith's confession, but we'll go with it for the time being."

"You mean until Sally wakes up?"

"Maybe she won't, and if she does she may not remember anything. We'll have to do another review of the Friedman case. Amanda may have fallen down the stairs without being pushed, but we still have to find out who moved her up to the storeroom and when and why. She and Sally ended up in the same place and the same people were on the loose—Hume, Hamilton and Smith. It's hard to believe that there's no connection.

"You didn't mention Thornbury. I guess he's out of it as far as Sally is concerned but he was here on Sunday. Do you think Fine's story about the key lets him out?"

"Not a hundred percent, but I think the others are much better prospects."

Amanda, her parents, Michael Schwartz, Hume, Hamilton, Sally, Elsie, Thornbury and Miller all came into the lengthy and unprofitable review, and finally Williams said, "We have to find Miller and we don't even have a decent picture of him."

31

A few hours after the cremation of her daughter, Chrissie Davis boarded a plane in Cleveland, Ohio. She would be back in her apartment by early evening and what she would do when she got there she couldn't imagine. Her relationship with Jill had not been very close, but they had liked each other and at least there had been another human being in the house and a point of focus. Now, at some point she would have to sort through Jill's things and decide what to keep and what to let go. She was thinking about this when she arrived at her apartment building, looked in her mailbox and found a letter from Jill. It was written in a neat hand on motel stationary, and it was a long time before she could bring herself to read it. When eventually she did, her immediate response was to telephone the police. She met Williams and Michelson at the door twenty minutes later, handed them the letter and led them silently to the living room. Williams was surprised to see that there was no drink on the end table. Following his gaze, Mrs. Davis said, "I feel too sick. I told her what I read in the papers about Amanda being found upstairs in the closet. It's my fault she killed herself."

Williams read the letter and passed it to Michelson.

Dear Mom,

I'm sorry about this but after you told me about Amanda I realized that I can't go on and I can't come back. We heard her fall down the stairs and Peter went and looked. I followed him and she was lying there in a heap. He said she was dead and we should leave immediately because nobody knew we were there and if we stayed we might get involved and wouldn't be able to leave. I wanted to get help for Amanda but he said there wasn't any point since she was dead. I was so much in love with him I did whatever he said. Now from what you told me I know he was lying, and if we had stayed to help Amanda maybe she wouldn't have died. Today, when I told him about Amanda, he said he thought I hadn't really decided about going away with him and this was his way of persuading me. He says he thought Amanda was OK except for a bump on the head and it was a good way of getting me to make up my mind. He seemed to think I should be happy about it and Amanda wasn't our responsibility. We went and rented another car and put all our things in it. I was supposed to drive the first one just around the corner and leave it but as soon as I was on my own I started thinking and I just kept driving. I thought he was so wonderful but it's all a fake like the rape with Amanda. All he cares about is getting money and avoiding the draft. Now that I know what he's really like, I can't bear to think about what happened on Sunday—any of it. It all seems so disgusting.

I'm sorry Mom. I know I haven't shown it much but I do love you.

Jill

"I'm sorry, Chrissie", Williams said. "You think that if you hadn't told Jill about Amanda she would still be alive. But this is all Miller's doing, not yours. There was no way you could have known what happened on Sunday."

"I know. The fact is I just didn't know enough about Jill—what she was thinking and what she was doing. When I told her about

Amanda I was just trying to make conversation—to keep her on the line a little longer."

"I know how hard it is with teenagers—how secretive they can be."

"Do you? Can I talk to you alone for a minute?"

Williams had mixed feelings about spending time alone with Chrissie Davis, but since it was in the line of duty he had to concentrate and see if there was anything new to be learned.

"Sergeant, go in Jill's room and see if you can find any photographs."

Chrissie Davis looked at Michelson's broad, retreating back and said, "I thought she was off somewhere having a good time. If I'd known about this, I wouldn't have . . ."

"I know—neither would I. But you're not the first person who ever wanted to use sex as a tranquilizer. And if things were different—well they would be different. Don't say any more now—you have my card and I think we're probably going to see each other again. I'll go and see what the sergeant's found."

But the sergeant hadn't found anything.

Michelson was feeling a little more optimistic.

"Well, that changes things—we can get him for depraved indifference as well as endangering the welfare of a minor."

"That's not the only thing it changes", Williams said. "We now know it wasn't Miller who moved Amanda into the storeroom, and that narrows it down a bit. Thanks to Fine we can also assume it wasn't Thornbury, since he didn't have a key, although that doesn't let him out altogether. Drive up to the school. We'll make our calls from there. I want to get them all together and see if we can get any more contradictions, and I don't care if it takes all night."

Williams had another idea about how Amanda might have ended up on the third floor, but he wasn't ready to talk about it yet.

Elsie Smith and John Hume were easy to find—Williams knew exactly where Elsie was and Hume answered his phone immediately. Thornbury and Schwartz were either out or just ignoring the phone, and it took several attempts before Jean Hamilton picked up. Told that her husband was needed urgently, she replied that he was in bed and asleep and she probably wouldn't be able to wake him up even if she tried, which she had no intention of doing anyway.

"OK", Williams told Michelson, "We'll put Smith and Hume on hold and we can get Hamilton when we want him. We'll send cars to Thornbury's and Schwartz's places—if they're not there they can try Vicky Picky and the Galaxy. I think in this case the sight of some uniforms might stir things up a bit."

The two officers sitting in their car outside Thornbury's town house were eventually rewarded when their quarry appeared, arm in arm with a smartly dressed blonde.

"We've got him, Sir", the report came to Williams, "but his girl friend insists on coming with him—she won't let him come without her."

"OK", Williams said resignedly, "bring them in."

They arrived at the same time as Schwartz, who, with a little help from the *Galaxy*, had been run to earth in a bar in Greenwich Village and was now vehemently protesting about police brutality and Gestapo tactics. Officers Kohn and O'Reilly, who had collected Schwartz, were sent to pick up Hamilton, who was brought into school after a great deal of fuss and protestation and, like Thornbury, had female company. With the arrival of Elsie and Hume, Williams had his whole company assembled. Kohn and O'Reilly were left in charge of the reception area while Michelson took the five witnesses into the auditorium and arranged nine chairs in a circle. Before going in, Williams had a quiet word with Victoria Picard and Jean Hamilton.

"You don't really belong here but it's just possible you can contribute something useful. You can go in, Mrs. Hamilton, but I'd just like another word with . . . with this young lady."

"Just remember, Mrs. Picard, that you're here on sufferance and if you start blurting, I'll either have you removed or I'll tell everybody who you really are."

Not waiting for a reply, Williams led Vicky Picky into the auditorium, where Michelson was sitting with Elsie, Thornbury and Hume on his right and Schwartz and Hamilton on his left. Jean Hamilton had taken the chair next to her husband and, faced with the choice of two seats, Mrs. Picard chose the one next to Hume. This put Williams between Picard and Jean Hamilton and gave him a good view of the all the people who had actually been invited. By the time everyone was seated, it was nearly midnight.

32

Eyeing his audience unsympathetically, Williams began with a formal and not very sincere apology.

"I'm sorry to have brought you here at such an inconvenient time, but we have new evidence concerning the death of Amanda Friedman and we need to act on it immediately. This also gives us the opportunity of looking into the fact that two of you gave contradictory reports of the events on Sunday afternoon, so the first thing will be to recap the evidence that you gave—starting with you, Mr. Schwartz. You told us that you came here with Amanda to see Mr. Thornbury. I'd like you to give us an exact account of your movements from the time you met Amanda until the time you left the building."

"Inspector Williams", Schwartz said, in the kind of tone that a person of exquisite taste might use when referring to a mess left by a dog on the drawing room carpet, "I strongly object to being forced to come here against my will. You have my statement already and I have no wish to repeat it."

Williams wasn't surprised.

"Sergeant Michelson, would you be so good as to bring in officers Kohn and O'Reilly?"

Two large policemen entered the room and Williams continued.

"Officer Kohn, what was Mr. Schwartz's attitude when you and Officer O'Reilly asked him to accompany you?"

"He seemed very scared, Sir, and at first he refused to come."

"What made him change his mind?"

"When we told him that he was wanted in connection with a murder investigation, the people he was with got very interested and started cracking jokes. They said they didn't think he had it in him."

Kohn looked at O'Reilly and Williams nodded.

"Yes, Sir. He was plain embarrassed."

"Did you use any physical persuasion?"

"No, Sir, we never laid a finger on him."

Williams turned back to Schwartz.

"Well, Mr. Schwartz?"

"I have nothing to say."

"Very well, that fact is duly noted."

Kohn and O'Reilly left and Williams continued.

"Since Mr. Schwartz is unwilling to speak I'll summarize what he told us on Monday. He and Amanda had made an appointment to meet Mr. Thornbury on Sunday afternoon at 3:45. I'll reserve for the moment what the meeting was about. They arrived on time and the three met in the headmaster's office. There was a heated discussion and Schwartz tried to persuade Amanda to leave. She insisted on continuing the discussion, so he left on his own and went home to write an article for his paper."

Jean Hamilton started to say something, but Williams silenced her with a gesture. He wanted Thornbury's statement to follow immediately.

"Now, Mr. Thornbury, give us your account of what happened."

"I was in my office when they arrived. I let them in and we went into the office. Amanda's idea was that if I didn't pay her off handsomely she would give all the details of the supposed rape to that miserable specimen of protoplasm sitting somewhere on my left and he—or it—would publish it in its nasty little newspaper. I told them to get lost, but I had a difficult time getting them out of the room. Amanda could see that there was nothing doing, but this unprepossessing organism kept on trying. I assume that Amanda had promised it a cut if the plan succeeded."

"So they left together?"

"Yes, still quarreling."

"This is a complete fabrication", Schwartz said.

"No, it isn't."

The voice was Jean Hamilton's. Everyone stared at her with reactions varying from mild surprise to blank amazement.

"I was here, standing just inside this auditorium doorway. The two of them came out of the office together and they were going at it hammer and tongs. He was saying something to the effect that since they couldn't get anything out of Thornbury she had to go home with him so they could write the story. He was trying to get her out of the front door but she got away from him and ran to the door to the basement stairs. He ran after her and I guess he thought he could get her out that way. I heard her shouting, 'I'm not leaving with you, so fuck off.' That door takes a long time to close and I could hear them clearly. He said something like, 'not till you give me every last detail.' After the door closed I could still hear something going on, but it was very muffled and after a minute or so it got very quiet."

"Did you see either of them again?"

"No."

"I want to get this absolutely clear, Mrs. Hamilton. Could Mr. Schwartz have come back up and left through the main entrance without your seeing him?"

"Absolutely not."

"And did you at any time see Mr. Thornbury?"

"Yes, I saw him let them in, but I didn't see him again. When they left the office the door closed after them."

"Did you see either of them again?"

"No."

"What time did this happen?"

"I can't say exactly but it must have been five or ten minutes after four."

"And what time did you leave?"

"About half an hour later."

"Did you see anyone else?"

"Yes. John Hume came down the stairs while they were still in Thornbury's office. He looked around and went down the basement stairs."

"Why were you here, Mrs. Hamilton?"

"I was spying on my husband."

"Did you see him?"

"Yes, he came down the stairs and left the building about four thirty."

"Was he alone?"

"No, Sally Evans was with him."

"Did you see anyone else?"

"No. They left together by the front door and I went home a few minutes later."

"And did you at any time hear anyone use the elevator?"

"No, and as you undoubtedly have noticed, it's a very noisy elevator."

"Thank you, Mrs. Hamilton, it would have been very helpful if we had known all this a few days ago, but I can understand why you didn't want to come forward. Mr. Schwartz, do you wish to say anything?"

Schwartz was still defiant.

"Only in the presence of my lawyer."

"Then we'll continue. The new evidence that I mentioned indicates that Amanda was seen, still alive but badly hurt, on the landing halfway down the basement stairs. Mrs. Hamilton's evidence helps to corroborate this. Now, Mr. Schwarz, if you left the building, it must have been through the basement door. That means you must have gone down the stairs and walked right by Amanda. Are you sure you don't want to say anything?"

Schwartz shook his head but he was visibly shaken.

"Well, then, maybe you didn't leave the building. Mrs. Smith, tell us again what time you left on Sunday."

"I don't know exactly, but it must have been somewhere around twenty past five. All I can say for certain is that it was quite a while after John Hume left, and I didn't see anybody."

"How do you know that Hume had left?"

"I went to see if he was still in the lab and he wasn't, so I sat on a lab stool and thought about things for a long time."

"That isn't what you told us on Tuesday."

"Oh"

Elsie looked confused.

"What did I tell you on Tuesday?"

"You don't remember?"

"After a day or two in jail, Inspector, you tend to see things differently. You should try it some time."

"This is just a matter of fact, Mrs. Smith, so how about telling us the truth?"

"I'm telling it now."

"So you must have sat in the lab for an hour. What were you doing?"

"Thinking, except when I wasn't."

"What were you doing when you weren't thinking?"

"Nothing."

"Did you see or hear anyone in the building during that time?"

"I heard footsteps on the floor above me."

"What time was that?"

"I really don't know."

"What did you do when you heard the footsteps?"

"Nothing."

Williams found this hard to believe, but he went on with his questions.

"How did you leave?"

"I took the elevator down and went out through the front door."

"Was it dark when you got outside?"

"Not quite—I saw the remains of the sunset across the river when I got home. I always watch the sunset when I have the chance—not that I'm likely to get the chance again."

Williams looked around the room. He had got something that he needed, although not in the way he had expected, and there was something weird about Elsie's testimony. Was it possible to believe that she had sat in the lab for over an hour, alternately thinking and not thinking, while someone waited all that time for the opportunity to move Amanda into the storeroom? It all needed a lot of consideration, so maybe this would be the time to close the session. If nothing further emerged it might be realistic to charge Schwartz with manslaughter or criminally negligent homicide, while Miller could be hit with depraved indifference if only they could find him. Once charged they might be more willing to talk, but it looked as if neither of them had been responsible for moving Amanda upstairs. Miller had left with Jill, and Schwartz presumably had no key to the storeroom. Furthermore, to get from the basement to the lab you had to use either the incredibly noisy elevator or the stairs, and if you used the stairs you had to pass through the front hall. So Amanda couldn't have been moved to the third floor until after Jean Hamilton left—unless, Jean was mistaken. And if Elsie was now telling the truth, Amanda couldn't have been moved until after 5:20, which would bring Hume and Hamilton into the picture; their movements were unaccounted for after about 4:30 and they had keys to the storeroom. He would have to have some more sessions with them, and not only about the Friedman case. He was still puzzling over the attack on Sally and very dubious about Elsie's confession, but he needed to give it some more thought before proceeding.

"Mrs. Smith, the officers will escort you back to your cell. Mr. Schwartz, I want a few more minutes of your valuable time. Everyone else is free to go, but I must still ask you not to leave the city."

Vicky Picky was disappointed.

"Well, that wasn't very exciting. I thought you would be grilling people all night."

Williams thought of asking her if she would like to be grilled, but he guessed that the pleasure would be entirely hers and decided against it.

"Mr. Thornbury?" he said.

Thornbury took the hint.

"Come on, Vicky, time to go."

"Thornbury!" Vicky hissed, looking daggers at him, and he realized he had dropped a brick. Nobody seemed to have noticed, however, and she allowed herself to be escorted from the room.

Jean Hamilton approached Williams.

"I thought I should tell you that I was waiting outside and saw them all arrive—all except the headmaster. Did you know that Peter Miller was here? He had a young girl with him, but I didn't recognize her."

This wasn't news to Williams, but he was deeply gratified to have it confirmed. While he took all the details of Jean's frigid vigil, her husband remained sprawled across his chair like a punch-drunk fighter who can't make it back into the ring for the next round. Jean looked across the room at him without much compassion.

"I guess I'll have to take him home. Maybe I'll like him better in the morning. Could you tell me about Sally? He wouldn't talk about it, and all I know is that she was hurt."

"Sally is in the hospital with a serious head wound and the prognosis is unclear. That's really all I want to say at the moment."

"But you think Jim may have been involved."

Williams shook his head and Jean wasn't sure whether this meant "No", "I don't know", or "I can't talk about it."

"Did you see your husband when he got home on Sunday?"

"No, but I heard him."

"What time was that?"

"It was a little after 5:30. I was very anxious as well as angry, and I kept looking at my watch."

She crossed the room and helped Hamilton to his feet.

By now, Elsie was on her way downtown with Kohn and O'Reilly, and soon Williams, Michelson and Schwartz were the only ones left in the room. Schwartz was still in his chair, his cockiness apparently dissipated. The policemen sat on either side of him and Williams did the talking.

"Now, Sir, if you're willing to help us here we may be able to get something settled. Otherwise we'll have to take you in, pending a charge of manslaughter or possibly murder."

"Murder!" Schwartz gasped.

"Exactly! First you push her down the stairs and then you walk right past her, leaving her to die."

"It wasn't like that."

"OK", Michelson said, "so what was it like? We have two witnesses who contradict your story, so this time we want the truth. You and Amanda left the office together, right?"

Schwartz still seemed to be weighing up the situation, so Michelson repeated, "Right?"

"All right—we left together."

"And you quarreled."

"Yes."

"What about?"

"The deal was that if Thornbury wouldn't come across, I would blow the whole cover-up in the Galaxy."

"You mean the cover-up of the alleged rape."

"Yes—the real reason why Miller had to leave and the payments to him and the Friedmans.

Williams took over again.

"How did you know Miller had been paid off?"

"I didn't, but it was obvious."

"OK, go on."

"I wanted her to come home with me so we could write the story, but she changed her mind. She said that if we did that it would kill her part of the deal—the easy A's and the college recommendation."

"So?"

"I tried to make her come with me. We struggled at the top of the stairs and she fell."

"Or maybe you pushed her."

"No, I was just trying to make her come with me."

"And then?"

"She fell all the way to the landing. When I got there she called me a bastard and told me to fuck off. I didn't realize she was that badly hurt and I heard someone coming, so I left through the basement door."

"Did you see that she was bleeding?"

"There were a few drops of blood on the floor and she was holding her shoulder. I thought she must have landed on it."

"Was she lying down, sitting up or standing?"

"She was sitting up and apart from her shoulder there didn't seem much the matter with her."

"So you went home and wrote your article."

"Yes—it was what we had agreed beforehand."

"And, just to be clear about it, you tried to make her leave with you and she refused to go."

"Yes."

"OK, Mr. Schwartz, I think that will do. We'll take you downtown and get you to sign a formal statement."

"But . . ."

"Or we can arrest you on suspicion of murder. Which would you prefer?"

Schwartz preferred not to be arrested and was allowed to go home after giving his statement, but he wasn't offered a ride and couldn't get a taxi, so he had to endure a midnight trip on the subway in order to get back to West 89th Street.

Vicky and Thornbury had been taken home in a police car but Jean Hamilton had declined the offer on the grounds that it was only a few minutes' walk and her husband would benefit from some fresh air. Hamilton had made it out through the front door and was now sitting on the bottom step while Jean questioned Hume a few paces away.

"How much do you know about all this, John? I read the papers on Tuesday but I hadn't seen Jim since Sunday and I didn't know anything had happened to Sally. I want to know if Jim was involved and I couldn't get anything out of the inspector. Don't spare my feelings—I just want to know."

"I don't think I know any more than you do about Amanda—well, except that I found her behind the lab and nobody knows how she got there. The terrible thing is that I found Sally in the same place last night, so obviously I'm under suspicion even though Elsie has confessed to attacking her."

"Elsie? That's ridiculous."

"That's what I thought, but the police seem to be taking her seriously and if it wasn't Elsie . . ."

"I said, 'Don't spare my feelings.' If it wasn't Elsie it was probably Jim. Isn't that what you were going to say? Why?"

"He broke it off with Sally on Tuesday. Yesterday he asked her to call him and she was on her way to do so the last time I saw her. And as far as the police are concerned, if it wasn't Elsie or Jim, it must have been me."

"Which is equally ridiculous. I'll have to see if I can get the truth out of him. You know, when we were married we used the old-fashioned ceremony and we said, 'For better or worse . . .' Now look at him—I never imagined it could be as bad as this."

Her husband was stretched out with the back of his head against the top step and he had fallen asleep. Hume hailed a passing cab and he and Jean frog-marched Hamilton over to the cab and pushed him into the back seat without, apparently, waking him up.

"Thanks, John", Jean said. "I wish . . . Oh, never mind."

Hume was glad Jean hadn't finished her sentence, which had sounded like the beginning of a request to stay in touch or exchange confidences. He didn't really believe Elsie's confession, and that led to only one conclusion. It was a very odd conclusion, however. If Hamilton did it, why was Elsie shielding him?

33

At nine o'clock on Friday morning the main building of the Benjamin Thompson School was occupied by six people. Bobby Fine had been recruited to act as receptionist and a uniformed officer sat at his elbow. Andrew Johnson was at work in the business office, but half of his mind was still trying to figure out the meaning of Bobby's greeting, which had been, "And the second hippopotamus said, 'It's a funny thing, but I keep thinking it's Thursday.'"

Lydia Schmidt was helping the registrar with the rising tide of requests for transcripts and recommendations, and Aloysius Thornbury was in his office dealing with calls from parents, faculty and reporters. All other members of the school community had been given confirmation of the closure of the school until further notice, and more than a third of the families had already applied to other schools. The next thing would be the task of writing references for teachers and staff looking for new jobs. Between phone calls, Thornbury thought longingly of his whiskey bottle, but so far he had resisted temptation.

While all this was going on at the Ben Thompson School, there was activity of a different kind at Mount Sinai Hospital. Sally Evans had regained consciousness, and this had started a lot of bustle among the hospital staff and the police. Inspector Williams received the news from the policeman on duty outside Sally's room at half past nine and within a few seconds the phone rang again, this time with the news that a young man believed to be Peter Miller had been taken into custody in Des Moines, Iowa. The hospital had said that Sally was not very coherent and might not stay awake very long, so Williams left a message for Michelson to keep in touch with Des Moines and drove uptown with lights flashing and siren blaring.

Having received the inevitable warnings that he could only have a few minutes and mustn't excite the patient, Williams looked down at Sally and said, "Hi, how are you?"

Sally said, "Ask a silly question and . . .", and promptly fell asleep.

Williams sat down on the bedside chair but the nurse said, "It's no use waiting—she'll probably sleep for several hours now. But it looks as if she's going to be OK."

"Did she say anything?"

"Yes, she was asking for somebody called John."

"It's definitely Miller", Michelson said when Williams called him from the hospital. "He was in one of those rental cars and he had a fake driver's license, so they charged him with that and went through the car. There was stuff with his name on it and the girl's too. I told them we were ready to charge him with depraved indifference and endangering the welfare of a minor, and they said they'd send him here under guard as long as we agree to pay."

"OK, you can tell them to go ahead."

"And the full post mortem report on Amanda came in."

"Anything significant?"

"Yeah—they say from the state of her brain she probably took several hours to die."

"OK, that's satisfactory—from our point of view, I mean."

"How about Sally?"

"Nothing from her yet, but the prognosis is much better. We're probably not going to get anything for another twenty-four hours, but I want to know what Smith and Hamilton will say when I tell them that I've spoken to her and that Miller's in custody."

"What about Hume?"

Williams sounded slightly embarrassed.
"I just called him."
"You mean you told him about Sally?"
"Yes."
"Why?"
"I thought he wanted to know."
"What did he say?"
"'Thank God!'"
Williams didn't mention that he had had an idea about Hume and was about to meet him at a café on Columbus Avenue. He also didn't mention that Hume enquired about Jill Davis.

The Benjamin Thompson School had been in existence for more than half a century before Hume arrived, and as far as he knew no one had ever died on the premises; but in the short time he had been there, there had already been two deaths and an attempted murder. There was no reasonable cause for the feeling that he was responsible, but it had seeped into his already overloaded conscience and now he had to work very hard to emerge from an abyss of self-loathing and self-pity, in which he saw himself as a creature designed by fate or the gods, or whatever forces controlled these things, to engender death and destruction wherever he went. He had to remind himself firmly that he didn't believe in any such supernatural entities, and that the whole sequence of events was in train before he arrived in New York.

Rationalizing didn't help much, but now, at least, he had a plan. Sally was going to get better. He would go and see her as soon as he was allowed. He would say goodbye and perhaps she would let him kiss her. Then, at the earliest possible moment, he would book a flight and go back to England. The trip to America had been a disaster but maybe it was a necessary one. Realizing that before he could proceed with his plan, the police would have to bring their investigation to the point where they might conceivably let him leave the country, he made an effort to think coherently about the situation. Elsie was already in jail for the assault on Sally, and that might or might not stick. Turning his mind to the question of Amanda, he went over the information he had received from Williams, and it seemed to him that when the process of elimination had been carried as far as possible only one suspect remained. It wasn't a pleasant thought and he could see no motive, but if it would help to bring the whole episode to a conclusion he would be grateful.

He took a shower, shaved and put on some clean clothes. These were things he hadn't bothered with for the previous couple of days, but now he had a clearer idea of where he was headed. Thanks to Williams, instead of going to his customary seat in the park, he walked over to Columbus Avenue and sat over a cup of tea and an English muffin while he waited for the inspector to appear.

Hamilton had changed his mind about the benefits of having his wife in the house. The problem was that she kept bringing him back to the actual situation. Thinking about it was bad enough and as long as he was on his own he could try to push it away—but talking about it was the supreme agony, and Jean really had no idea of the effect her questions had on him. Having been plentifully supplied with information by Andrew Johnson, she seemed to have accepted Elsie's guilt in the matter of Sally Evans, but she insisted on going over the events of Sunday afternoon in minute detail, as if in the back of her mind there was the unpleasant suspicion that her husband was somehow responsible for Amanda's being found in the storeroom.

"I can understand how you could get involved with Sally. It's despicable, but you're at the silly age and that sort of thing happens all the time. She was probably flattered that someone like you would pay attention to her—but what I don't get is how you could be involved with Amanda. When I left, Thornbury was the only person still in the school and he had no idea there was anything going on in the basement. Somebody must have come back later and that means that if it wasn't you, it must have been Hume or Sally, which I don't believe. So what am I supposed to think?"

"Sally wasn't flattered. I was flattered. And what about you, spying on me like that? Wouldn't you call that despicable?"

"I had a good reason, didn't I?"

"Maybe, but you didn't know that, and anyway, how did you get into the building?"

"The way you've been behaving, I did know it. I just borrowed your keys and had copies made."

"All of them?"

"Yes—if you want to know, I thought I might catch you in the act."

"Good God! So for all anybody knows you could have put her in the storeroom yourself. I wonder if the police have thought of that."

"Don't be a fool, Jim. Can't you see I'm trying to help you?"

"Really? I thought you were trying to convict me. Well, I wish you would just shut up and leave me alone."

Jean took him at his word and Hamilton soon had the house to himself again.

By the time Williams arrived at the café, Hume was on his third cup of tea and his second muffin. He didn't see what use any further discussion would be, but the combination of caffeine and carbohydrates was helping to put him in a better mood and at least he might find out if the inspector's thoughts were going in the same direction as his own. It came as a mild surprise when, once coffee had been ordered, the first question was, "How well do you know Jean Hamilton?"

"Not very well—I've only met her twice. She made a very good impression. Why do you ask?"

"Because there's no one to confirm that she left the school when she says she did. She could have gone down to the basement to see what had happened, and for some unknown reason pulled Amanda into the elevator and taken her upstairs. She had copies of all her husband's keys, so she would have been able to lock her in the storeroom. And I think it's plausible that covering her with her raincoat was a woman's touch."

"But why would she do that?"

"I don't have the faintest idea—but the trouble is I don't have a concrete idea why anyone else would do it, either. It could have been Hamilton or Sally or both of them together, but they couldn't have known that Amanda was in the basement and I can't think of any reason why they would have gone down there"

"Maybe it wasn't any of them."

"That's just what I've been wondering. But she didn't lock herself in."

"No, it just changes the problem and I don't know that it makes it any easier."

"OK, but here's something else. Amanda was a blackmailer. She tried it on Thornbury and it didn't work. Can we take that a stage further? I mean, who else was doing something that they didn't want people to know about?"

"Hamilton, I suppose."

"And Sally—we don't actually know where either of them went after you saw them."

Earlier in the day, Hume had been under the impression that he had solved the problem. Now it had opened out again and even his beloved Sally was under suspicion. Suddenly he found that he had lost his appetite.

"That's absolute nonsense", he said angrily. "Can you really see Sally lugging a body round the school? And, in any case, Sally doesn't seem to care two hoots whether people know who she's carrying on with."

"She might have cared on Hamilton's behalf."

"Not that much—certainly not enough to commit a major criminal act."

"They could have done it together."

"So, according to you, they left school, went for a long walk, came back and for some unknown reason went down to the basement, found Amanda, carried her upstairs and locked her in the storeroom. What possible advantage would there be in doing that? If you had heard the way Sally talked about Hamilton you'd know what a ridiculous idea this is. It certainly wasn't a grand passion—not on her part, at any rate, although it may have been on his."

"OK, it certainly sounds ridiculous, and that brings us back to the fact that we have no reasonable explanation for Amanda being found on the third floor."

"So why don't you arrest me? I'm sure the British police have told you that I'm not to be trusted with young girls."

"Yes, they have, but we have absolutely nothing that connects you with Amanda and no evidence that you returned to the building after you left around four o'clock. I don't think you had anything to do with it. One reason for meeting you here was just to get you to talk, and everything you say tends to confirm that opinion."

"Well, you're right, but I don't know what else I can tell you. You think Hamilton was involved, don't you?"

"Apart from Thornbury, he's the only one I can think of with even a faintly plausible motive. Well then, here's another possibility. Maybe Amanda managed to crawl as far as the elevator. She thinks Thornbury is still in his office, so she gets that far and collapses. He doesn't want to be found with her body on his doorstep, so he thinks of a convenient place to hide her. It sounds plausible, sort of, but the problem is that while this was going on, Bobby Fine had the spare key to the storeroom in his pocket."

Hume remembered the old books in the storeroom and what Hamilton had told him about the headmaster's interest in chemistry.

"That may not be a problem", he said. "Thornbury probably had a key of his own."

Hume explained and Williams found the idea very interesting, but he didn't say much and moved quickly on to the assault on Sally.

"I'll bear all that in mind but, going back to Hamilton, if he left Amanda in the storeroom, Sally may have known or found out about it without having been actually involved. He decides Sally knows too much and is too dangerous to him, so he splits up with her, arranges to meet her in the lab and tries to kill her."

This was beginning to sound almost plausible and for a moment Hume had nothing to say. Williams hadn't finished.

"Elsie Smith saw something—we don't really know what—and for reasons that we can only speculate on, says that she did it.

Maybe she's still in love with Hamilton. I admit this is flimsy and there's no evidence, but Hamilton is the only one that makes any sense at all as a suspect. You must have seen quite a lot of him in the short time you've been here—what kind of impression do you have?"

"It's difficult to say—when I first met him he was very kind and seemed calm, steady and completely professional."

"The kind of person you could tell your troubles to?"

"Yes—in fact I found myself telling him things that I had expected never to speak of again. But now he seems like a completely different person."

"When did this change take place?"

"I wasn't really aware of it until after I found Amanda, and then not immediately. I talked with him on Friday afternoon and he seemed more or less normal. What I don't understand is why you're talking to me about all this? Do you normally discuss your theories with one of the suspects?"

"It depends", Williams said. "Maybe I just wanted to see what you would say. It's amazing how people let things out when it's not an official interrogation."

"Will I be allowed to see Sally?" Hume asked.

"Not yet—we don't want anyone to talk to her until after she's well enough to make a statement to the police."

Nevertheless, Hume paid his bill and walked across the park to Mount Sinai Hospital. He sat in the waiting room for a long time.

34

"I don't get it", Michelson said to his superior officer. "Why go and talk to Hume like that when he's just as much a suspect as any of the others?"

"That's exactly what Hume wanted to know."

"OK, so what did you tell him?"

"That I wanted to get a reaction from him."

"You mean you thought he might confess or you might get some more information out of him. Maybe if you had pushed the Sally possibility a bit more . . ."

"It certainly crossed my mind, but I wasn't counting on it. I thought he might have something useful to say. He sees a lot and he's the odd man out."

"Why—because he's British?"

"He's also new—there's no history with all these other people. And he comes across more as an observer than a participant, at least until Sally pulled him into the game. Anyway, I did get something new out of him."

"You mean about Thornbury's key? As far as I can see, that only complicates matters. It means he could have taken Amanda straight up in the elevator."

"Which would mean that he waited in his office until Jean Hamilton left, and then for some reason went downstairs and found her. He finds her unconscious, and thinks he'll be incriminated as he's just had a big quarrel with her, so he takes her upstairs and palms her off on Hume. Well, it's possible, I guess, but I wouldn't bet a nickel on it."

⚯⚯

By the time Thornbury went home on Friday afternoon, the number of defections from the school had risen to more than fifty percent of the student body. He was looking so exhausted and woebegone that Victoria, who met him at the door in her glamorous persona, felt some slight stirring of sympathy inside her blond wig.

Greatly to Thornbury's surprise, she said, "You could just resign."

It was her turn to be surprised, when he replied, "I could, but I don't want to. What would I do all day, apart from being pushed around by you?"

"I could give you a job."

"Me? Work for Vicky Picky's fashion factory?"

He began to laugh and, once he had started, he couldn't stop.

Victoria looked at him quizzically for a moment and then she began to laugh too.

"Come on, Thornbury", she said eventually. "I'll get some drinks and tell you my great idea."

Thornbury abruptly stopped laughing. He was looking rather apprehensive as he followed Victoria into the living room. He had abstained from alcohol ever since waking up in his office on Monday morning, but after the shock of Victoria's suggestion he turned gratefully to the scotch bottle.

"The first thing", Victoria said, "is that we have to get married."

Thornbury choked on his drink.

"What do you mean, 'have to'?"

"Not *that*, you numbskull!"

Thornbury was used to Victoria's habit of using of terms of abuse as endearments; it was the next part of her proposal that really staggered him.

"I'm giving up the Mrs. George M. Picard the Third, slash, Vicky Picky, slash, eccentric-old-lady image. I shall be Victoria Picard, keep my wig and show off my company's latest fashions. I shall marry you and commit all my company's resources, including public relations, to bringing Ben Thompson back to life."

Thornbury shuddered.

"What happens if I don't want to marry you?"

"I thought of that, knowing you as I do. As a member of the Board I can bring my proposal at the next meeting. I'm sure they'll be able to see the advantages of it."

"Do you want them to vote on your marriage proposal?"

"Listen, blockhead! I may have been joking when I suggested a job for you at VIP Fashions, but I'm dead serious now. If you dislike the idea of marriage so much, why have we stayed together so long?"

Thornbury had sometimes wondered the same thing, but he didn't want to say so. In any case, Victoria hadn't finished.

"You know the school is going under unless something dramatic happens. Well, I'm offering something dramatic. And you know what else? I was doing this double act long before I hooked up with you, and you're the only one who knows about it. Does that tell you anything?"

Thornbury wasn't sure, but he had an inkling of what Victoria was driving at. The fact that no one else knew Victoria's secret suggested something about her feelings about him that he hadn't considered before. He had always thought it was mostly an alliance of convenience, in which the good sex made up for the frequent quarrels, but now he was forced to face the question of whether there was anything in his feelings about her that he hadn't bothered to think about before.

"I'm too tired to figure it out now. Let's go to bed."

"OK", Victoria said with a smug smile.

Later that evening, Sally woke up again. Inspector Williams was summoned to her bedside, and this time she didn't immediately fall asleep.

"Hello Sally—are you feeling better?"

"Well, I wasn't feeling at all until a little while ago, so I guess I must be. I'd smile at you if I didn't have these bandages."

"Do you know what happened to you?"

"Not really—all the nurses will tell me is that something hit me on the head. They told me you were coming to see me and you would explain."

"I'll explain as much as I can, but can you stand it if I ask you a few questions first?"

"I'll try, but everything is still a bit fuzzy."

"OK, and when you've had enough, just tell me. It's now Friday evening, and you were found behind the third floor lab on Wednesday evening. We know you were at your desk until four o'clock that afternoon and we need to know where you went and what you did after that time."

"I haven't been awake long, and things have been coming back to me in a random kind of way."

"I understand, and we wouldn't be bothering you except that we need to know whatever you can remember before other people start telling you their versions."

"Some of it is a little bit private", Sally said, and she couldn't help smiling, in spite of her bandages.

"We know a bit about that already. The person involved didn't want to talk about it but, in the circumstances, we had to apply a little pressure. It would be helpful if I could hear about it from you."

"OK—I remember that I went to see John Hume in his apartment."

"How long were you there?"

"It was a long time . . . And then I had to leave."

"Why did you have to leave?"

"I don't remember."

"Do you remember seeing anyone else?"

"I think I saw Elsie."

"Where did you see her?"

"I don't know. It's all mixed up, like she was following me around."

"Did you see anyone else?"

"I don't remember—I'm getting very sleepy. Oh, there's John."

Williams looked around and saw Hume standing in the doorway with the policeman who had been Sally's doorkeeper throughout the day.

"Let him in", the inspector said.

Hume went hesitantly to Sally's bedside. She was almost asleep, but she managed to say, "It would be OK to kiss me."

Her forehead wasn't available, so he kissed her lips very gently.

"I think I told you something wrong", she said, as sleep took her.

Williams wasn't sure whether she was talking to him or to Hume. Hume had an idea that he knew what Sally meant, but it wasn't the sort of thing he wanted to discuss with a policeman, so he hugged the thought to himself.

35

Peter Miller arrived at La Guardia Airport late on Friday evening and spent an uncomfortable night on a cot in a prison cell. Early on Saturday morning, when Williams and Michelson confronted him in an interview room, he was tired, depressed and puzzled, but his innate cockiness had not completely deserted him. What was puzzling and depressing him was that he didn't know what had happened to Jill. She must be out there somewhere, and maybe the police had found her—and then what? All the Des Moines police had said was that there was a warrant for his arrest on a charge of second degree murder from the New York City police and, unless he wanted to hire a lawyer and fight it, he was being sent back immediately. Well, Jill would tell them that he hadn't murdered anyone.

Williams had conceived a great dislike of the prisoner before even meeting him, so he didn't bother with conventional greetings. Knowing that the charge of murder would be virtually impossible to sustain, he went straight to the point.

"Tell us what happened on Sunday."

"You haven't asked me if I want a lawyer."

"Didn't they ask you that in Des Moines?"

"Yes, but we're not in Des Moines now."

"OK, do you?"

"Since I don't intend to answer any questions, I don't need one."

"OK, then, I'll tell you some things. Last Sunday, you and Jill Davis entered the Benjamin Thompson School through the basement door at about three-thirty. You went to the infirmary and we won't talk about what you did when you got there. You thought you had the building to yourselves, but some time later you heard a noise on the stairs and you went to see what was happening. Amanda Friedman was lying in a heap on the half-landing. Jill was right behind you and you told her that Amanda was dead, although you knew she was still alive. You didn't want to get involved, because it might interfere with your plans, so you persuaded Jill that you should leave immediately, even though she wanted to get help for Amanda. You left by the basement door and arranged to meet early the next morning at the car rental on West 96th Street. The point is that if you had summoned help instead of running, Amanda would probably still be alive. We call that depraved indifference—that's why you're being charged with murder."

Miller's mood changed abruptly. So, instead of following the plan, Jill had simply driven to the police and told them the whole story. It didn't seem like the kind of thing that she would have done, since she had often spoken derisively about the cops and even referred to them as pigs; but that seemed to be the way it was and it upset him very much. He thought they must somehow have coerced her into talking, but the trouble was that it was all perfectly true. Now either he had to admit that the facts were as they had been presented or he had to find some way of lying his way out of the situation.

"I assume you got all this from Jill. I want to talk to her before I say anything else."

"Why? Do you want to get her to change her story? I can tell right now that you won't succeed. And I should tell you that we have several other witnesses who substantiate parts of Jill's evidence."

This was true. Jean Hamilton, Hume and Schwartz had all witnessed fragments of the drama, and there was no need to mention that one part of Schwartz's report contradicted one part of Jill's.

Sensing that Miller was losing his poise, Williams pushed a little harder.

"We think that someone threw Amanda down the stairs, and we want to find out who it was. I can promise you that it will be greatly to your advantage if you tell us the truth at this point."

Distrusting the police as he did, Miller took this last remark with a large pinch of salt. Further denials seemed pointless, but he still managed a little show of bravado.

"OK—the murder charge is absolutely ridiculous, but what Jill says is true. Amanda was breathing normally and I thought she had just been knocked out. I'm not a doctor, and you can't blame me for being mistaken. Now I want a lawyer. And I still want to see Jill."

"One other thing first—did you hear or see anyone else in the basement or on the street."

"We heard the basement door close just after we left the infirmary."

"That's all? You didn't hear anyone talking?"

"No."

Williams had felt only contempt for Miller ever since he first heard of him. Having finished the extraction of information, he looked at him with profound distaste.

"We'll provide a lawyer, unless you have one of your own, but I'm afraid you won't be able to see Jill."

"Why not?"

"I'll tell you in a minute. Isn't it true that you left New York in this clandestine fashion because you wanted to evade the draft?"

Taking silence for consent, Williams went on.

"That being the case, why did you take Jill? You must have known that with her along the police would be looking out for you in every state of the union. If you'd gone on your own it might have been weeks before anyone even noticed you were missing."

Now there was a response, not verbal but in the form of a deep flush, and Williams wondered whether it could possibly be that Miller had never thought of this.

"So maybe you thought you were really in love with her and it was a great romantic adventure."

Miller was stung into speech.

"Jill feels exactly the same way about Vietnam as I do. We love each other and we had to be together."

"Then I guess you'll be sorry to hear that she killed herself just after leaving you in Akron. That was your real murder, but unfortunately we'll never get you for it. Come on, sergeant, we'll get him a lawyer and leave him to think about it for a while."

What Miller was thinking was that his interrogator had just taken police brutality to a new level.

The news from Mount Sinai Hospital was a little better. Sally was sitting up and eating a little. Williams and Michelson discussed Miller's story as they drove uptown.

"What do you think, Sergeant?"

"When you put his statement and Jill's letter together, I think it's the truth."

"So?"

"Schwartz is lying—Amanda couldn't have been sitting up and telling him to fuck off and then out cold five seconds later. That's what Jean Hamilton heard her tell him before she fell down the stairs. If she said it after she fell, Miller would have heard her, unless there's something wrong with his ears as well as his brain. She was unconscious and Schwartz just left her there. How many people can you get for depraved indifference in the same homicide?"

"I don't know, but we'll never get him for anything else. We can't prove he pushed her down the stairs."

"One thing I don't get—how did he know about her shoulder? If we're right, she couldn't have been sitting up holding it."

"My guess is that he knew about it because it happened while they were struggling at the top of the stair—he threw her against the wall, or something like that. Then he thinks it will make his story more convincing if he mentions it."

"Trouble is this leaves us mostly where we were."

"Maybe not—at least we know that none of these people had anything to do with Amanda getting upstairs. And as far as what happened to Sally is concerned, I'm beginning to get an idea. It may be crazy, but I like it. Did you ever play billiards, Sergeant?"

"No. It's some kind of pool, isn't it?"

"Kind of—how about bowling?"

"Yeah—once in a while."

"Well?"

Michelson thought for a moment.

"OK, I agree."

"You like the idea?"

"No—I agree that it's crazy."

"OK, well maybe you're right, but that doesn't necessarily mean it isn't true. And getting back to Amanda, after you drop me off at the hospital you can go and get Schwartz. If he doesn't want to come, you can tell him we have new evidence and arrest him on suspicion of murder."

When Williams arrived at Mount Sinai, Hume was sitting in the waiting room.

"Good morning, Mr. Hume—any news?"

"Good morning, Inspector—only that the patient spent a restful night and is feeling better. I think they've concluded that I'm her grandfather—anyway they say I can talk to her if I get police permission."

Williams looked sympathetically at Hume. Being mistaken for the grandfather of the young woman you're in love with is probably not the happiest way to start the day.

"All being well we won't keep you waiting very long."

Some of Sally's bandages had been removed and she was sitting up and looking much more like her usual self.

"I've remembered quite a bit more", she told Williams.

"Good—so start again at the time you finished work in the afternoon."

"Well, like I said, I went up to John's apartment and I met him on the top stairs—he was just coming down to look for me. We went up and we were in bed until some time after seven o'clock. Then I remembered I was supposed to call Mr. Hamilton, so I thought I'd call from school, only when I went in, Elsie was sitting at my desk. She was going through all my things. I decided to call from John's office, but Elsie followed me upstairs and we had a big scene in the lab. She had something in her hand and I think she was threatening me, but it's all a bit hazy. Oh, I went into the back and called Mr. Hamilton."

"Can you remember why you had to call Hamilton?"

"He asked me to."

"When?"

"I don't know exactly—some time earlier in the day."

"What did you talk about?"

Sally closed her eyes, and Williams thought she had fallen asleep, but after a few seconds she said, "He wanted me back."

"What did you say?"

"I said 'No.' And later on I saw him and Elsie."

Sally opened her eyes.

"I think they wanted to hurt me. They both seemed kind of crazy and I was very frightened. I tried to run away and something hit me."

Seeing that Sally was becoming agitated, the nurse who had been hovering in the background whispered, "Careful, Inspector."

"Just two more questions, Sally. Do remember seeing anyone else after leaving Mr. Hume's apartment?"

"No."

"And can you remember what it was that you wanted to tell him about Amanda?"

Sally looked bewildered.

"Tell him about Amanda? I don't know what you mean. Can I see John now, please? I need him to hold my hand."

Williams looked at the nurse, who nodded.

"I'll go and get him", the inspector said.

"OK, and tell him on no account to get the patient excited."

"Don't worry—he's a kind of walking tranquilizer."

After dismissing the policeman who had been on duty outside Sally's door, Williams passed the nurse's message on to Hume and added, "I want you to be available at school this afternoon, from about two-thirty on. And anything Sally tells you about the assault must be kept strictly to yourself. No questions now—I'll call you before then."

Hume thought that Sally was asleep, but after a few minutes she squeezed his hand and said, "I feel safe now."

From his perch on cloud nine, Hume murmured something inarticulate. Sally kept talking and now she sounded wide awake. She described the scene in the lab as far as she could remember it.

"They were both crazy. He was going to rape me and she wanted to kill me. I was terrified. Only, I don't know what happened at the end. I wish I could remember."

"Elsie says she hit you with a clamp stand."

"Did she say anything about Hamilton?"

"Not in my hearing—she may have, to the police."

After another long pause, Sally asked, "What's happening at school?"

"Nothing much, I'm afraid, except working on transcripts and recommendations. Most of the parents are finding other places for their children."

"Is Mr. Thornbury OK?"

"He seems to be. We met his girlfriend the other day."

Sally smiled.

"What's she like?"

"Blonde, smart and fortyish—I suspect that she wears the trousers."

"Poor Mr. Thornbury! I wish they would let me get up."

Hume was momentarily worried in case Sally wanted to get up so that she could comfort Thornbury, but her next words relieved him of that anxiety. They also almost doubled his pulse rate.

"Can I come and stay with you when they let me out?"

Hume's reply was almost instantaneous, although a lot of thoughts had flashed through his mind in a few milliseconds—the good advice he had given Hamilton, the fear of getting hurt, no fool like an old fool.

"Yes, of course—but I only have one bed."

"That's good—I don't expect we'll have any visitors."

Sally pressed a button at her bedside. The nurse who arrived a few minutes later was surprised to find the patient sitting on the edge of her bed.

"I want to go home", Sally announced.

"You'll have to ask the doctor about that, but I doubt if he'll let you. You're supposed to be here for at least a week. And you only started walking on your own yesterday. Now be a good girl and get back into your bed."

"Where's the doctor?" Sally asked, without moving.

"He'll be making his rounds in an hour or so."

"Do I have anything to wear?"

"Only what you had on when they brought you in. Anyway, he's not going to let you out."

The nurse departed with a loud sniff.

"What was I wearing, John?"

Hume made a deep, U-shaped gesture over his chest and drew an imaginary horizontal line just below waist level.

"There was a fair amount of blood", he said.

"Oh. Well, I probably won't need clothes for the first day or two. Do you have a spare bathrobe?"

"No, but your overcoat and handbag are still in the lab. I could go and get them and be back in twenty minutes. You could just put the coat on over your hospital things."

36

Dr. Goldin did his best to persuade his patient that it would be much better for her to stay in the hospital for the full week, but eventually he gave up. He made his final point just as Hume walked in with Sally's coat over his arm.

"Well, Miss Evans, if you insist on going home, I can't stop you. I know you said your father would look after you, but he has no medical training. If you have a relapse I won't be answerable for the consequences."

For a moment, Hume experienced acute disappointment, as it seemed that Sally wasn't going to stay with him after all. Then, as the doctor turned to speak to him, he caught Sally's broad wink and remembered that her parents had died.

"Mr. Evans?"

"Yes, Doctor?" Hume responded bravely.

"I gather that you have tried to talk some sense into this young woman and she won't listen. She says that you were a naval officer and know a lot about first aid, but the complications of concussion go a long way beyond ordinary first aid . . ."

After continuing for several more paragraphs, Goldin gave up and left. When Sally had signed several forms indicating that she knew what she was doing, which was only partly true, Hume helped her on with her shoes and her overcoat. It was a long walk to the main entrance and the taxis, and by the time they got there he was practically carrying her.

Trying to explain, she said, "I never felt scared like this before. They both seem to hate me so much and I keep dreaming that he's chasing me around the lab while she stands there waving that clamp thing. I just have the feeling that when I'm with you nothing bad can happen."

Hume wasn't so sure about this, but he didn't want to say so. He was wondering how he was going to get Sally up the final flight of stairs to his apartment. In that narrow space it would probably have to be the fireman's lift. Halfway up the staircase, with his left hand on the rail and Sally's amazingly light body draped over his right shoulder, he stopped for a brief rest, and she said, "John, I've remembered what it was I wanted to tell you. You know, about Amanda. Only now I'm not sure I want to talk about it."

This was meaningless to Hume, so all he said was, "Let me take you up and put you to bed and then you can decide. It's all ready—I got the bed out when I came for your overcoat."

The reason for Sally's reticence was that she had remembered what she had been doing the last time she saw Amanda, and she didn't want to tell Hume about anything that involved details of her intimacy with Hamilton. In any case, within a few seconds of her head touching the pillow, she was fast asleep, so the problem was shelved for a few hours. When the phone rang and Hume talked to Inspector Williams, she didn't even stir.

"In the lab at two-forty-five, Mr. Hume—I want to talk to you again before getting the others in."

At midday, Williams was sitting at Sally's desk at the Ben Thompson School with the phone to his ear.

"You got Schwartz?" he asked Michelson.

"Yep. We just got back. He was still in bed and he didn't want to come, but I convinced him that it would be in his interest to cooperate."

"OK—keep him in reasonable comfort till two-fifteen and then bring him up here. "I think I've got it sorted out."

After giving Michelson a brief account of his conversation with Sally, Williams gave some instructions.

"Get the relevant personnel in Hume's lab this afternoon at three—that's Smith and Hamilton. I'll have Hume there already. After that we'll meet with the whole gang in the auditorium. We'll have to do without Sally, but I want to get this thing wrapped up. And we'd better have Higgins along, in case there's a problem with Smith."

Michelson looked uneasily at his phone. His boss wasn't usually given to flights of imaginative fancy.

"Are we going to play billiards?"

"Not unless you're a really good shot with a clamp stand."

"Oh—well don't say I didn't warn you."

"If it's a fiasco, I'll make sure everybody knows it was my idea. Higgins and a couple of uniforms—everybody there half an hour early.

"No, Vicky, I won't marry you", Aloysius Thornbury said, as he poured two cups of coffee, twelve hours after the queen of *haute couture* had made her proposal. "At least, not yet. If you want to bail out Ben Thompson, that's wonderful, but I want to see how long your transmogrification lasts. And couldn't you do something nice with your real hair? I mean I can't imagine it's beyond your ingenuity to find some way of getting rid of the wig—I don't want to be married to a woman who takes her hair off every night when she goes to bed."

"You know what, Aloysius?"

Vicky only called him that when she was in her Mrs. George M. Picard the Third mode—otherwise it was just "Thornbury" or a selection from her stock of mildly abusive endearments.

"I liked you better when you weren't so goddamn sober."

She pulled her wig off and threw it at him, but at that point the exchange was interrupted by the telephone.

Thornbury draped the wig over his head and picked up the phone.

"Yes, Inspector, I'll be there . . . No, I understand perfectly and I'll make sure she does, too. Two-thirty? OK."

"Give me that wig", Vicky demanded.

"You won't need it. You're not invited."

⦾⦾-⦾⦾

By Saturday morning, Elsie was getting used to being in prison. She hadn't changed her story and she hadn't asked for bail, but on the advice of a lawyer supplied by the City of New York, she had pleaded "Not guilty" to the charges of attempted murder and assault. In view of the fact that she had admitted hitting Sally on the head with a clamp stand, it didn't make much sense, but this seemed to be beside the point. As a mathematician, she knew that most equations have no real solutions—so why should it be any different for life situations? She blamed herself for her present predicament, for which there was obviously no solution at all, real or imaginary. The events of Wednesday had been the disastrous close of a long chapter in her life, and the next one would be shaped by other people's decisions. Whatever happened would happen. She had been relieved to learn through her lawyer that Sally was recovering, but she found herself absolutely without curiosity about any of the other participants in the drama. The only feeling she had was that she never wanted to see any of them again, which was why she would not have applied for bail even if there had been any way of raising the money.

The news that she was to be taken once more to her old work place, for a meeting with Inspector Williams and certain other relevant people, caused very little anxiety, but it aroused a strong sensation of distaste. Fundamentally, they were all assholes—well, all except Hume—and, if she was being perfectly honest, she was an asshole too. The only real difference between her and the others was that she knew it, whereas they apparently didn't; but she took no credit for this realization, since she hadn't arrived at it through insight, but through the brute force of circumstance.

⦾⦾-⦾⦾

Hamilton's thoughts were still swimming around in an alcoholic fog, so they lacked the clarity of Elsie's. He was very confused about what had happened, and he told himself that basically he hadn't done anything wrong, apart from cheating on his wife and trying to avoid being blamed for something that really wasn't his fault. He had eaten nothing since Jean left for the second time, so when the police came for him on Saturday afternoon he didn't have the strength to protest or ask for an explanation.

At half-past-two, Williams sent Officer Kohn to the auditorium and stationed Officer O'Reilly at the front desk.

"You have the list", he said. "Send them in to Kohn and buzz me upstairs when they've all arrived. Then I want Sergeant Michelson to take Smith and Hamilton up to the lab. When we've finished up there I'll meet with everybody in the auditorium. If anyone else shows up, detain them here."

O'Reilly looked at the list.

"Those two women who were here last time . . . There's only one here."

"Right—I don't need the blonde one. If she shows up you might have to handcuff her to a chair."

At twenty minutes before three, Sally was still asleep. Hume kissed her into semi-consciousness and said, "I have to go and talk to Inspector Williams in the lab. And then there's supposed to be some kind of meeting. I don't know how long it will take."

Sally woke up a little more.

"Who's going to be there?"

"He didn't tell me, but I suppose it will be everybody who's been involved—Hamilton, Elsie and everyone else who was in school last Sunday."

"I'm scared, John. I know it's stupid and they can't get at me here, but . . . I guess it's the bang on the head."

Hume couldn't think of anything sensible to say. He could lock the apartment door and the door to his private staircase, but he could see that her anxiety was too deep-seated for that kind of assurance to be very helpful. He moved the telephone as close as possible to the bed and told her he would call whenever he had the chance.

Williams and Hume sat on opposite sides of one of the long lab workbenches.

Williams asked, "What exactly did Mrs. Smith say when she found you in the park on Thursday?"

"She said, 'I came to tell you I'm sorry.' I asked her what she was sorry for, but she didn't say anything else until you came along."

"What did you think she was apologizing for?"

"The only thing I could think of at the time was that she was apologizing for pursuing me or, more likely, for the way she spoke to me on Wednesday evening."

"And what do you think now?"

"Well, the most obvious possibility is that she was apologizing for what she did to Sally, although my impression was that it was really about something that she had done to me personally."

"Yes, I think that fits. Well, that's all I wanted to ask you about. Now here's the important thing—as far as anyone here is concerned, Sally is still in critical condition and can't remember anything about what happened to her. At some point in the first couple of minutes, I'll mention Sally and I want you to interrupt and ask if there's any news about her. Can you make it sound spontaneous?"

"I'll try."

"OK, don't forget. We'll have the others up now."

Williams called downstairs from Hume's office.

"They're all here", O'Reilly reported, "but there's a problem. That blonde woman showed up, only she isn't blonde today. She's done something else with her hair, but I recognized her anyway. She tried to get into the auditorium with the others, so we had to restrain her."

An awful picture appeared in Williams's mind.

"What do you mean, 'restrain her'?

"Well, we did what you said, and now she's walking around with a chair handcuffed to her arm."

Williams tried to see the funny side of the situation. Police officers were trained to obey orders, and it would have been difficult for the authorities to include special provisions for those with literal minds and no sense of humor.

"OK—tell Michelson to make his announcement and bring Smith and Hamilton up here—and then you'd better let Mrs. Picard into the auditorium."

"Mrs. Who?"

"Victoria Picard. Make sure that she knows that you know who she is."

There was a long pause before O'Reilly found his voice.

"Victoria Picard—the fashion lady?

"Yes."

"Holy shit . . . Sir. Wait till I tell my wife. Oh—should I take off the cuff?"

"Yes, and for God's sake pull yourself together. Tell her if she's a nuisance we'll arrest her for obstruction and make sure it's fully reported in the press."

"And, by the way, Sir, Hamilton looks kind of ill."

"Good!"

37

Michelson's carefully prepared announcement was short but not sweet.

"Mr. Thornbury and Mrs. Hamilton are here at our request and are free to leave. Mr. Schwartz is also here at our request, but if he decides to leave he will be arrested for the murder of Amanda Friedman. Mr. Hamilton, likewise, is subject to being arrested as a material witness in the attempted murder of Sally Evans. Mrs. Smith is under arrest for the attempted murder of Sally Evans and has been informed that she is entitled to have her lawyer present at any proceedings connected with that charge. We have brought you all here because we believe that these investigations can be brought to a satisfactory conclusion today—satisfactory to us, that is. Mr. Hume is already in the chemistry lab with Inspector Williams, and I'll ask Mrs. Smith and Mr. Hamilton to accompany me there now. This may take some time, and I can only ask the rest of you to be patient."

Williams had no intention of using the blackboard, but he stood in front of it, looking across the demonstration bench and facing his audience of four adults, who were arranged on uncomfortable lab stools as if they were students awaiting instruction. From left to right, he saw the red-eyed, gray-faced Hamilton, the massively reassuring Michelson, Elsie Smith—bolt upright and tense—and Hume, whose outward calm was his customary disguise for inner turmoil.

"Mrs. Smith", Williams began, "I want you to recall what you told us about your movements last Sunday afternoon—a week ago today. You said that you sat in the lab for a long time and heard footsteps at a certain point, but that you didn't see anyone. Is that still your testimony?"

"Yes, it is."

Hamilton had been sitting with his feet up on the rung of his stool, his eyes closed, his elbows on his knees and his chin in his hands. Watching him out of the corner of his eye while he spoke to Elsie, Williams saw no movement and wondered if he had fallen asleep. He continued with his questions.

"We know that the people upstairs were Mr. Hamilton and Miss Evans, but you didn't know that at the time. From what I've heard about you, Mrs. Smith, I can't believe that you didn't go and look."

Elsie wasn't impressed.

"Frankly, I have no interest in what you can or can't believe. You'll just have to accept the fact that I have nothing further to tell you."

"Well then, let's consider some facts. According to your statement, you got home several minutes after sunset. It's about a ten minute walk from school, and sunset was at five-twenty-nine that day. Being generous about the time, you couldn't have left school before about five-twenty, and that agrees exactly with the time that you told us on Tuesday. Assuming that your story is correct, Amanda couldn't have been moved into the storeroom until after that time unless . . ."

"Unless what, Inspector?"

Hamilton opened his eyes for a moment.

"Unless you did it yourself, Elsie. That's obvious, isn't it?"

Elsie looked at Hamilton in astonishment. After a moment she turned back to Williams.

"Listen, Inspector—over the past couple of days and nights, I've had ample opportunity to think about things and realize how stupid I've been. One thing that I've figured out is that people get the kind of friends they deserve, and if I hadn't realized that before, I would now. Part of the stupidity is that I put myself into a position where I couldn't very well add anything to my original statement. Now I'm beginning to think that I'll have to change my mind. When I do, I'll tell you, but for now I'll just have to let things take their course, and you'll have to manage without any more help from me."

"That might be an improvement—so far you haven't been particularly helpful. Unfortunately, I can't just leave it at that, since you're not only under arrest for the assault on Sally Evans, but you are also an obvious suspect in the murder of Amanda Friedman, which is an even more serious matter. One reason . . ."

"Inspector!"

Hume's prearranged interruption sounded rather diffident, but Williams stopped anyway.

"I'm sorry to interrupt, but is there any news about Miss Evans?"

"The last I heard was that she is still in critical condition and unable to recall anything about the events of Wednesday. They're pretty sure that even if she recovers she still won't remember anything."

Williams paused for a moment to let this sink in.

"Now, as I was saying, one reason why you're all here is that we've got to the point where we have a pretty good idea why Amanda was left to die and why she was left in Mr. Hume's storeroom, which has always been the weirdest element in this case. Mrs. Smith—how much do you know about Hume's past? Did he tell you about an encounter with the British police over the death of a young girl?"

This was a question that Elsie was willing to answer.

"When I tried to get him to talk about anything personal, he more or less told me to get lost—politely, of course."

"Is that correct, Mr. Hume?"

"Yes, I suppose it is."

"So, if Mrs. Smith didn't know about it, I'd like to know who did."

Hume started to speak, but now Hamilton stirred and interrupted Hume.

"She did know—I told her."

For the second time, Elsie stared at the speaker in amazement. Finding her voice, she said, "There's a name for creatures like you. I guess I've been even more stupid than I thought."

"And who told you", Williams asked Hamilton.

"Hume told me."

Turning to Hume, Elsie said in a hurt voice, "You told him that? Why him, and not me?"

Hume looked very embarrassed.

"It seemed safer, somehow."

Elsie's face turned almost the color of her hair.

"Stupider and stupider", she muttered, while Williams went on with his analysis.

"I'm sure you all see that this provides a possible answer to the question of why Amanda was left where she was. The object was to throw suspicion on Hume, which would make sense if the murderer knew about Hume's past. Mr. Hume, did you tell anyone else about this?"

"No."

"Are you sure you didn't tell Mr. Thornbury?"

"Yes."

"And when did you tell Hamilton?"

"It was on the Friday afternoon before . . . before this all happened. We were supposed to have a chat at three o'clock every Friday."

"Where was this and how long did it go on?"

"In Hamilton's office—I don't know how long, but at a rough guess I'd say it was about a twenty minutes. I was feeling very depressed and he encouraged me to talk. He had been fairly frank about certain things and I thought talking might help. I really don't think he had anything in mind beyond that."

"So if Hamilton told Mrs. Smith, it must have been some time after about 3:20 on Friday."

"Yes, but I don't understand why he would do that. It's not what I should have expected."

Williams turned back to Elsie.

"Did you see Hamilton later on Friday afternoon?"

Elsie looked at Hume and decided that she couldn't expect him to lie on her behalf.

"Yes. I was waiting in the biology lab while they had their so-called conference. John saw me there when he left."

"What did you want to see him about?"

"Ask a silly question . . ."

"Yes, that's what I thought. Did you have a good time?"

"Yes, if you must know—short and sweet and, at the time, very reassuring."

"How was it reassuring?"

"I thought he had been losing interest, but it seemed I was wrong. I guess you haven't been in the little conservatory behind his office. It's very cute and convenient—do I have to explain?"

"No. Why was it short?"

"He said he was meeting his wife downtown, so we went out together. He went down the subway and I walked home."

"What time was that?"

"I don't know exactly—probably around ten to four."

"Did you see Miss Evans on the way out?"

"No—we took the elevator and left through the basement."

"Why was that?"

"He accidentally pressed the wrong button—or so he said. Obviously it was really so that Miss Evans wouldn't see us together. And, in case you're still wondering, he didn't say a word about Hume."

Turning back to Hume, the inspector asked, "Did you see Mrs. Smith in the lab when you were leaving?"

"Yes."

"And when you were talking to Hamilton, was the office door open?"

Hume thought for a moment.

"I think so. At any rate, I don't remember having to open it when I left."

"So Mrs. Smith could have overheard your conversation with Hamilton."

"Could have, but didn't", Elsie butted in.

Hamilton was sitting up and a little of his normal color had returned to his face.

"She didn't have to", he said. "All that stuff about having a good time is sheer wishful thinking. The reason I told her about Hume is that neither of us could think of anything to talk about. In the end I had to shoo her out because I had a lot of correcting to do."

"So it would be no use asking your wife to confirm that you were meeting her downtown?" Williams asked Hamilton.

"Of course not—Elsie just made that bit up."

"Why would she do that?"

"Your guess is as good as mine."

"I'd like to hear your guess, anyway."

"All right, if you must. I hate to say this, but isn't it most probable that Hume is responsible for leaving Amanda in the storeroom and Elsie is trying to protect him. It's the space that he has easiest access to, and she knew that he has a history with young girls. He could easily have come back on Sunday after everyone else had left. He found Amanda unconscious or semi-conscious and took her upstairs for whatever purpose he had in mind. Elsie figured this out . . ."

Elsie interrupted in a cold, hard voice.

"You unutterable bastard! Well, now I don't have to keep your dirty secrets any more."

"My secrets? What about yours? Listen, Inspector. This woman has slept or tried to sleep with every male object on the faculty of this school. It wouldn't surprise me if she's had a go at Luis, or even some of the students. There's certainly been gossip to that effect. I admit that what I said about Hume was pure speculation, but if you dig around a bit you may find that Mrs. Smith had a very good reason for wanting Amanda out of the way. So maybe she did it and thought she could put the blame on Hume."

"Do you have evidence for any of these theories, Mr. Hamilton?"

"Nothing concrete, but we know that Amanda was a blackmailer and she had a habit of prying. She could easily have tried it on Mrs. Smith as well as Thornbury."

"Or, of course, on you."

"I suppose so, but the fact is that she didn't."

"Inspector Williams", Elsie said, with an obvious effort to remain calm. "I wish to make a statement about my actions on Sunday afternoon."

"I'll bet you do", Hamilton blurted.

"Quiet, Mr. Hamilton—go ahead, Mrs. Smith."

"First I have to state that in spite of all your pleas, I haven't been telling the truth. As you will shortly see, the reason for this is something very stupid. Everything I told you is true up to about four-thirty. At that time I was sitting almost where I am now and I heard footsteps on the floor above. I went to the stairway and saw Hamilton and Sally Evans on their way down. I came back here and then I went to office in the back and sat at the desk. I won't tell you what was going through my mind. Being the kind of person I am, I investigated the drawers pretty thoroughly, but the only interesting thing I found was a matchbox with a Yale key inside."

"Very interesting", Miller said. "Go on."

"I was about to leave when I heard the elevator. As far as I was aware, it had been on this floor ever since John Hume and I arrived. I didn't want anyone to find me hanging around in here, so I went and stood in my classroom door and awaited developments. I had the impression that it went all the way down to the basement and then came back up again. It's hard to tell with that elevator since it's always very loud whatever it's doing, but I thought it stopped on the fourth floor. I assumed that Hamilton had returned, and I was just about to go up and confront him when the elevator went down again."

"What time was this?"

"At a very rough guess, just about five o'clock. The elevator came up again, passed this floor and stopped upstairs again. A short time later it came down to this floor. The next thing I saw was Hamilton carrying Amanda's body into this lab. I came a few steps inside here and saw him coming back from the office. He seemed a little surprised to see me."

Elsie stopped, as if for a round of applause after this essay in meiosis. The attention was so concentrated on her that nobody noticed that the lab door had opened an inch or two. Williams was not as impressed as Elsie had evidently hoped—she could certainly tell a good story, but maybe that's all it was.

"Go on, Mrs. Smith. What happened next?"

"Nothing", Hamilton growled. "It's a complete fabrication."

"Mrs. Smith?"

"He said, 'Oh, hello, what are you doing here?' I said, 'Watching you dispose of a body. You'd better tell me about it.' This may be hard to understand, but I still found this man sexually attractive, so instead of calling the police I sat down with him and asked him what had happened. He said that he had returned for something that he had forgotten and had found Amanda lying dead in the doorway of the biology lab. I asked him why Amanda was up there and why he didn't call the police. He said he had no idea and didn't want to be implicated and it would be better if the body wasn't found until later. He said he put it in the storeroom because it probably wouldn't be found until some time on Monday. He would be out of it and there was no reason why Hume would be suspected. I didn't really follow his reasoning, but you have to take into consideration that we had had sex in his office twenty-four hours previously and I wasn't thinking very clearly . . ."

Elsie paused, as if some kind of inner struggle was going on.

"Well, since I'm trying to tell the truth, I guess I should admit that in the back of my mind there was the idea that I might get some kind of hold over him if I played my cards right. I also knew that if Hume came under serious suspicion there might be something to be gained from my ability to clear him. Hamilton was looking very shaky, so I told him he'd better clear out immediately. He said there might be bloodstains on the floor above. I said I'd take care of that and he left. I went up there and I couldn't find anything. I went home, but I'm not quite such an unscrupulous person as you might think, and I couldn't get the picture of that girl lying in the storeroom out of my mind. The thought came to me that maybe she wasn't dead. Eventually I couldn't stand it any more and around nine o'clock I came back to see. I opened the door with the key from the matchbox and there wasn't any doubt that Amanda was dead. She was very cold, she wasn't breathing and there was no pulse. I covered her with her raincoat, which he had left in a heap beside her, and I left again."

Elsie's voice died away and she looked as if she might faint at any moment.

Hamilton said, "Do I really have to sit here and listen to this nonsense?"

"Yes, you do Mr. Hamilton?" Williams responded. "Go on when your ready, Mrs. Smith."

Elsie seemed to be very far away, and Williams had to repeat his request.

"Sorry, Inspector, I was just wishing I was back in my cell where I don't have to talk to anybody. OK, I was about halfway home when the full stupidity of my actions began to dawn on me. I was almost as deeply involved as Hamilton in whatever had happened, and it seemed to me that he had just as much of a hold over me as I had over him. I never believed that he had actually killed the girl, but the idea that she might still have been alive when he locked her in wouldn't go away. If that was so, I was almost as responsible as he was. I thought he was depending on me to keep quiet about seeing him here, which is why I was so surprised when he went for me just now. Now, of course, it's just my word against his. That's all."

At the mention of possible bloodstains on the fourth floor, Williams had caught Michelson's eye and pointed to the back room. Michelson had nodded and left his position between Hamilton and Elsie. Now he returned and said, "They're on their way, Sir."

"OK, so maybe we'll get something useful. Now, Mr. Hamilton, you have not been officially accused of anything, and you're not under any compulsion to speak. It's up to you."

"Thank you, Inspector. I'll only repeat that Mrs. Smith's story is a complete fabrication. As I told you before, I left school at four-thirty, walked into the park with Sally, left her near the Delacorte and walked home. I got there before five-thirty and stayed there for the rest of the day. As far as I know, Amanda was not in a position to blackmail me about anything, and in any case, she had not made any attempt to do so."

"That's not quite true, Jim."

The door had opened fully and Sally, still bandaged and wearing her overcoat over her hospital things, walked unsteadily into the room. She was still talking.

"Don't you remember? She walked in on us just as you were making a minute examination of my right nipple. Of course, I didn't know at the time that you had just finished making love to Elsie, but I'll bet you anything Amanda did."

38

Hume helped Sally to a stool next to his own and put his arms around her so she wouldn't fall off.

"I couldn't stay up there on my own", she told him. "I was too scared. Very silly, I know . . . And then I was afraid something would happen to you."

Michelson, who had been about to sit down, stood there with his mouth open. Elsie said, "Well, I might have known you'd show up." Hamilton had turned several shades grayer and appeared to be groping for words.

"I won't apologize for the slight deception, Mr. Hamilton", Williams said. "I may have exaggerated the gravity of Miss Evans's condition, but I'm just as surprised as you are to see her here—I thought she was still in the hospital. I was just wondering if you had any more to say, but you seem to be having trouble speaking. What I'd really like to know is how Amanda arranged to meet you on Sunday. Did she call you at home?"

"I don't think she had to", Sally said. She was near the end of her resources and barely audible. "There was a note taped to the front door when we left on Friday. He read it and shoved it in his pocket. He said it was just a student wanting help with an assignment. I was going to tell John all this stuff about Amanda catching me and Jim in the act, but I didn't want to spoil things. Later on I couldn't remember."

Hume tightened his grip on Sally. He understood perfectly what she meant about not spoiling things.

"I think I should take Sally back to bed", he said, ignoring the snort that his choice of phraseology drew from Elsie. "I expect she'll be willing to make a formal statement later."

"Could you possibly hold on a couple more minutes?" Williams asked Sally. "There's a lot here that we'll have to come back to, but I'd like to ask if you've remembered any more about what happened on Wednesday."

"All I can remember is that I was trying to get away and something hit me on the head."

"Who were you trying to get away from?"

Sally looked around the room.

"Him", she said, pointing at Hamilton. "Now it's coming back—he had me by the wrists and Elsie told him I'd been sleeping with John. He screamed something about ripping my shirt off. I got a hand loose and tried to run . . ."

"One last thing—you said before that Mrs. Smith had something in her hand—can you remember what it was?"

"Yes, it was a clamp-stand."

"Thank you, Miss Evans. We can excuse you now, but we still need Mr. Hume. Sergeant Michelson, please call downstairs for Higgins."

Sally looked very apprehensive, so Williams explained.

"Jane Higgins is a very experienced officer. She'll take care of you until we've finished here. In the meantime, could you just explain how you got past Reilly downstairs?"

"He was very charming but he wouldn't let me up. So I went outside and came in again through the basement. I didn't want you to hear me, so I took the elevator to the second floor and came up the stairs."

"Amazing", Williams said. "No wonder you're exhausted."

Higgins was a few years older and a few inches taller than Sally, and her skirt came down almost to her knees, but she had a ready smile and a twinkle in her eye. Sally suddenly felt very relieved and allowed herself to be led away, but only after kissing Hume and telling him to come home as soon as possible.

"Home?" Elsie muttered, and there was a brief silence while the word seemed to resonate around the room. Elsie thought about her seven-room apartment on Riverside Drive and her tiny prison cell; Hamilton was momentarily back in his house on West 85th Street, now empty and dead; Hume had a few seconds of acute homesickness for his cozy flat in the West of England; Williams thought of his bachelor pad and, in an aberrant moment, placed Chrissie Davis there; and Michelson hoped that this session and its anticipated aftermath would be over in time for him to have supper with his amiable and long-suffering wife.

Williams quickly returned to business, the sharpness of his tone quickly dispelling all these images.

"Well, Mrs. Smith?"

"What do you mean, 'Well'?"

"You're standing here with a convenient object in your hand. Hamilton has played fast and loose with you and Miss Evans has stolen the affections of both of the men you're interested in. There they are. What do you do?"

Getting no reply, Williams went on.

"We're pretty certain that your story about hitting Miss Evans isn't true. You said that she turned away and you hit her with the clamp stand—but the injury was on the left side of her head and you're a right-handed swinger."

"You've been reading too many detective stories, Inspector. I have a very strong backhand."

Williams was not disconcerted.

"I don't think so. I've tried it—a clamp stand, with all its weight on one end, is a very different proposition from a tennis racket. So I tried imagining myself in your place. Miss Evans is struggling free from Hamilton. She's trying to get to the telephone and he's close behind her. I'm furious with both of them, and I'm standing ten feet away with a heavy object in my hand. So what do I do?"

There was a harsh laugh from Hamilton.

"You throw the damn thing and you don't care which one you hit."

"Exactly, Mr. Hamilton. The problem was that you and Miss Evans both had head wounds and you were unable to give a satisfactory explanation of yours. That's why I asked Sergeant Michelson if he had ever played billiards."

"Good Lord", Hume murmured, "a perfect cannon. Two points."

"Yes, Mr. Hume, except that we call it a carom in this country. In fact, Miss Evans and Mr. Hamilton each have two wounds—one where the clamp stand hit, and one where the head hit the corner of a bench in one case and, presumably, the floor in the other. What I don't understand, Mrs. Smith, is why you admitted responsibility for the assault on Miss Evans but gave a less than plausible description of how you did it. Since you are a person of considerable intelligence, I imagine that the last item was deliberate."

"All right, Inspector, I'll try to explain, but you must remember that people don't always understand their own motivations. I was, of course, extremely angry with all three of them."

"Three?" Hume said, involuntarily.

"Yes, John, I was very angry with you—surely I don't have to explain why."

"No, I understand now. You got back at me by leaving Sally in the storeroom, and that's what you were apologizing for the next day."

"Yes. 'Frustrated middle-aged woman goes berserk.' Amanda's reporter friend would love it. Actually Hamilton is wrong about one thing. Their heads were quite close together, but I was aiming at him and I got him somewhere around the left ear. It was very satisfactory, and the fact that it bounced off and hit Sally on the back of the head was icing on the cake. Sorry, John, I'm just saying how I felt. Hamilton got his legs tangled and went down on his back. Sally's head hit the corner of the workbench. They were both out cold. It was quite a shot . . ."

Elsie stopped for a moment and the ghost of a smile appeared on her face.

"I had seen John working on the storeroom door earlier and I thought I'd leave a surprise for him, except I didn't realize how badly she was hurt and I thought she would probably come to and leave before he had the chance to see her. By the time I got back to the lab, Hamilton was sitting up and asking what had happened.

He was still in a daze, so I told him that Sally slipped and fell while he was chasing her."

"You mean he never knew what hit him?", Williams asked.

"Right", Hamilton said thickly. "I can't believe that I could have known this woman so long . . ."

"And so intimately", Elsie interposed. "I know what you're going to say. 'Without realizing what a bitch she is.' So, for the second time in four days, I told him he'd better get out and I'd take care of things. I told him Sally was dead, just as he'd told me that Amanda was dead. He was terrified and he went like a lamb. I felt very calm, but I think I must have been drunk on adrenaline. I washed the clamp stand in the sink, and I knew there would be blood on my shoes, so I went to put my boots on, only the zipper was jammed. You know all about that. Then I went down and finished the search of Sally's desk that had been interrupted earlier. Then John came in and I thought, 'Oh, he's going to get his surprise after all. I was high for the rest of the evening but by the next morning it had turned to self-disgust and what you might call Hamilton-disgust . . ."

Hamilton interrupted.

"Isn't this enough, Inspector? Surely you've got all you need."

"Not quite, Mr. Hamilton. We can arrest you now or a little later, but one way or the other you'll have to stay. Go on, Mrs. Smith."

"It's like this, you see—people need sex but they also need love, and ever since my husband died I've generally been able to get sex but not love. They look at me and think, 'I know what she wants', and usually they're right. I thought for a while that it might be different with Hamilton, but it was mostly wishful thinking and on Sunday I knew he'd just been keeping me warm while he went after Sally. So I thought, 'Well, I can play that game too.' After watching him dispose of Amanda, I let him think I was helping him and I thought either I'd get what I wanted from him or I'd turn him over to the police. It was the same with Sally, just another string I could pull, and yes, the left-right business was a spur-of-the-moment thing—kind of semi-deliberate. You were very clever to get at me by suggesting that John was under suspicion, but being the bitch that I am, I managed to confess in such a way as to keep my option on Hamilton. I knew you would get it and eventually everything would have to come out, but I thought I would enjoy prolonging the agony."

"And did you?"

"Not very much. Sitting in that little room for all those hours, I couldn't help seeing myself as if I were someone else, and I came to the point of despising myself almost as much as I despise Hamilton. Basically I'm just as bad as he is. While I was still involved with him, I was fishing for John Hume and feeling that there was someone who might be capable of love as well as sex. The fact is I was in love with you, John, and that was what made me so crazy in the end. After it was all over and everything was totally pointless, I thought I might just as well let things take their course."

Hume seemed to be struggling to say something.

"What is it, Mr. Hume?" Williams asked.

"It's really nothing to do with your investigation, Inspector—still trying to understand about love, I suppose. It's like religion—if you get it right it's wonderful, but if you get it wrong it turns you into a monster. And I was remembering my first impressions of all these people."

Elsie laughed.

"Such nice people weren't we?"

"So I thought."

"And now you know we're all assholes, every one of us. All except you—you're too nice-minded to be an asshole, but you're still a fool. Don't bother about love—there's no oasis in this desert. Just go back to England and leave Sally to continue her adventures over here."

"No, Elsie", Hume said quietly. "I'm an asshole too—a fool and an asshole. It's an unfortunate combination."

Michelson coughed politely.

"Yes, Sergeant", Williams said. "Time to get back to business. James Hamilton, I am arresting you for the murder of Amanda Friedman . . ."

39

O'Reilly and Klein were on their way downtown with Hamilton and Smith. Downstairs in the auditorium, Jean Hamilton had sat in silence for more than half an hour, and Michael Schwartz had spent the time filling page after page of his notebook. Victoria Picard was not so patient.

"What are they doing up there, all this time", she wanted to know.

"It's none of your business, Vicky", Thornbury said. "You weren't invited, you arrived late and I can't imagine why they let you in."

He had been tempted to add that it certainly wasn't for her looks, but realizing that she had actually tried to follow a suggestion that he had made a few hours previously, he relented. In his opinion, her hurried attempt at a new hairdo was not a success, the basic problem being that she didn't have quite enough hair. At least she had made an effort, but the result was that she looked rather like a cross between her two selves. Maybe she'd better keep the wig after all. What was really exercising his mind was the question of whether he should accept all or part of her offer to rescue the Benjamin Thompson School. Vicky might be a handful, but he had grown accustomed to her funny face, and when he tried to imagine life without her, all he got was a large image of a scotch bottle. The big question, which scared the hell out of him, was whether he would actually have to marry her. He had just decided to stop thinking about it when Inspector Williams appeared at the door.

"Mrs. Hamilton, I'd like a word with you outside, please."

When they were outside, Jean said, "I think I know what you're going to say, but you'd better go ahead and say it."

"I'm sorry to tell you that it may be worse than you think. Your husband has been arrested for the murder of Amanda Friedman and may face charges in connection with the assault on Sally Evans. You will be able to arrange to see him later, after the initial formalities are complete."

"There's no need to apologize, Inspector. Last time I saw you I was thinking that I might be able to help him and maybe there was still some future for the two of us. Now I don't even think of him as my husband any more. Frankly, I can't see that my being here serves any useful purpose, and if you don't need me for anything else I'll leave."

"It's entirely up to you, Mrs. Hamilton. I thought we might have to go over some of your evidence again, but as it turned out, that won't be necessary. As of now you're absolutely free to go."

"Thank you—I'd like to make a brief phone call before leaving—not to my lawyer. It's not private—I can make it from the desk here."

Williams nodded and went into the auditorium. The phone rang in Andrew Johnson's apartment, and a few minutes later, Delia Johnson was saying to her husband, "Was that the Hamilton woman again? There's something going between you and her, isn't there."

Andrew Johnson wasn't defensive about it.

"Yes, there is. Her husband has been accused of murder and I'm helping her to cope with the situation."

"I've been wondering what helping her includes. Have you realized that she's at least ten years older than you?"

"Six years", Andrew said, "and I didn't think you worried about things like that. After all, you're seven years older than Robert Fine."

Delia stared at him.

"I didn't think . . ." she began.

"No, I don't suppose you did—if you had, you might have realized that you weren't as clever as you thought."

Meanwhile, Michelson and Hume had joined the company in the auditorium and Williams was talking to Thornbury and Schwartz.

"I asked you to be here because it might have been necessary for you to repeat or amend some of the evidence you have given. This has turned out to be unnecessary, so I apologize for taking up your time. Mr. Schwartz, your case has been turned over to the DA's Office and for the moment you are free to go. In fact, I'd appreciate your immediate absence."

"What if I choose not to leave?"

Williams could see what was going through the reporter's mind.

"You'd love to be forcibly ejected, wouldn't you? It would make such a nice story. So we'll do things the other way around. Mr. Thornbury, may we use your office?"

"Of course."

"Then I'll see you and Mr. Hume there very shortly."

"What about me?" Vicky asked plaintively.

"Oh, I guess you'd better go along with Mr. Thornbury—as long as you behave yourself."

Williams stood over Schwartz, barring his way.

"OK, Sergeant, now there are no witnesses."

Williams and Michelson each took an arm and propelled Schwartz through the front door.

"There you are, safely outside without a bruise on your body. Put that in your report."

When Williams and Michelson re-entered the building, they were very surprised to see Higgins sitting at Sally's desk.

"She wouldn't let me take her home", Higgins said, a little defensively. "She said she wanted to lie down in the nurse's room and listen for the elevator. Now she's in the office with the others."

"OK. Don't worry about it—you can go off duty now."

Williams watched her leave. Chrissie was more of a willow wand and Higgins was more of an hour glass—amazing how women of totally different proportions could press the same button with the same effect. Thinking what a shame it was that she was his subordinate, Williams turned his mind back to business.

Thornbury was sitting at his desk with a glass and a scotch bottle in front of him.

"No ice, Inspector, but if we're celebrating the end of your investigation we can drink it neat. No proper glasses either, except mine, but I've always taken the precaution of keeping a few plastic cups in my bottom drawer. How about it?"

Michelson looked hopefully at Williams.

Vicky, who had positioned herself in the background by the window, said, "Come on, Williams, let's get him drunk—he's more tolerable that way. Only don't get him started on those filthy cigars."

Sally, who was sitting on his lap, said, "You know, I think a little drink might make my head feel better. I'll share a cup with John."

The bottle and the cups were passed around the room, and Williams was soon sipping appreciatively.

"We're here", he said, "partly because it's important for Mr. Thornbury to know the exact situation as it affects the future of the school, and partly because some of you have been under suspicion and you can be assured that that is no longer the case. So here are the salient points. We are satisfied that James Hamilton was responsible for moving Amanda Friedman into the storeroom. Medical evidence makes it highly probable that she was still alive at the time, so Hamilton has been charged with her murder. We are also satisfied that Elsie Smith bears the primary responsibility for the assault on Sally. She had already admitted this but had given a fictitious account of how the assault took place. She has now amended this and we know that Hamilton was involved too. Hamilton has given what amounts to a confession for both crimes, but it remains to be seen whether this will be formalized. I hope that Hamilton and Smith will plead guilty. If they don't, you can all expect to be called as witnesses at their trials—all, I should say, except Mrs. Picard."

Thornbury looked behind him.

"Don't feel bad, Vicky", he said, with a grin.

"Idiot!" Vicky muttered. "Don't you know there's no such thing as bad publicity?"

"I'd have to disagree, as far as the school is concerned."

"I don't know if my impression is worth anything", Sally said softly, "but I think there's a fairly big group of parents who want the school to continue. Not all the phone calls I received were from people asking for transcripts."

Williams took another sip from his paper cup.

"Here's to the future of the Ben Thompson School. I think I've told you all you need to know. We'll need to be able to keep in touch with you, so please report any changes of address . . ."

"But inspector", Sally objected. "Aren't you going to explain things a bit more? I have no idea what really happened to me, and I'd like to know what happened to Amanda. I was . . . very close to Jim Hamilton."

"I was, too, in a different way", Thornbury said. "I still can't picture him as a murderer."

Williams sighed heavily.

"A lot of murders are committed by people who aren't really murderers. They seem like ordinary decent people until they get into a situation that they can't deal with. It's usually sex or money."

It struck Hume that apart from the thing about money, this was exactly right. Jessica's intelligence, wit and idealism had hooked him in the first place, but it was her physical body that had finally sent him over the edge. No, that couldn't be right—it was his own physical body that had sent him over the edge. But that didn't seem right either—it sounded too much like an excuse . . .

Williams was still talking.

"And when it's over, they may be decent people again, only, of course, it's too late. If you steal, it's possible to make restitution, but murder can't be undone."

Hume's thoughts ran on.

I don't know—can you be a decent person again? They talked about extenuating factors, but I still feel like a murderer—so what am I doing, holding Sally like a lover when she doesn't know what I really am?

"Well", Williams was saying, "Mr. Hume was present for the whole session in the lab, and there's nothing to stop him from giving you all the details, so I'll just give you a few basic facts. Mrs. Smith says that she saw Hamilton carrying Amanda into the chemistry lab shortly after five o'clock on Sunday. According to her, he said that he had returned to school, found her dead body outside his lab door and left her in Hume's storeroom because he didn't want to be involved. He denied the whole thing at first but later implicitly admitted it. The difficult question for us was always how Amanda got up to the third or fourth floor. The medical evidence is that the bleeding in her brain was slow and she took a long time to die. It's quite plausible that after lying unconscious in the basement for forty minutes or so, she woke up sufficiently to remember that she had made an appointment with Hamilton. That, presumably, is why she had refused to leave with Schwartz. Thanks to Sally, we know that Amanda had seen things that she wasn't supposed to see and was probably intending to put the screws on Hamilton. So she makes it up to the fourth floor and collapses on Hamilton's doorstep. If this reconstruction is correct, the next bit shows a particularly nasty streak in Hamilton's character. A couple of days previously he had heard about an incident with a young girl in John Hume's past that would almost certainly make him an object of suspicion."

Hume groaned so quietly that only Sally heard him. He had already decided that he must tell Sally the whole story of Jessica's death, but it was still a shock to hear Williams referring to it in front of her, even though the reference was an oblique one.

"He thinks that if Amanda's body is found in Hume's storeroom, the police will make the association. That didn't work out, so if this comes to trial he will undoubtedly maintain either that Smith's story is a complete fabrication or that it's true and he was quite sure that Amanda was already dead. Now that we have Smith's story, we're doing a more concentrated search for bloodstains on the fourth floor. I don't need to tell you how important it will be if we find anything. I don't want to talk about personal relationships, so

I'll just say that Smith took the opportunity to establish a hold over Hamilton. Now, as far as Wednesday's events are concerned . . . '

"Wait a minute", Vicky interrupted. "Can't you explain what happened to Amanda in the first place?"

Williams frowned at her and might have refused if Sally hadn't said very quietly, "I'd like to know too."

"OK—you all know Schwartz's story."

"I don't", Sally said. "I don't even know who Schwartz is."

"You probably read an article by him in last Tuesday's *Galaxy* and you can get the details from Mr. Hume. Schwartz admits that he and Amanda struggled at the top of the basement stairs and she fell to the half landing. He says she was still alive and cursing when he left, but we have evidence from another quarter that she was unconscious, so he must have just walked past her and left. We've pondered trying to get him for manslaughter or depraved indifference, but frankly I doubt whether we can make the charges stick. That's really all."

"But what about Jill Davis? Wasn't she involved in this somehow?"

Williams felt that he had already gone on too long and said too much, but Sally was irresistible. He told the whole story, from the rape that hadn't been a rape to Jill's suicide and her letter to her mother, and he wasn't surprised when Sally began to cry. Hume tightened his grip on her and she said, "I'm sorry—it's just that everything is so horrible, including me. I've been sitting at that desk every day, taking everyone at face value, having a good time and not caring that much whether anyone got hurt . . . I mean, is there anyone kind of clean and straightforward in this school, or do we all have mean streaks and dirty secrets?"

She stood up abruptly and would have pitched forward on her face if Hume hadn't held on to her. Now he knew that his whole adventure was even more of a disaster than he had thought, and there were tears in his eyes, too. If Sally wanted someone clean and straightforward, with no dirty secrets, she would have to look elsewhere.

"She ought to be in the hospital", Williams said.

"I want to be with John", Sally whispered. "I'm not going back to the hospital."

"I don't know whether I can get you up the stairs", Hume said. It seemed to him that she was in worse condition now than when she had left the hospital.

"Come on", she said. "We'll manage somehow."

⚭⚭

Williams and Michelson departed, feeling that the aftermath might well be even more trying than the investigation. Left to themselves in the headmaster's office, Aloysius Thornbury and Victoria Picard looked warily at each other.

Eventually Victoria spoke.

"What are you going to do?"

"I haven't decided. Do you still want to marry me?"

"I don't know—I'll have to think about it. What about the school?"

"Damn the school! Let's have another drink."

"Good idea—then we can go out and get something to eat."

"OK, only not one of your Brazilian messes—there was an ear in the last one I had."

"Blockhead!"

⚭⚭

Half an hour later, while Sally was in a deep sleep, Hume sat by the bed and tried to figure out what he must do. He thought that Williams's reference to Jessica's death might not have registered with Sally, but one way or another she would have to know, either to make it possible for them to be together or so that she could understand why he was leaving. It seemed to him that the decision was easy, although acting on it would be an excruciating ordeal. Sally might possibly be in love with him now, but when she was thirty he would be sixty, and when she was forty, he would be seventy; and she still didn't know that he was a murderer.

He didn't have much to pack and he didn't care if he left things behind. The important thing was to leave before Sally woke up, but first he had to make a difficult phone call. Then he had to write a note for her, and that would be difficult too.

40

When Sally woke up it was pitch dark. She knew exactly where she was and who would be with her, but she was too exhausted to reach for the bedside lamp. She heard someone stir in the chair next to her bed, and remembered what it was that had been worrying her as she was falling asleep.

"John? What was it that the inspector said about you and a young girl?"

"Hello, Sally. John isn't here."

The voice was Jean Hamilton's.

"I'm very sorry", Jean went on. "He asked me to stay with you till you woke up. He left a letter for you."

Sally hadn't recognized Jean's voice.

"Who are you? And why isn't John here?"

"Jean—Jean Hamilton. Not the person you would have chosen to help you, I'm afraid. Is it OK if I switch the light on?"

"Not yet."

Sally knew in an instant what had happened, and thought she knew what would be in the letter. It would have taken a thousand words to explain it, but she already had a picture that was complete except that she couldn't fit Jean Hamilton into it.

"He's gone, hasn't he?"

"Yes."

"And he asked you to help me? But . . ."

"You don't understand why I would. Neither do I, really. I guess it's partly because I don't have anything else to do at the moment. But I don't hate you, if that's what you're worrying about. You weren't the first and I'm sure you wouldn't have been the last. I'll probably give you a Scottish accent and put you in one of my books when I get around to writing again. Do you want the letter?"

Sally didn't answer the question.

"Did he tell you anything?"

"Not much—just what's in the letter. All I can tell you is that he's in love with you and he's scared stiff of getting hurt. He didn't say that, but it's obvious. For some reason he thinks I'm a good person and he asked me to look after you until you're well enough to manage on your own. I said I would and here I am. Now I'm going to put the light on, give you the letter and go away for half an hour."

Dear Sally,

I love you very much and I think, perhaps, that you love me. I thought for a while that it might somehow work out for us, but after what happened this afternoon I see that I was wrong. I am not the person you thought I was. You said something about everyone having dirty secrets and I have to tell you that I have a secret that is dirtier than anything in the past of anyone in this school. Being in love with you helped me to forget it for a while, but it won't go away. My just punishment is that I shall carry it with me for the rest of my days. I am going back to England as soon as I can get a flight. It's just possible that I may be able to get my old job back.

Jean Hamilton has promised to take care of you as long as you need her.

John

Sally only cried for a minute or two. When Jean got back precisely on the half hour she was sitting up in bed and looking unexpectedly cheerful.

"Good Lord", Jean said, "What's come over you?"

"I'm going to England. If you come with me we can probably leave tomorrow—otherwise I'll have to wait till my head's a little better."

Hamilton's defence against the murder charge was that on the Sunday afternoon in question he had done exactly as he had originally stated. He had walked into the park with Sally and then gone straight home. As far as Elsie's version of events was concerned, it was simply his word against hers. He specified that he and Elsie had been lovers and that he had ended the relationship when he took up with Sally. Obviously Elsie had made up her story as a way of getting back at him, and this contention was supported by her subsequent attack on Sally. Williams was at first very gratified to hear that bloodstains were found on the floor outside the biology lab, but Hamilton surprised everyone by producing the note that Amanda had left for him on Friday afternoon and using it as evidence in his favor.

"I was sorry you were too busy to talk to me when I looked in on Friday", it said, "but I could see that you were doing something really important. So meet me in your office on Sunday afternoon around five o'clock, and we can discuss the matter—unless you would like to have it reported in the Galaxy."

Hamilton said that he had decided to ignore the threat and that Amanda had presumably gone up to the biology lab to look for him. Remarks he had made later on, that sounded like admissions of guilt, were the results of unfair tactics on the part of the police. Asked to explain how the body had made it into the storeroom, he said that as he hadn't been there at the time he had absolutely no idea. Further than that he had nothing to say.

This stonewall defence was very effective. Everyone concerned was morally certain that it was Hamilton who had left Amanda in the storeroom, but eventually the case had to be dropped because there seemed to be no prospect of a conviction.

Elsie had been planning to change her plea to "Guilty" in the matter of the assault on Sally, but when she heard about Hamilton's manipulation of the situation, she changed her mind. A "Not guilty" plea would necessitate a trial, forcing Hamilton to appear in court to testify. Sally could testify that Hamilton had grabbed and threatened her, and Elsie would corroborate Sally's evidence, so it was quite possible that he might be charged with some form of sexual assault. Since no one had seen Elsie throw the clamp stand, she thought she might possibly get away with it, in spite of her two contradictory confessions and other odd things like the fact that someone had washed the clamp stand. Unfortunately for everyone involved, except Hamilton, the proceedings had to be put on hold because the key witnesses, Sally and Hume, had disappeared.

Tuesday's *Galaxy* carried an unusually restrained follow-up to its previous report on the state of affairs at Ben Thompson. It mentioned the arrests of Hamilton and Smith, but readers who were expecting more intimate revelations were disappointed. There were two reasons for this, one being that the details of Jill's suicide and of Sunday's sessions in Hume's lab and the headmaster's office were unknown to Michael Schwartz. The other was that Schwartz was living in fear of being arrested at any moment. When the police did appear at his apartment, however, it wasn't to arrest him but to question him further as a potential witness in the trial of Peter Miller. Schwartz was his usual unhelpful self and, even when faced with the evidence of Jill's letter, refused to change his story. Miller maintained that he really did think that Amanda was dead and that Jill's subsequent report was the result of a misunderstanding. Once again it was a matter of one unreliable witness's word against another's, the result being that eventually Miller was released with a stain on his character but no convictions on his record. Another result was that Miller received his draft papers a few weeks later and realized that, on the whole, he would rather have gone to prison.

The one good thing that came from the interrogation of Miller was the admission that his "attempted rape" of Amanda had been carefully worked out beforehand and that Amanda's parents, who were up to their eyes in debt, had been deeply involved. Jill had not been informed of the plot—Miller had planted her in the storeroom so that she could be a witness in case one was needed. The Friedmans, of course, denied the whole thing.

On the Friday after Williams had apparently wrapped up the case in Thornbury's office, several unobtrusive announcements appeared in the New York Times. One reported discreetly on the state of affairs at the Benjamin Thompson School.

"In spite of the recent unhappy events, the headmaster, Mr. Aloysius Thornbury, assures us that the school will re-open on Monday. 'We understand that many parents have felt the need to enroll their children elsewhere, but we shall continue to provide a full program for those who elect to stay, and those who have left can be assured of a warm welcome if they choose to return."

In the fashion section, a slightly more flamboyant article announced that Mrs. George M. Picard III, who was the owner of VIP Fashions and a member of the Board of Trustees of the Benjamin Thompson School, was creating a multimillion educational foundation with the object of improving the quality of private education in New York City. Schools would be able to apply for grants, so that they could attract highly qualified teachers and improve their facilities, especially in the area of science.

Neither of these reports made a whole lot of sense to anyone who knew anything about Ben Thompson and Victoria Picard, but if such a person had happened to glance at the society page, the explanation would have become clear.

"Victoria Picard to wed Aloysius Thornbury"

Two items that weren't announced were that Chrissie Davis had moved in with Inspector Williams, although she had wisely decided to keep the lease on her own apartment, and that Sergeant Michelson had had supper with his wife on three consecutive evenings.

41

On a bright morning in late February, Colin Woodcock, headmaster of the Nave School in the City of Gloucester, England, was sitting at the back of a large chemistry lab, observing his new teacher. As far as Woodcock could tell, he was a good chemist, but he had the unfortunate habit of talking to himself instead of to the boys. What he said made abundant sense to anyone who listened carefully and knew any chemistry, but most of it never penetrated the ears, let alone the brains, of his students. He had been engaged to complete the school year as a temporary, but the headmaster had no illusions about the prospect of finding anyone better.

Returning to his office, he bumped into his secretary.

"You have two visitors", she said. "They're looking for John Hume."

"Did you tell them he's gone to America?"

"They've just come from America. They say he's come back to England and, more to the point, he said something about possibly getting his old job back."

"Really? Well, I'd better talk to them. If he's back we know exactly where to look for him."

When Hume opened the door of his apartment and saw his two visitors, he almost fainted. It flashed through his mind that he had sailed to America to get away from Jessica and he had flown back to England to get away from Sally, and it hadn't worked in either case.

Sally was more composed.

"Well, aren't you going to ask us in and make some tea?"

If you wish to know how things developed from this point, you will have to await the publication of the next episode.